CHARITY

THE DISTINGUISHED ROGUES
BOOK 3

HEATHER BOYD

LLD PRESS

One

"THE CHILD IS asleep now, Miss Birkenstock. You should put her into bed."

The nurse's curt voice dragged Agatha from her rebellious thoughts of running away to a simpler world where people kept their promises.

Wearily, she opened her eyes. "Yes, I believe you are right, Mrs. Bates."

She looked upon tiny Betty Smith lying peacefully in her arms at long last, and her heart fluttered. No matter how tightly the babe clutched Agatha's fingertip, or how much she longed to stay, she couldn't remain at the Grafton Street Orphanage overnight to oversee the child's care. The trustees would never stand for it. Nor would her grandfather.

Slowly, Agatha rose to her feet. The babe in her arms startled at the movement and Agatha pressed a kiss to her cheek. "Hush, sweetheart, all is well."

Betty grumbled and, instead of giving the sleeping infant up to the nurse's outstretched arms, Agatha carried the child to bed, tucked her snug into the linens, and then placed her favorite rag doll beside her. The nurse clucked her tongue in disapproval at the toy.

Agatha fingered the little girl's pale curls and smiled that Betty rested easily. "Please send word if her night should be disturbed again, Mrs. Bates. I will be here early tomorrow morning to visit with her."

"As you wish, miss."

No matter how harmless the words, the old nurse's tone hinted she'd rather Agatha be gone from the orphanage, never to interfere with her charges again. Well, that wasn't going to happen. Not a chance of it.

After smoothing her hand over the child's pale curls one last time, Agatha straightened to look about the chamber. Six narrow beds hugged the imperfect walls of the chilly room, each containing a peeking set of eyes belonging to a child in need of warmth and kindness. She'd love to drag each of them from the covers, smother them with affection, and stay until they were all sound asleep. If she could take them from this depressing place and home with her tonight, she would be perfectly happy.

But her grandfather and the board of trustees wouldn't allow *that* either.

Agatha paced the length of the room, doing her best to ignore the cheerless severity of the chamber. The children's bodies under the frayed covers didn't so much as twitch. A fear of Nurse Bates' displeasure kept them still as statues, she was sure. Such strict adherence to rules saddened her. These children needed the freedom to run about on cool, green grass, to smile and be silly instead of being expected to appear perpetually grateful for the bed space they occupied.

She would promise them everything would be well, if she didn't harbor a kernel of doubt that she could live up to her own promises. The sting of disappointment was the hardest emotion to conquer. She would promise them no more than she could vouchsafe: her time, her affection, and a game of cricket in the tiny, rear walled garden if the weather allowed.

Even though the children showed no sign that they were awake, she made a point of checking each one to be sure they would be warm enough for the coming night.

As Agatha reached the end of the room where the drafts were at their worst, the nurse cleared her throat. Nurse Bates always appeared anxious for her to leave, but Agatha refused to hurry. She checked the remaining children and left the room when she was ready.

Her maid waited in the front hall, hands clenched over Agatha's cloak. Nell rushed forward. "It be a frightful night outside, Miss Birkenstock. The fog is thicker than pea soup."

Since Nell was such a fanciful creature, often prone to exaggerate the mildest of events into the worst possible calamity, Agatha disregarded her words. She donned her cloak, secured her reticule about her wrist, and then turned for the door. "It's just a bit of fog, Nell. It hardly signifies. Come along."

The butler opened the door for them and then stepped back. Pea soup, indeed. Agatha couldn't see the street clearly from the top step. Her confidence slipping a little, she hurried down the stairs and turned right into the mist. The orphanage door closed with a heavy thud.

Rushed, light footsteps behind her confirmed that Nell was but one pace away. "People get lost in the London fog, miss," Nell whispered.

"That shall not happen to us. I know my way home perfectly well."

Nevertheless, Agatha clutched her cloak tightly about her and kept her eyes fixed on her path. She followed the high front fences along Grafton Street, ignoring the disturbing way nearby houses appeared out of the thick fog only to disappear from view a moment later. It was eerie and quiet and, with Nell crowding her left shoulder, Agatha's heart raced in a foolish rhythm.

The maid's nervousness tainted Agatha's mood. She turned left at the corner of Dover Street, chiding herself that she knew this route like the back of her own hand. The landmarks between the orphanage and home were distinctive. If she paid the proper attention, instead of panicking as Nell appeared to be, they'd be home as quick as if walking about on a clear, sunny day.

As she approached the next corner, Agatha's gaze drifted to the left. A faint glow burned from the windows of a tall townhouse, signifying that some amusement might be underway within. A deep sadness gripped her. Could she hear laughter from Lady Carrington's house? She slowed her steps. With the thick fog muting all sound but their breathing, it was impossible to tell with any certainty where the laughter came from. Perhaps there was a dinner party in progress. After all, Lady Carrington was very fond of entertaining, and she had her son's position in society to maintain. The viscountess must be so happy that Oscar had secured such an advantageous match with an earl's daughter.

The hot sting of jealously burned through her body. She pushed the sensation down, leaving only her teeth to unclench. Perfect Lady Penelope. Wealthy and titled Lady Penelope. Desirable attributes for the image-conscious viscount.

The front door of Lady Carrington's townhouse opened. Dark shapes—a man and woman, judging by their attire—descended the steps and clambered into a waiting carriage. Agatha expelled a sharp breath. She should not be interested in the goings-on of the Carrington family. She was far removed from their business now. Determined to forget them, she started off again, but her eyes strayed to the departing grand carriage, and she wondered who it had contained.

Agatha stumbled off the pavement onto the Hay Hill crossing and pulled up sharply. Her steps had propelled her faster than she'd thought. Woolgathering on a foggy night was foolish in the extreme. She needed to keep her wits about her in order to avoid becoming turned around.

Nell clutched at her arm. "Are we lost?"

"No, of course not. I just stumbled, is all."

The maid yanked her fingers from Agatha's upper arm. Agatha hadn't meant to snap, but agonizing over past mistakes was a futile endeavor that no amount of tears or self-recriminations could fix. She was angry at her own foolish gullibility, not the maid.

With that thought firmly in mind, Agatha turned right and hurried along the deserted street, pleased to be almost halfway home. She turned right again and peered into the mist, looking for the next cross street on her left. The comfort of Berkeley Square should be very close.

~ * ~

If ever a man was in need of the understanding and affection from his own woman, then Oscar Ryall, Viscount Carrington, was clear out of luck tonight. He stood amid the chattering gaiety of his mother's drawing room, his breathing shallow and fast. For just a moment, he had imagined Bartholomew Barrette had entered the room. His pulse raced. His palms slicked with sweat.

But Barrette was dead.

Oscar had killed him himself.

Determined to again push the terror into the quiet recesses of his mind, he skirted the room, searching for better company. A bigger distraction than the inane chatter of the woman he would soon marry would restore his balance.

However, before he had gone too many steps, a hand caught his arm. "Lady Penelope will do very well for you I think, Oscar. Once she and I become better acquainted, I would enjoy taking her under my wing to ensure she is accepted everywhere."

"She's an earl's daughter, Mother," Oscar murmured. "She is already accepted everywhere. She's very agreeable to everyone else."

"She might be accepted everywhere, but she must make a bigger impression if she is to rise with the cream as she should. And she should be agreeable to her future husband too. Does she not please you?"

The urge to blurt out the truth maddened him. "Of course she does," he lied. "Forgive me. I am merely fatigued tonight."

His mother, a shrewd and determined woman, peered hard at his face. "You said that yesterday and last week, too, at the Belmont Soiree. Are you certain you're in good health, my dear?"

Again, he had the urge to blurt out the truth. Only this time he would scream it out loud. He didn't trust himself not to cause an embarrassing scene in his present state of mind. He'd have to leave another entertainment early again. "There is nothing wrong with me that a good night's sleep couldn't fix. Leave me be, Mother. It will all come to rights in the end." Oscar desperately wished that might be so. But the dreams, the remembrances of that fateful night one month ago, only grew in strength until he'd begun to fear for his sanity. When he closed his eyes, he imagined the slow slide of blood across Barrette's forehead.

A light touch landed on his arm, and he startled.

Lady Penelope fluttered her long lashes at him. "Forgive me for the interruption, my lord, but Lady Prewitt desires to take her leave of your mother. She has developed a megrim and requires immediate rest."

Oscar forced a smile to his face for his betrothed's benefit. "Of course, Lady Penelope. It was good of you to come. I do hope your sister recovers swiftly. A sore head is a terrible affliction and can linger for days, I've heard."

Lady Penelope's lips turned up in a sudden smile. "They can, can't they? I will pass along your good wishes."

When his mother fluttered off to do her duty as hostess, Oscar scanned the guests. None paid him the slightest attention, so he slipped into the adjoining dining room and listened to the soft conversation in the hall. There seemed to be some debate over leaving. However, he wouldn't interrupt to smooth their departure. He simply couldn't face another tedious farewell with the woman he had to marry. Not tonight. Tonight he needed so much more than empty pleasantries.

Once his betrothed and her family had departed, Oscar slipped along the quiet hall, only noticed by the butler. Quite used to Oscar's habit of stealthy escape, the butler retrieved Oscar's hat and cane without a word. Just to be sure that his betrothed had truly left, he eased the front door open an inch and peered outside. Lady Penelope's carriage remained below the stairs. Oscar snapped the door closed an inch and listened until it finally drew away. He let out a relieved breath and stepped out into the thick fog.

As if the cloying cheerfulness inside wasn't bad enough, now he had to traverse through oppressive fog. Hopefully this experience wouldn't add to his nightly dreams. As it was, almost every encounter, large or insignificant, blended into his oft-repeated dream of killing another man.

The fact that Bartholomew Barrette's reason had slipped toward madness remained a cold comfort during Oscar's lonely nights. He still wondered if there might have been another way to disarm Barrette without killing him. Yet his actions had spared his best friend, Daventry, and the earl's future wife, Lillian, from suffering any injury that might have resulted in death. He'd had to act quickly to save them. Although Daventry had later embraced him as a brother for his timely arrival and quick intervention, doubt over his actions still filled Oscar with dread.

Oscar descended the stairs, shoving his hands beneath his arms to calm the shaking. Such jitters caused people to stare and ask questions. Thank heavens he'd hidden his misery while inside his mother's house. With so many influential members of society gracing her drawing room, any appearance of distress would turn into a fast-running rumor.

Soft sounds in the distance lifted his head. He peered forward and saw two slight forms moving away from his location. Two more people foolishly abroad on a night better suited to staying indoors and making love.

Oscar shook his head to dispel the yearning. He was a betrothed man, and as such he'd committed to marrying Lady Penelope. Making love to her was well down on his list of desires. Perhaps he should engage a mistress.

Perhaps he should run away and avoid the marriage altogether.

But he was committed. The contracts were signed. The blessings of the *ton* had rained down upon his head. His future was set in hard, unforgiving stone.

He was to marry a woman he didn't love.

Oscar set off toward home at a leisurely pace. He had nothing and nobody waiting, so there was no need to rush. Ahead of him the fast footfalls of the women moving toward Berkeley Square echoed off the buildings. Perhaps they were some of his neighbors. But being out on a night such as this was foolish. Dangers hid in the shadows of London.

A thrill of purpose thrummed through him, and Oscar lengthened his stride to catch up to them.

Two

AS AGATHA NEARED the next crossing, a prickle of heat swept her skin. The unusual sensation caused her heart to race again. Afraid someone was following, she peered behind them. But there was no movement, no disturbance or dark form stalking toward them.

Nell's fanciful imagination had indeed gotten the better of her. Agatha squared her shoulders, stepped off the curb, and onto the street.

A hand closed upon her elbow in a bruising grip. Agatha shrieked right along with her maid. A greasy, cold hand slapped tight over her mouth, muting her cries for help. A man's arm wrapped tightly around her waist— forcing her hard against a large body. She tried to pry herself free with her fingers but was hoisted into the air. She swung her feet, kicking out at the man who held her until someone else captured her legs. Held captive like a trussed lamb, Agatha was carried deeper into Berkley Square.

"'Git her purse," a gravelly voice urged.

The hand over her mouth slacked, and another fumbled at her wrist. She bit down as hard as she could. Her toes touched the ground as her assailant cursed. But instead of releasing her as she'd hoped, Agatha's attacker changed his grip, winding an arm about her neck and squeezing.

"Do tha again, and I'll let you have a taste of something else of me, ye vixen. Sommat I'll enjoy more tha you will. Be still."

Terrified, she obeyed the command. She didn't want to provoke them so far that they'd fall upon her like ravenous beasts. Perhaps if she stopped fighting and gave them what valuables she had, they'd let her be. She hoped Nell did the same. Agatha whimpered her agreement.

A grubby, toothless face appeared before her from the mist and she shrieked in surprise, recoiling against her captor.

Behind her, the brute chuckled. "He isn't a pretty sight, is he?"

The other man cackled, but then ripped Agatha's reticule from her wrist. Toothless stuffed it down his gaping shirt front and reached toward her chest. Agatha whimpered again, desperate that Toothless not lay his hands upon her.

The arm at her neck tightened, lifting her chin until she had to stretch to remain touching the ground and keep breathing. "We git our payment one way or tuther. Ya got plenty to satisfy me without touching ya scrawny hide. There be a chain about her neck. Git it, too."

Rough fingers slid up Agatha's chest and her necklace was snapped from her neck. Her eyes watered as the rough fingers returned to bite cruelly into her breasts.

Toothless leaned close. "You'll come ta like tha, missy."

The air to the right of her whooshed, and a loud male groan of pain rang through the square. Was Nell fighting against her attacker? She'd hardly believe the girl capable of defending herself. But if she was, then there might be hope for them both. Agatha fought against the hands that held her as more grunts echoed through the square.

But then all fell silent. Agatha's attackers turned to face the threat, dragging her with them as a shield. "This one's ours. Be off with you," her attacker warned, pulling her against his chest, but stepping behind the toothless man for protection.

The square remained silent.

Toothless turned to them, uncertainty clear in his movements. Her assailant shuffled and then backed away as a dark arm appeared from the mist to wrap around Toothless' throat. He disappeared into the mist, a desperate gasp of breath the only indication that he was still near. Then nothing. Silence. Toothless didn't reappear, but a loud thump echoed around them.

Agatha whimpered as the brute holding her tightened his grip on her neck. He shuffled back a few steps, turning her every which way as he sought the location of Toothless' attacker. Another loud crack broke the silence. The brute holding Agatha stiffened and then she fell, slamming hard into the ground. A heavy weight fell upon her and she scrambled away, rising to a crouch quickly to see what was happening.

The sounds of fighting grew louder. She couldn't see more than the blur of dark shapes coming closer then disappearing again as fists hit flesh. Agatha didn't know which way to turn. Nothing made sense in the gloom. She scrambled to the left and ran her hands over the ground, feverishly searching for a weapon she could use to defend herself.

Just as her fingers closed over a thin, hard stick, a loud thump signaled the demise of one of those fighting. Agatha curled as small as she could and clutched the stick with both hands.

"Now the odds are even, you bastards," an unfamiliar male voice growled. "The type of men who attempt to accost women in this neighborhood are vermin with a very short lifespan."

A sickening grunt signaled someone had landed a good blow and Agatha cringed as a low moan of pain rang out.

"What I don't understand," the speaker continued, "is how you can bear the knowledge that you're good for nothing but the beating I'm giving you. When you hit the ground, I suggest you stay down. I truly don't need much more of an excuse to thrash you senseless."

Another blow sounded, and then two more. After each punch, the groans grew in volume. She covered her ears.

There was one more sickening thump, and then the fighting sounds stopped.

She stayed where she was, barely daring to breathe lest attention turn in her direction. Someone large moved around in the fog, but she couldn't tell who. She tightened her grip on the stick. A muffled groan and scuffling some distance away hinted that her attackers had quite given up in the face of this unknown brawler's intimidating presence.

"I'd slink away too, you worthless excuse for men," the deep voice muttered from close by. Agatha jumped as the sound grated along her nerves. She'd never heard such masculine aggression before.

"Accosting women? Come into this square again and be prepared for more than bruises. You know, maybe you *should* come back. I'm still of a mind to beat better manners into you."

The distant sounds quieted, but the stranger moved around in the dark park, his boots shuffling across the earth. Agatha shivered, more wary of this one man than the two villains combined. There was something strangely familiar about the way he talked while trouncing her two attackers. It wasn't so much the words he spoke, but the way he said them sent shivers racing across her skin.

"Now, where did you go? You had better come out before they come back. Devil take it! Where *did* I drop my cane? It should have been right here. Have you picked it up?"

Agatha bit her lip to stop herself from answering. She had a cane in her hands. That explained the smooth wood. She inched her fingers along the shaft until she found a solid, cold metal lion's head. That was good. That could hurt. She adjusted her grip so she could use it if necessary.

"Are you still not going to speak to me?" The stranger blew out a loud breath. "I had hoped we could get around this little problem, but not even risking life and limb will please you now, will it? You have the cane, don't you? And you're planning on clobbering me with it? I suppose

I do deserve a good beating from you, but do you think we could do it somewhere more private?"

How did he know she had the cane? Where was home? She was all alone in the dark with a strange man who could read her mind. Even the fact she had a weapon in her hands did not make her feel very confident. The attack had completely turned her around.

And there was Nell to worry about. She needed to find out what had become of her maid. Had she managed to escape and return home for help?

Silence stretched between them.

"Did they hurt you?"

The concern in the stranger's voice surprised her. She started to stand, hopeful that her pale gown was still hidden beneath her darker cloak, keeping her invisible to the stranger. When she was upright again, she took a tentative step backward. Gravel crunched beneath her boot. She froze.

"So, you're not hurt. You just don't want to talk to me." The stranger groaned as Agatha took another step back. "You do know you're going the wrong way, don't you? Your house is to your left. And another thing, what the devil are you doing out here alone? A foggy evening is not a safe place for you. Actually, when I think of it, nowhere is particularly safe for you, especially alone. What were you doing walking home without a proper escort? Your grandfather will be livid."

Agatha froze as she tried to place the bitter voice. It was familiar, but she'd never been introduced to someone as cheerless as this. She had to get away.

"Agatha, stop, or you will hit the—"

"Ow." Pain sliced through her head as she encountered something hard. She clutched her head with one hand and the tree with the other, letting the cane slip through her fingers.

"Tree," he finished. "Are you still upright?"

"Yes," Agatha supplied angrily, appalled by her clumsiness.

"She speaks! I think I need to sit down, but perhaps not in the middle of Berkley Square. Your friends might come back at any moment, and they may bring reinforcements." Gravel crunched as the speaker drew closer. "While defending your person is my greatest delight, my knuckles already sting quite a bit. Thank you for giving me the opportunity to apply my boxing skills. Although, I must say, they were not very sporting about it. I don't believe they know the rules of proper behavior. Two against one is hardly fair. At least my arrival at your side improved the odds, but I should have caught up to you sooner. Forgive me."

The regret in the stranger's voice startled her. Whoever he was, he sounded as if he believed he had a responsibility to protect her. Well that was certainly untrue. She didn't need a man in her life. Not anymore.

"I hate to rush you, but we really should get you home," he said. "We don't want anyone to hear of this escapade, do we, precious?"

Precious.

Only one man had called her that.

This time Agatha trembled for an entirely different reason. She *did* know this rambling gentleman. She just hadn't heard him speak recently. And he'd changed; his voice was now so devoid of his usual warmth that she hadn't recognized him at all. Where had the gentleman hailed as the most charming lord of London gone?

Agatha slumped against the tree, mostly to keep from flinging herself into the deceptively safe haven of his arms. He could lie for a living and still be seen as a charming innocent. "Oscar! You cannot be here. You promised to stay away."

His footsteps drew closer. "I never did promise. How could you think I'd let any harm come to you?"

A dark outline appeared before her and then he was there. Oscar Ryall, Viscount Carrington, filled her vision until she saw none but him. Hands—strong, firm, and terribly warm—wrapped around Agatha and pulled her from the safety of the tree. She shuddered as she was settled against the fine linen and brocade covering Oscar's body.

"I have you now, precious. I have you."

Agatha lifted her face away from the warmth of his chest. A quick pant of breath crossed her cheek before

Oscar attempted to claim her mouth. She turned her face aside. "You cannot."

Shifting her hands between them to push away from his body, Agatha ignored the familiar rush of longing to wrap her arms tighter about him. She'd missed him. She'd missed the charming liar far too much.

But the cold rush of reality sobered her. He was a man engaged for an advantageous match. He was to marry an heiress. A woman hailed as a diamond of society. By comparison, Agatha had no place in Oscar's life except for a sordid one as his mistress.

Oscar groaned, attempting to drag her close again. "Change your mind."

His ardent whisper brought tears to her eyes, but she pushed against his embrace until there was some space between them. "I cannot be your mistress."

Oscar's fingers closed about her hands and trapped her firmly in place. "Please."

Agatha shook her head and tried to extract her hands from his grip. But he curled his fingers about hers, lacing them together as he had done so often.

The tears in her eyes fell at the familiar gesture. "You know it's impossible. I cannot be the woman you want."

"The woman I want is you. Exactly as you are. How can you deny us our only chance for contentment?"

Agatha took a deep breath and let it out slowly. She'd had a lot of time to consider her past behavior, to see that she'd been swept away by an unbecoming lust and lulled by the intimacy of frequent proximity. She should have taken greater care with her heart and kept him, a man far above her station in life, at arms' length.

But she'd been foolishly smitten by his charm and had missed the obvious signs that they had no *proper* future together. Oscar held opinions that were so very different from hers. He'd wanted her to warm his bed, but didn't want to marry her. Why would he? He lived a charmed life, dined among the best circles in London, and frittered away his time with meaningless pursuits. To her horror, she'd discovered his goal had always been to marry to better his estate, to marry a daughter of a peer and elevate his family in his rarified world. Marriage to a merchant's granddaughter hardly fit in with his grand schemes.

He must have been vastly amused with her feeble resistance to his seduction.

She pressed her hands to his chest and shoved hard. "You ask me to fulfill a role that is held in low regard. I cannot be your mistress. I would become a pariah in good society. I won't risk being denied the right to work with the orphans if rumors of my fall were to spread. Thanks to our past familiarity, I already have a somewhat questionable reputation. But I won't give up the chance for a meaningful life because you cannot take no for an answer."

Across from her, Oscar stiffened. "You spend too much of your time thinking about those damn orphans."

Agatha pressed the point of her finger into his breastbone. "And you, my lord, think of nothing at all and no one but yourself. You do exactly what is expected of you, instead of what you should. Now get out of my way. I'm going to find my maid."

Three

YET AGAIN, AGATHA Birkenstock's tart tongue left Oscar speechless. He dragged in a heavy breath, intent on calming his frantic heart. How dare she label him a heartless bastard? Hadn't he just fought tooth and nail to keep her safe? Usually her direct way of speaking was one of the things he enjoyed about her. But not today.

Not when his blood was still coursing with a wild desire to thrash the life out of the men who had dared touch his precious Agatha. Not when Oscar was still shaken by his own recent behavior. Behavior that he wished no one would discover. But secrets were hard to keep from society at the best of times, and he was biding time until the news reached the *ton's* flapping ears. How society would regard him then was anyone's guess. How Agatha Birkenstock took the news was another matter entirely.

Ahead of him, Agatha was calling for her maid and creeping through the square with outstretched arms. He caught up to her. "You go too far, Agatha."

She blinked. "Well you, my lord, have not the right to tell me what I should or should not do. Kindly stay out of my business."

"You *are* my business." Oscar dragged her into his arms. She could have been hurt. He could have lost her. He forced a large breath into his lungs and let it out slowly. She appeared unhurt, but it had been a very near thing. What if he hadn't become so frustrated with his mother's party and escaped early? Who knew what he would have found.

Oscar ran his hands over her cloak, molding her tighter against him, discreetly attempting to gauge her state of health. It had been too long since he'd seen her without a crowd or closed window between them. Too long since he'd held her in his arms. Yet when she forcefully resisted his embrace, he let her go. He'd never force Agatha to stay, but her need for independence worried him.

As she stepped around him, Oscar caught her arm again and dragged her to his side. "We are not finished speaking about your lack of a suitable escort. Why is a footman or such not with you?"

Agatha stiffened. "Do you listen to me at all, Lord Carrington? Stay. Out. Of. My. Business."

Her blue eyes blazed with defiance and Oscar's heart pounded harder in his chest. She was, in a word, a formidable woman. Much like his own mother, with her determination to steer her own path. But the path Agatha had chosen would separate them, and Oscar, despite knowing it was in her best interests, was no longer sure he could bear that.

A groan to Oscar's right startled them both.

Agatha pulled from his grip and rushed toward the sound. "Nell, where are you?"

"Damn it, Agatha," Oscar hissed, frustrated all over again by his inability to continue a conversation with her. Just when he thought he had a chance to plead his case, she darted away.

"Here, miss. I'm here."

The weak call turned him around until he stumbled over Agatha crouching low to the ground.

"Oscar. Nell is hurt. You have to help me."

The young woman at Agatha's feet groaned. Poor girl. He'd been too late to prevent her from coming to harm.

Agatha tugged on his trouser leg. "What are you waiting for? Help her up so that I may have her seen to."

"No," the maid squeaked.

Oscar took a step back. While he was more than happy to carry out Agatha's request, as any gentleman should, he understood better than Agatha why the maid might not wish him to place his hands on her. The scoundrel that had accosted the girl had been very free with exploring her body, despite her vigorous protests. She might see any assistance he tried to give as another threat against her.

Oscar gripped Agatha's arm and dragged her a few steps away so he could speak freely. "She's been handled in the worst way possible, Agatha. Be gentle with her. It would be my honor to help you, however I think she fears me."

Agatha blinked up at him for a full minute as she assessed his words. Then her blue eyes widened with understanding. She flew to her servant's side. "This is all my fault, Nell. I'm so sorry. So very sorry, indeed. I should have allowed George to accompany us."

The maid's tears started as soon as Agatha helped her stand and made a fuss of straightening her gown. "We do not look too bad. If asked about our mussed attire, we will say we were almost struck by a carriage and fell to the hard ground. However, instead of returning below stairs or to your chamber, Nell, you will come straight to mine. I will say I have need of you, so there shall be no prying eyes until you feel better."

Oscar grimaced. Agatha involved herself in matters best left to the servants far too much. She should hold herself aloof from their contretemps. But no matter how often Oscar had warned her that her efforts would be resented, she persisted in thinking them her friends.

Agatha lifted the maid's chin to look in her eyes. "Nell?"

The maid sniffled. "Thank you, miss."

Agatha slung her arm about the girl's waist and moved off slowly without waiting for him.

Frustrated to be summarily ignored again, Oscar rushed to stand before them, his arms outstretched. "Agatha? My cane?"

Her huff of annoyance was loud. "Beside the tree."

After a few turns about the tree base, Oscar spotted it and then hurried to catch up. But by then the women were at the edge of the park and, without a backward glance, they limped across the street.

Careful to remain out of sight, as they ascended the front stairs of the building beside his and disappear inside. He leaned against the wrought-iron fencing as his heart squeezed. For all the annoyance Agatha brought to his life, he missed her dreadfully. Her sudden smiles, her infectious laugh, and the way her gaze had once fallen upon him with a steady acceptance, despite his flaws.

And he had many. Society might claim him to be the most charming man in society, but his inner thoughts were oftentimes less than graceful. Especially now, when society expected so much from him and gave nothing back to help him accept this loveless match in which he'd been bound.

He needed someone to confide in, yet he couldn't bear to open his heart. Not when the one who still held it looked upon him with such disdain. What Oscar wanted most was to ease her hurt, but he feared that losing Agatha was a suffering he'd never be free of.

Oscar tucked his hands under his arms and rocked on his feet. Months of unanswered questions stirred within him. He needed to speak with Agatha privately, but he dreaded hearing her responses.

Oscar pushed off the fence and crossed the street, hopefully appearing as if he hadn't a care in the world, should he pass anyone foolish enough to be abroad on this wretched night. He hurried up his front steps, pulled the key from his pocket, and let himself inside the quiet house. But he couldn't hope to evade his butler.

"You have an urgent message, my lord."

His butler held out his little tray. *Mother?* What new scheme she had hatched in the last half hour? Oscar headed for his tiny bookroom, breaking the seal as he went.

He swiftly read the elegantly worded note. Another inescapable invitation to another tediously dull luncheon. And tomorrow no less. Why hadn't she mentioned it tonight? A quick glance at his appointment book showed he had promised to take his future wife driving in Hyde Park at five, but he should have enough time to fit both outings into his schedule.

Oscar ran his finger over his engagements for the rest of the week. Penelope, Penelope, Penelope. How dull. He groaned and dropped his head to the open page. Life was not going the way he'd planned.

But there was nothing to be done now. Only make the best husband he could and forget about Agatha Birkenstock. Except that was proving more than difficult.

Of course, living in the house beside Agatha was certainly responsible for keeping her uppermost in his mind. That place should be occupied by Lady Penelope, a socially acceptable earl's daughter.

Yet no matter how hard Oscar tried, he couldn't dredge up the necessary enthusiasm for the chit. The dark-haired beauty didn't affect him at all. Her conversation didn't draw him into a greater understanding of her character. Her smile, when she chose to bestow one in his direction, lacked warmth. And unless matters changed and she stepped from her family's shadow long enough to speak with him alone, he'd be just as oblivious on his wedding day.

At least her father, the Earl of Thorpe, hadn't pressed for an actual wedding date as yet. Indeed, her brother-in-law, Lord Prewitt, was very quick to suggest a long engagement so they could become better acquainted. But how Oscar was supposed to do that, when Lady Penelope never left her family's company, stumped him.

Oscar rubbed a hand across his face. He'd thought to make a proper marriage to the advantage of his family. He'd thought to marry a woman with impeccable breeding and decorum. What he got was being discovered in a state of dishabille beside Lady Penelope. But he'd not been the one to muss her prim gown.

No, that was the worst of it.

Lord Thorpe had concluded, quite wrongly, that Oscar had been responsible for his daughter's state. Yet all Oscar had done was stumble upon her straight from having Agatha Birkenstock in his arms. But Lady

Penelope had claimed firmly that he'd been the one to do the deed, as it were.

Of course, with no repeatable explanation for his less-than-pristine appearance, matters had quickly spiraled out of his control. He couldn't very well say that he'd tumbled Agatha over Lady Archer's pianoforte. So, his planned slow courtship of Lady Penelope had become a quick engagement, and then, to his shock, he'd lost something more precious than gold.

Agatha wasn't fearless. Despite his extravagant offer of *carte blanche,* she refused to become his mistress. Instantly. The memory of that painful interview haunted him, because he had discovered that Agatha had presumed to be his wife. Offering her the position of mistress, when she'd assumed otherwise, had turned her cold to him. When she'd walked away without a backward glance, he knew he'd made a grave mistake.

Oscar leaned back in his chair and considered what he'd so foolishly thrown away. He and Agatha had become friendly not long after her arrival in her grandfather's house. Her sad, pinched face and darkly hued mourning attire had tugged at his heart, sitting as she was tucked into her windowsill. But when she had realized he was so close, she had hidden herself from view.

For a month of Tuesdays, he had placed a bag of sweets on her windowsill, determined to wipe the unhappy frown from the grieving girl's face. When at last she didn't throw the bags back over the railing, he caught a glimpse of her smile. After that day, he'd gained her trust, gained her friendship, and the desire to never see her so unhappy again.

He'd thought everything was perfect.

But then he'd never spoken a word about their future, so he didn't know they each had a far different plan in mind.

Now he was engaged to marry a woman he didn't know, didn't care for, and certainly didn't trust, while the one he wanted shunned him. So far, he'd been unable to detect one glimmer of embarrassment in his future wife's eyes. If she suffered from a broken heart at her separation from her own lover, he certainly couldn't sense it.

He stood suddenly, morose resignation weighing heavily on his shoulders. Perhaps he should attempt a fresh start after the wedding away from Town. He couldn't continue to live beside Agatha Birkenstock every day of his marriage. Despite her demand that he stay away, Oscar didn't know if he could maintain a distance between them. That irked him.

And to hell with the betrothal clause stating he had to reside in the Earl of Thorpe's residence upon his marriage to Lady Penelope. Such a restriction to his life was not to be borne without resistance.

Perhaps a home in the country would be best. The Berkley Square townhouse was entailed, but his fortune was enough to purchase a little place in the country. Of course, given the townhouse's position, he'd have no trouble renting it out during the season, freeing him of the temptation to return to London and see Agatha just one last time.

The thought gave him no joy.

These last months since the engagement were the worst of his life, and he could see no happy ending in sight.

Cast down, he made his way up the narrow staircase to an upper floor rear door and stepped onto the dark balcony. He walked to the rail, slung one leg over carefully, mindful of the spikes atop the metal work, and stepped onto Agatha's adjoining balcony.

Someone moved about inside her bedchamber. Objects clanked against wood, or was that a scraping of a chair? Was Agatha still attending to the poor maid? He tapped on the glass once, dropped a sack of sweets on the windowsill, and then settled in to wait until she doused the light. After a little while the window rattled, and then Agatha's head popped out into the night. "You have to stop doing this."

"Come out, precious."

The sack of sweets landed at his feet. "I can't." She ducked her head back inside.

"Please, Agatha. We need to talk and then I'll leave you be."

She huffed another breath. "Oh, all right. But you must mind your manners."

The window inched higher and, after a slither of sound, she stood beside him. Oscar reached for her hand and brought it to his lips. Her smooth skin and the sweet scent of her perfume made his blood run hot. He quickly led her to the rail, stepped over, then turned to help her, intent on swinging her nightgown clear of the spiked rail.

As his hands settled about her waist, desire made his palms sweaty. When she was on her feet on his balcony, he was very quick to lead her inside before they were seen together.

Despite his earlier decision to leave her in peace, Oscar gathered Agatha into his arms to hold her tight against him. After a moment's hesitation, Agatha returned his embrace, wrapping her arms low around his hips.

God, he was so unbelievably stupid.

Giving up Agatha was going to kill him. He let her go with reluctance, clutched her hand in his, and led her to his bedchamber where a fire burned hot enough to ward off the chill of the foggy night.

As they crossed the threshold, Agatha's hand slipped free of his. "What do you want, Oscar?"

Instead of answering immediately, he crossed the room to sit and regarded her. So far he could see no change to her body that hinted she might be carrying his child. But he had to be sure. Despite the surge of desire sweeping him at the sight of her in his bedchamber again, dressed for bed in familiar white linen, he steeled himself to remain at a distance. But with her hair unbound and lying thick about her shoulders, she was everything he'd ever wanted and more.

"How are you, precious?"

His question appeared to take her off guard. She stared at him a long time. Her gaze flowed over his face. A frown line appeared between her eyes. "Better than you, it would seem. You look dreadful."

Oscar nodded. He couldn't explain his weary appearance without telling her what he'd done—what circumstance had forced him to do in the name of friendship.

"Are you unwell?"

"I am very well, but I've not been sleeping the best. No doubt there are peas hidden under my mattress."

Agatha scoffed and rose to her feet. Fearing she was about to bolt, Oscar started to stand, but she closed the distance between them to press her hand to his head, keeping him in place.

"You are no warmer than usual. Does something trouble you?"

Oscar closed his eyes, drinking in the concern in her voice. Her fingers slid into his hair in an intimate caress he'd missed. Oscar shuddered. "Aside from missing you like the devil, what could be wrong?"

Her fingers cupped his jaw and then slipped away. "It's more than that, isn't it?"

Agatha resumed her seat, but she sat forward, apparently eager to hear his confession. Was she as starved for the sound of his voice as he was for hers?

No matter the reason, he couldn't tell her the truth. "I asked you here to speak about you." Now that the moment had come to ask his question, he was afraid of the answer. "I am most particularly concerned that there might have been consequences from our nights together. A somewhat awkward expectation. You never wrote to me as I asked."

"Awkward?" Agatha's face filled with hot color as she understood the significance of his question. "Oh, there are no *consequences*. I knew that almost immediately."

Oscar hung his head, filled with deep sadness. In the back of his mind, he'd begun to formulate a plan to set Agatha and the child up somewhere. Somewhere he might visit often. Somewhere with green fields to take picnics upon. As he looked up, Agatha swiped her fingers across her cheeks, brushing away tears. He dropped to his knees and crawled across the room to pull her into his embrace. Sweeping her hair aside, he pressed his face against the smooth skin of her neck and waited for her to compose herself again.

When she eventually raised her head, Oscar sat beside her, clasping her fingers in his grip. "It's for the best, then."

Agatha nodded, but he could tell she didn't agree. He didn't believe himself, either.

With her neck exposed to the candlelight, an angry red mark upon her skin was revealed. "You were hurt. Why didn't you tell me?"

His fingers grazed her skin, then he dropped kisses beside the mark to make her better. For a moment or two, Agatha allowed it, but too soon twisted away from him.

Her eyes, when he met them, were twin pools of pain. "I must return home before Nell frets."

Oscar let the sight of her fill his vision, let the precious memories of her friendship fill his mind, until his heart settled into a deep, steady rhythm. "I know. How is she?"

Agatha twisted her fingers together nervously. "Quite shocked, I fear."

"Give her time to come around." He stood and held out his hand. After a moment, Agatha came to him, let him wrap her in an embrace, and finally let him kiss her as he'd dreamed.

Distance and longing heated the exchange, until they were both grasping for breath and each other. The thin nature of her nightgown proved little barrier to his questing fingers, and he felt every contour, ever delicious dip and sway of her body.

But she had refused him. He wouldn't seduce her into breaking her word. "Agatha."

She whimpered, threading her fingers into the waistband of his trousers in a manner that drove him insane. "Yes, Oscar."

Ignoring the husky quality of her voice, he pressed his lips to her hair. He would not make a mistake tonight and take her to his bed. He couldn't lie with her again. The risk was simply too great. "I've not slept with another woman since our first kiss. I want you to know that."

"If you had, it is no longer my concern." Agatha sniffed. "Let me go."

He deserved that, he supposed. But Agatha needed to know the truth from his lips. He should have been honest with her from the start. With an ocean of regret on his shoulders, Oscar led her to the back of his house, lifted her over the railing, and watched her take his heart away.

Four

LIVING WITH HER grandfather had, at one time, been very easy. When she'd been younger and still distraught over her parents' sudden deaths, Thomas Birkenstock had set his business affairs aside to soften her heartbreak. He'd been gently patient with her wish to remain apart from the world. Unfortunately, such sympathetic treatment hadn't lasted much beyond her sixteenth year, the time when he realized she was of an age to need a husband. The once gentle prodding had grown to become a daily lecture—an interview where Agatha struggled to be an agreeable, dutiful grandchild, but not commit herself to any man he favored.

Agatha surreptitiously watched him scanning the London Times while he dug into a heaped plate of fried beef and cabbage with a saucer of mead to wash it down. Normally, she could ignore the combination. Today, however, she was hard pressed to keep her countenance when he belched into his hand. Meal times were the worst of living with him.

The flick of the paper signaled an end to his silence and the continuation of his routine. He was a man of exact habits, neat to a fault, and growing obsessed with seeing her married now that she was an old maid of one-and-twenty years.

She counted the times he folded the paper: in half, then thirds. As he stood and tucked it under his arm, she felt the weight of his stare settle over her. Her grandfather's lips had compressed, signaling his thoughts had probably turned to her unwed state again.

"Shall we meet at eleven today, child? I have some letters of business to write before our discussion."

A brief reprieve, but certainly not an escape from the inevitable. "Of course, sir."

She smiled until he disappeared from view then let her ladylike pose crumple. How was she supposed to commit to marry a man of his choosing? It wasn't that she disliked the idea of marriage, a home, children, or the happy slide into comfortable old age. Yet her foolishness three months ago had made that respectable future utterly impossible.

Agatha lifted her teacup to her lips and sipped, glancing about the morning room with a critical eye. The chamber was in a bright, sunny position, being at the rear of the house, and she'd gathered her grandmother's best possessions together to make the room feel homey for her grandfather. She was a good housekeeper for him. Couldn't he be happy to let their situation remain a long-term arrangement?

She let the cup clatter noisily onto its saucer. No, he wouldn't let the matter rest, but she had an hour in which to enjoy her life before the lecture began again. She had temporary freedom. Leaving the morning room behind, Agatha hurried to her little corner of the house— a narrow slice of room that she'd taken over completely. The cluttered space held her favorite things: books, needlepoint, a soft quilt belonging to her mother that she liked to tuck about her legs on cold days. The dark walls and lavender-scented chamber offered Agatha more comfort than any other part of the house these days.

Dragging out the heavy, cushioned chair before her writing table, Agatha sat to write out the menu for tomorrow night's dinner then wrote a reply to her newly married friend's letter, being sure to make her life sound more wonderful than it really was. Virginia, Lady Hallam, didn't need to know the truth of her situation.

She didn't need to know that Agatha's heart had shattered into a million pieces the night Oscar became engaged after compromising the incomparable Lady Penelope. The wealthy debutant possessed a healthy dowry and an equally angry father. Agatha's lips curled into an unladylike snarl. Damn that conniving strumpet. Lady Penelope had insinuated that she had given herself to Oscar that very night. And by the time Agatha had returned unobserved to the ballroom, neat and once more respectable after *she'd* succumbed to Oscar's affections, he was being threatened by Lady Penelope's irate father.

When Oscar's gaze had fallen upon her across the ballroom, her heart had stopped. He'd appeared unconcerned with his entrapment. He'd smiled and had immediately agreed to the match. Heartbroken, Agatha had clapped along with the other guests, and then escaped as fast as her grandfather could be convinced to leave.

It wasn't until later, when Oscar had knocked on her window as if nothing had changed between them, that she'd discovered her error.

Oscar's marriage to Lady Penelope was in the wind all along. He'd been courting her behind Agatha's back. She'd only been a diversion from boredom.

Furious over his duplicity, of his plan to marry Lady Penelope and keep her as his mistress, she'd sent him away. But later, as the enormity of her mistake became apparent, she grieved for what might have been.

Her only consolation now was that Oscar appeared miserable too.

A shadow fell upon Agatha's table, blocking the light filtering in through the window as her butler, George, passed by on his way through to the kitchen garden. Nell, standing in a patch of bright sunlight, was gathering lavender stalks by the far wall.

Agatha dropped her quill to the table and stood. After yesterday, she wasn't sure how Nell would react to the male servants in the household. She'd been considerably distressed last night, and it had taken all of Agatha's powers of persuasion to convince Nell that she was not about to be let go. After all, the assault was hardly her fault. She was an innocent victim of a lustful man. Just as Agatha had been three months ago.

She pulled the curtain aside and peered out. With the window closed, she couldn't discern what the conversation was about, but so far Nell seemed to be holding her own. George took a step forward, closer to Nell, and blocked her view. Anxious that he not question Nell about her late night duties, Agatha headed outside to intervene. The cool morning air gave way to the warmth of sunshine, but with George towering over Nell now, Agatha didn't linger to enjoy.

"Have I done something to offend?" George asked, a hard edge to his tone.

Nell took a step away. "No, of course not." The maid retreated another step, and George followed.

The anxiety in her maid's voice tugged at Agatha's heart. She stepped to the side, letting Nell see her approach. Her maid's eyes widened.

George turned to take in Agatha's approach. "Can I be of assistance, Miss Birkenstock?"

"No thank you, George. I am here to speak with Nell. You may go about your usual duties." The butler looked about to say something more to Nell, but he clenched his jaw over the words, nodded, and then turned on his heel to return to the house.

"Nell?" Agatha took a step and caught the miserable expression in her maid's eye. Oscar claimed she should hold herself aloof from the servant's contretemps, but Nell needed her support, at least for the moment. The girl certainly needed a distraction. "I believe the flowers would do better with a little less pressure around the stems."

As hoped, Nell glanced down and made a show of checking the poor flowers.

"What did George want?"

Nell shrugged. "He wanted to know if I was ill. I missed dinner last evening and picked at my breakfast since my stomach just churns over and over. It was remarked upon below-stairs."

"A pity he didn't know that my late supper last night was for you, but no matter." Agatha picked a few more sprigs and tucked them into Nell's drooping bunch. "The less he knows about last night, the better, am I correct?"

Nell looked up, yet her misery remained as clear as day. If she kept up that sort of mournful expression she would be faced with many more questions below-stairs.

"Try to push the memory from your mind." Heedless of the impropriety of behaving with such familiarity to a servant, Agatha stroked Nell's arm. The maid nodded just as the clock began to strike.

Already eleven! Dash it all. Now she had to face her grandfather.

Agatha picked up her long skirts and hurried inside. Punctuality, or lack thereof, was also another favorite topic to be discussed at length. At her grandfather's study door, she smoothed her hair, then tapped on the wood and waited. Just as the final chime rang through the house, he bade her enter.

Almost at once, Agatha was cast back to her first day in the house. The decidedly masculine chamber had intimidated her then, just as it did now. Striving to appear placid, to be the dutiful granddaughter he expected, Agatha crossed the room and took her usual seat.

He waved a letter at her. "I've received a letter of invitation from the Marquess of Ettington to spend Christmas at his estate in the country. However, given certain changed circumstances, I am undecided on the value of whether to accept."

Concerned, Agatha leaned forward. "What has changed?"

He scrubbed his hand across his jaw. "Given the recent spate of marriages amongst his set, I fear the time and unnecessary disturbance to attend would not be worth the effort. It doesn't do you any good to associate with gentlemen already committed in marriage. I can hardly imagine the marquess would widen his circle with eligible men just to be sure you had the opportunity to be properly admired."

Agatha pressed her lips together to keep from crying out. He would refuse an invitation to spend Christmas with her friends simply because there would be no marriageable gentlemen in attendance? Was that the only reason he had forced her into society, into the presence of peers far above her expectations when the invitations had come from Ettington House? She longed to see Virginia, Lady Hallam, and Constance, the Marchioness of Ettington, again. But if he said no today, his decision would be final.

Determining it best not to let her anxiety show, she said nothing while he paced the room. If she spoke up with too much enthusiasm for the trip, he'd try to make a bargain with her. A typical businessman, he'd press her into committing to meet another gentleman of his acquaintance in return for indulging her.

Abruptly, he threw the letter to the desk. Agatha exhaled slowly, certain, given his rushed gesture, that he hadn't made a decision as yet.

He circled the desk and sat as if he were negotiating a difficult meeting. "Now we have the orphanage's charity tea tomorrow, and I want you to wear something pretty. There's many a lady there with sons in want of a wife who should be greeted with the utmost civility. After that, we shall take a turn around Hyde Park in the new carriage, eh?"

Agatha clasped her hands together to hide her nervousness. "As much as I would like to please you in this, Grandfather, I am already committed with duties during the performance. I am to escort the children and provide the accompaniment on the pianoforte."

Behind her, the footsteps halted. Agatha waited. She'd given her word to help convey the children to Ascot House. If she changed her plans at this late stage, her actions would reflect badly on her grandfather. Perhaps it would be enough that she was to play the pianoforte in public, a feat he was always attempting to arrange. Usually performing in public would set her nerves to chaos, but for the children's happiness she was prepared to endure the embarrassment.

"Very well, but do your best to be agreeable during any introductions. You will have little time to make an impression with your conversation. Let us hope there is a gentleman in the room with the ability to detect your superior playing under the noisy racket the children will strike up. I'd not like the occasion to be a disappointing waste."

"Yes, of course. I will do my best to make a good impression."

When her grandfather nodded and picked up his paper again, Agatha made her escape. With luck, she'd go unnoticed by the guests attending the concert. And with more luck, the unmarried gentlemen seated for the concert would be tone deaf.

Five

ESTELLA RYALL, LADY Carrington, liked nothing better than to be the center of attention at any society gathering. However, today she wasn't as keen on the sensations caused by the warm regard afforded her as usual.

"Mother, could you remove your fingers from my arm? Your grip is causing me considerable discomfort."

Estella glanced at her rigid fingers gripping her son's arm and made a greater effort to calm herself. She was one of the *ton's* most influential hostesses and should be above being ruffled. But the vexation of having her lover and her oldest acquaintance in the room was proving a real point of contention. Having them both watch her so closely, with exactly the same predatory expression, proved unsettling in the extreme. Flustered, she smoothed her hand over her gown like a green debutant then silently scolded herself for her foolishness. She raised her chin. "The performance is almost ready to start, Oscar."

His eyes lit up. "Yes, that was what I'd mentioned several times already. Perhaps we should sit."

As Oscar unwittingly tried to maneuver her close to both men, Estella managed to direct him to an unoccupied row some distance away. Her son's eyebrows rose in query as he settled in his chair. "Well, Mother, you have me all to yourself. You must have a somewhat urgent matter to discuss to shun your friend's company."

Estella opened her reticule to withdraw her fan. "I just wanted to enjoy the performance in peace with you. Really, some of them will think nothing of chatting through the entire performance." Aghast at her blunt words, she snapped open her fan while she glanced at her neighbors to determine if anyone had overheard. After a few anxious minutes, she blew out a relieved breath.

"That was rather boldly said, Mother. Are you feeling quite the thing?" Oscar chuckled. "So, to what torture am I to be subjected today? The screech of violin or harp, the latest debutant wailing about her lost love? You know that lost love will be a lucky man, don't you?"

Estella smacked Oscar's knee with her fan. "You do go on with a lot of nonsense. I'd thought you had outgrown your impatient nature. You will sit and do your best to listen with polite interest. We are here for the orphanage, as you well know."

Oscar shifted in his chair. "No, Mother. I don't believe you mentioned that fascinating tidbit in your note."

Estella glanced up at her son's face and found it dark with . . . Well, she wasn't exactly sure what emotion he was feeling at that instant. But he definitely glanced toward the door as if to judge whether he could escape.

Surely the orphans couldn't be that bad.

"I'm told the children have been practicing with Miss Birkenstock for months. Why, I think they have positively blossomed under her greater influence. She has devoted many hours to their wellbeing in recent months and has a very good way with them. As a patron, you should be keen to see how your generous contribution has improved the children." Alarmed at the way her son's face had paled, Estella placed a comforting hand on his arm. "Oscar?"

Her loud tone turned a few heads in their direction and, after another long moment, his smile returned. "That sounds wonderful, Mother. I am glad the orphans have such good care."

The patter of many tiny feet drew Estella's attention to the stage. Six children stood upon the small, raised dais——the youngest and last orphan absent from their ranks being too young to do more than wail—nervously waiting to perform. She smiled her encouragement, but doubted the poor dears noticed. Their faces turned as one to a side curtained area where the scrape of wooden chair or stool could be heard.

As the audience settled, Estella cast a quick glance at her son. Although his face appeared impassive, as was most always the case, there was a tension, a new strain upon Oscar's features that hadn't existed until recently. Given his usual even-tempered disposition, she worried for him. Becoming engaged to an earl's daughter should have eased Oscar's concerns, but the improvement in his connections appeared to have produced a new gravity. Although he'd been the toast of society for an age, he didn't seem happy within himself anymore. Restlessness seemed to grip him, and Estella had found no way of discerning exactly what had altered.

Parties and dinners certainly hadn't cheered him.

Although discovering the start of his disquiet was important to her, the soft notes of a pianoforte swept over the room and the children began to sing. The orphans held the tune well. They pulled her into the sweetness of the song and the superior accompaniment kept her enthralled until the very last note. The audience clapped enthusiastically and the children sang two more songs.

During the third set, she glanced at Oscar, sure that he would be yawning his boredom. But he sat with his eyes closed, head dipping in time with the tune. She'd never seen him so absorbed in a concert. Indeed, judging by his lack of enthusiasm for past performances, Estella feared she'd be abandoned after the first note.

As the last words faded, he stood to clap for the children, causing others about them to do the same. Such a reaction was unprecedented for Oscar, but she rose to her feet and clapped for the giggling children.

As the orphans were ushered out of the room, Oscar's eyes followed them with an intensity she found disturbing. When they were gone, his animation died.

"I see you enjoyed the little performance."

Oscar led her to the buffet set along a side wall. "Yes, an altogether tolerable performance. I shouldn't mind hearing them again one day."

Tolerable performance! Whatever blue-devils plagued her son were not to be easily banished by a heart-warming melody. As she added chicken and little sandwiches to her plate, she wished he would confide in her. But no matter how she'd phrased her questions these past weeks, he'd avoided any kind of meaningful answer. He worried her. "Then I shall be sure to demand your escort again."

His lips twisted into a shallow smile. He turned to fetch her tea, led her to a little grouping of table and chairs, then left to fill a plate for himself.

"May I join you, Lady Carrington?"

Estella looked up and forced a smile to her lips. "Of course, Mr. Manning. Do please join my son and me. He will return momentarily."

With supple grace, Manning drew a chair out to her right and settled his teacup before him. From a seated position, Estella found Manning's greater height easier to bear. Age had peppered his pale hair with grey, but a boyish quality, a reminder of him as a youth, remained. Despite holding the position of Rector of St. George's he still cut a fine figure.

His long but damaged fingers, still gloved to protect feminine sensibilities from shock, fiddled with the teacup until she could stand the silence no longer. "Didn't the children acquit themselves well today? Such wonderful voices should definitely be heard more often."

Manning nodded, took a sip of his tea, and settled back in his chair, stretching his long legs before him as if he planned to stay awhile. "I'd rather hear your voice, but I've discovered to my considerable disappointment that you no longer perform."

Estella smothered a laugh. "Manning, it's been many years since I've had the desire to sing in society. There are so many younger, fresher voices to be heard nowadays."

A scowl crossed his face. "You only stopped when your husband disapproved of the adulation you received. He never could share your company."

Estella pressed her lips together. *Here we go.* Another round of veiled complaints aimed at the memory of a dead man. Her late husband hadn't been the most agreeable man in the end, but did Lynton Manning have to constantly bring up his flaws?

Manning touched the back of her hand with the tip of his leather-gloved finger briefly. "Still blindly loyal to his memory, I see."

Really, what did he expect her to say to that? No matter what had happened in the past, Estella was determined to never become a bitter woman as her years advanced. If she harbored ill feeling toward the man who'd stolen her youth, no one would ever know of it. She'd worked hard to forget her life with Charles Ryall. "Really, Mr. Manning, you sound very unlike a man who holds the position of Rector of St. George's. I had hoped your calling might have settled your prickly temperament, but it seems you are still given to flights of fancy."

Manning set his cup down with a clatter. He didn't speak immediately, but his silence spoke volumes. If five-and-twenty years hadn't passed since their last disagreement, she might have tried to appease him. "My memory is surprisingly clear about certain events. Should I remind you?"

Estella swallowed, shocked to the core that Manning would bring up his ridiculous assertion after all this time. Revisiting the past would change nothing.

"Ah, Mr. Manning. A pleasure to see you again, sir," Oscar said as he fell into a chair on Estella's left.

"Carrington." Manning met her son's gaze and she blanched at his intense scrutiny. She shouldn't care what her oldest acquaintance thought of her eldest offspring, but she was holding her breath. She forced herself to breathe normally again.

Oscar's lips lifted in amusement. "Is there a problem, Manning?"

Manning shook his head slowly. "No, nothing. It's just you . . ."

Estella laughed to distract the men. "Did you forget breakfast this morning, Oscar? I think you have enough there to feed a regular sized person for a week."

Oscar slanted a quick smile in her direction and promptly fell silent as he ate. When Manning discontinued their conversation too, the silence at the table grew uncomfortable again. Between bites, Estella was aware that her son's gaze flickered between her and the rector. If she had an explanation she cared to share, she might enlighten Oscar as to her estrangement from her oldest acquaintance. As it was, Oscar was better left in the dark about their tangled past.

Manning shifted in his chair, his leg rubbing against hers under the table. An unfortunate flush of heat swept her cheeks. Damn the man. Could he not leave her be?

Manning chuckled at her immediate reaction. "When you have a moment, Lord Carrington, I wonder if I might have a word with you," Manning asked with a quick glance in her direction. "In private, perhaps."

Oscar pressed a napkin to his mouth and then threw it over his unfinished plate. "Of course, I am at your immediate disposal."

Manning spared her a wry glance. "Forgive me, my lady, I hate to deprive you of your son's company, but if you can spare him this instant my business should only take a few minutes."

In an attempt to hide her irrational nerves, Estella nodded her head rather than question them. The men departed, leaving her with a sinking feeling. This could be very bad, indeed.

"Why the long face, my dear lady?" The seat to her right creaked as her lover unwittingly settled where his rival had sat moments before.

"I was just wishing the children were to sing another song, but they've all gone back to the orphanage haven't they, Thomas?"

Her gaze settled on the big man. She was determined to forget all about Lynton Manning. Thomas Birkenstock was kind, a generous man who made few demands on her time except for their infrequent rendezvous. She *should* be content.

Thomas rolled his eyes. "Agatha took them back immediately after the performance. She's got a bee in her bonnet over the sick, little one and cannot abide being apart from the babe."

Estella smiled and patted his hand quickly. "Her compassion does her credit. The children are getting along so much better with her influence."

"Perhaps her playing will have affected some unattached gentleman here today," he grumbled. "Her performance on the pianoforte was exceptional, but I do not like that she refused to linger and take advantage of it."

"Was that Agatha, today? She certainly plays beautifully. Oscar appeared enthralled with the performance. Perhaps the other gentlemen noticed too."

"My granddaughter should be thinking of her own children by now, but the stubborn minx is dead-set against the idea of marriage. I fear she always has been and hid her discontent behind polite smiles. I might have to resort to a matchmaker to see her wed securely." Under the table, Thomas knocked her knee with his.

Although Thomas mimicked Lynton Manning's earlier gesture, Estella's body didn't respond the same. Her cheeks remained stubbornly cool, her heartbeat at a regular plodding pace. She swallowed at the discovery. Why didn't she react more to Thomas?

Estella forced a smile to her lips. "Surely the situation is not as bad as all that." She sighed and set her chin in her hand. "I'm sure all that's required is for the right man to sweep her off her feet. Agatha is a very pretty young lady. I'm constantly surprised that some clever gentleman hasn't recognized her worth and married her already."

A hand pressed hard to her shoulder and she looked up to find her son hovering. His expression appeared pained.

Estella stood. "Is everything all right, son?"

His lips twisted into a grimace. "Everything is fine, but I appear to be very popular today. Several members of the orphanage's board of trustees wish to speak with me as a matter of some urgency. Do you mind if I leave you in Mr. Manning's care for the afternoon?"

Estella frowned, wondering at the trustee's agitation. Yet her unease at being left in Manning's company stirred too. She didn't want to be anywhere near him. "Mr. Birkenstock is entertaining me, Oscar. I do not need to be coddled."

"Nevertheless, I have asked Manning to escort you home in my place if I do not return within the next half hour. We were coming to inform you, but I think Manning was delayed by Mrs. Whittaker."

Estelle glanced around her son and found Manning indeed trapped by the notoriously chatty lady. Poor man, but still, she wouldn't be going to rescue him. "I hardly need an escort, Oscar. I'm sure you will be free again in due time."

Oscar raked his fingers through his pale hair, disturbing his usually neat appearance. "Would if that were true, but I am promised to take Lady Penelope driving in the park this evening." He pulled out his pocket watch and checked the time. "As it is, I may be inexcusably tardy in my arrival. It would help me a great deal if you let Manning escort you home."

Damn her son's need to keep everyone happy. As a child, she'd liked the trait. However, as an adult his constant need for approval drove her to distraction. Not everyone needed to be pleased. "Of course." But inside, Estella dreaded the drive.

It didn't take long for Manning to grasp her arm after Thomas took his leave. He whisked her out the door quickly. As she approached his gleaming coach, she tried not to appear concerned to be all alone with her former beau. However, the lingering hand that pressed against the small of her back as she entered the carriage proved just how interested Manning was in improving their acquaintance. A flush of heat swept her cheeks again and she dipped her head to hide the reaction.

Determined to quell the impulse to bolt from the carriage, Estella drew in a deep breath to calm herself. "Do you know what the trustees wish to speak to my son about? It is not like them to involve him in their petty squabbles." There, she could be civil with Manning and forget all about those distressing reactions.

Manning pursed his lips, as if considering whether to share his thoughts. The board members frequently failed to share most reasons for their decisions with her. Indeed, it was a lucky coincidence that anything happened there at all. She'd never met a group of men who bickered as much as they did. Estella held her breath, hoping Manning would trust her enough to share this confidence and tried not to think overmuch about those pursed lips, or past kisses bestowed from them.

"The board wishes for an evaluation of the orphanage to be conducted, but they do not want to bring in an outsider. Since your son's involvement has been minimal to date, they have agreed that he shall be judge and jury for its continuation."

Shock held her mouth open. Of all the hair-brained, foolish decisions. Having Oscar decide the fate of seven children seemed ludicrous. "He barely knows the place," she whispered.

Manning removed his leather gloves and flexed his fingers in a way that drew her attention. The ugly scar on his left hand and the missing little finger, an ever present reminder of times past, caused Estella's heart to race with renewed anxiety.

He clenched his damaged hand into a fist. "Exactly. He'll not be swayed by allegiances within the board. They expect him to make a fair decision."

Estella dropped her face to her hand. This was simply dreadful. The poor children. To be judged in such a manner, without any attempt to understand them or their needs. And Oscar's habit of trying to please everyone would fail him this time. She was sure someone would be disappointed with his decision.

The carriage dipped as Manning squeezed onto the bench seat beside her. Alarmed, she slid to the side to put distance between them again.

"You should not fret so, Essy. I'm sure your boy will do a fair job of it."

Despite the use of his old nickname for her, his smile chilled her to her core. "This was your doing. All of it."

He waggled his undamaged hand. "You have no idea of the pain listening to those pea brains causes me. An evaluation will finally put the matter to rest and then we can move forward. I have every confidence that Carrington will vote in favor of continuation. But no one need know that but us."

He reached for her hand, but she clenched them together and denied him a chance for improper behavior. His frown grew. "What are you about, Essy?"

"I am about nothing, Mr. Manning. You, however, are again attempting to overstep your bounds. Kindly return to the other side of the carriage."

Manning huffed but did as she asked. His eyes, however, held deep scorn. "You know I hadn't wanted to believe the whispers, but it appears they could, indeed, be true. Do you know they say you've taken that cit, Birkenstock, as your lover?"

Manning quirked one brow as he waited for her to deny it. While the rumor was true, she'd hardly confess her most personal affairs to a man of the cloth. Especially since that man also aimed to take her lover's place, most likely after a respectable wedding ceremony had been performed. Estella had no intentions of marrying again. She pasted a fraudulent smile to her lips. "What amazes me is that the *ton* haven't learned of your wicked past and shunned you for it."

He lifted his damaged hand in the air before her and waggled it. "I imagine that would relieve you, as anything questionable in my past almost certainly involved you."

How typical of a man, even a man of the cloth, to lay the blame for wickedness on a woman. She'd had nothing to do with the loss of his finger. She hadn't known of the duel that caused its loss until years later. To this day, it amazed her that he'd become a vicar. Given what she knew of his past, he was far too lusty a man for the role. How could he stand before a congregation and extol the virtues of thrift, compassion, and avoidance of sin, when he was so well versed in them? "Please. Spare me your lies."

The carriage drew to a halt before Manning could speak. When the door opened, he jumped to the pavement then held his damaged hand out. With no further wish to argue, Estella slid her palm over his lightly and then stepped from the carriage with relief. Manning tucked her arm tightly about his, led her up the stairs, and ushered her into her drawing room before she had time to object to his cavalier attitude.

The closing door sounded loud in the empty space. Manning crowded her against the wood, ducked his head, and pressed their lips together. At first, Estella pushed against him. But when his tongue slid along the seam of her compressed lips, she gasped, and he claimed her mouth in a way she'd forgotten. Fierce and total possession.

No one would believe a vicar could be a danger to a woman's virtue. Yet her reaction to Lynton Manning's actions proved otherwise. His kiss thrilled her. She touched his tongue with her own, and her body hummed. Lynton devoured her, eating at her mouth until she lifted her arms and threaded her fingers in his hair. He moaned as she clutched his skull, tangling her tongue with his until her body sang with pleasure.

She needed so much more.

Although any other man would have groped at her body, Lynton held himself apart, offering only the soul-numbing precision of his lips. She wanted hands and the press of a hard body against hers.

Estella arched off the door, but instead of embracing her, Lynton drew away. "No lies, Essy. The duel was over you, and I lost you, and part of my hand, due to that conniving bastard arranging a distraction that almost killed me." He pressed a quick kiss to her cheek, then the door handle rattled as he prepared to leave. "By the time the pain had diminished enough to regain my senses and venture out again, you were wed and gone. I never took up with an actress, as Carrington claimed. I was strapped to my bed while my hand healed. I wish my brother had told you the truth, but gentlemen never speak of duels of honor. I've been waiting nearly twenty-five years for you, and I believe it's past time I got my reward for patience. I'll prove my worth this time. This time you'll choose me."

Manning stormed out and slammed the door behind him.

She was glad he was gone, because she didn't know how to react to his version of events from the past. Estella wished she could remember the past more clearly. He'd left without word, and Charles Ryall had amused her and taken her mind from the disappointment. It had seemed the right thing to do to accept Carrington. He'd been a viscount, where Manning was only a second son. She shook her head. The past, and Carrington, was gone. She had greater problems to deal with.

The enormity of Estella's faithlessness to Thomas rose up to choke her. She stumbled into a chair. What had come over her? Estella dropped her head into her hand and pressed her temples hard. The pious and upright rector portrayed to London society was as much a devil as he'd been in his youth. How could he think to kiss a woman engaged in an affair with another man? Although she'd not confirmed his accusations, he'd have to suspect. Why would he want her after all this time? She had to be sure that kiss, and any others like it, could never happen again. She would not become a slave to lust. Not again.

Six

AS OSCAR'S CARRIAGE slowed before the steps of his future wife's home, he vaulted from the conveyance without waiting for his footman and hurried up the stairs. Although he'd rushed his agreement to assess the orphanage, he'd still ended up ten minutes late to take Lady Penelope driving in the park. He hated to be disobliging, especially to his future wife.

He refused the butler his hat and cane. He would only be staying a moment, after all. There was really no point in handing them off if he intended to hurry out again for the park. The butler led him to an empty drawing room to wait and pulled the doors shut behind him as he left, leaving Oscar alone with his rising trepidation.

Not knowing how his intended might react to his tardy arrival, he tugged on his sleeves, and took a stance close to the fire. The drawing room about him was opulently furnished, elegantly arranged, and a showcase of the Thorpe family's wealth. Penelope's mother had died some years past, and he wondered if the room about him was a product of Lady Penelope's taste or that of her married sister, Lady Prewitt, who still resided under her father's roof. If his intended had been instrumental in the decoration then Oscar could at least be assured of a comfortable home.

Lady Penelope swept into the room on her brother-in-law's arm. Although her polite smile, the only type she graced him with, should have comforted him, it didn't. Her dark brows neither rose in accusation nor in delight. Her face was a blank mask that concealed her emotions. As far as Oscar could tell, Penelope didn't appear to care one way or another about his late arrival.

Her brother-in-law, Lord Prewitt, however, scowled. "Thought you'd forgotten, Carrington."

Oscar accepted the rebuke. Clearly, he was in the wrong, but it was not to his future family that he would apologize. He wasn't here to see them at all. "I do owe your sister-in-law my apologies. Forgive me, Lady Penelope. Lords Carter and Brooke wanted to discuss the business of the Grafton Street Orphanage. I had the devil of a time getting away from them. And then, of course, their daughters interrupted and had to be acknowledged. They are such a lively pair."

Although Oscar's answer appeared to appease Prewitt, his betrothed's reaction startled him. She peeked at him from under her lashes and her lips stretched into a warm, flirtatious smile. "You are too good to indulge those pair. They'll never find a husband with their chatter."

Drawn by the warm smile, Oscar took a pace toward her. "They are harmless flirts. No harm in that."

"Perhaps we should sit, sister," Lord Prewitt growled suddenly.

Lady Penelope jumped and settled on the lounge. "Do sit down, my lord." She gestured to a chair opposite while Prewitt chose to sit at her side.

Oscar frowned but took his place, frustrated that the brief moment of warmth from Lady Penelope had been crushed by her brother-in-law. Perhaps there was a chance for them.

Penelope fussed with her skirts, keeping her gaze lowered. "Did you spend any time with the orphans, my lord?"

"No, not really. They performed on a little stage, a vastly entertaining concert for the patrons and such, and then returned to the orphanage. I'm surprised not to have seen you there. I was led to believe my mother sent you an invitation to join her and that you had initially accepted. She would love to further your acquaintance with family friends."

Penelope's glance slid to her brother.

Lord Prewitt cleared his throat. "A family matter prevented our attendance this morning. My wife would offer her apologies if she were well enough to join us."

Given that Lady Prewitt was often ill, Oscar was inclined to believe him. And yet, why would Penelope defer to him instead of answering herself. Was she not allowed to speak of her sister without permission?

Oscar shifted forward in his chair. "Lady Prewitt is very lucky to have you, Lady Penelope. Do send my best wishes for a speedy recovery."

Penelope nodded, but her fingers twisted in her lap. "I will."

They lapsed into an uncomfortable silence, but neither made any attempt to fill the gap. The sensation of intruding surfaced, but he shook it aside. He was determined to get to know his intended a little better before they were actually wed. He tapped his hat against his knee. "I hope you're still looking forward to our outing this afternoon. My greys and carriage stand ready to depart for our afternoon in the park."

Hyde Park was the place to be seen, especially for any newly engaged couple whose union had delighted the *ton*. He'd received more congratulations just that morning—discreetly suggesting he'd made a wise choice. But no one came right out to say he'd stalked an alliance with the earl's daughter for the connection.

Lady Penelope glanced at Prewitt again. When he nodded, she rose to her feet. "Yes, of course we should go. Please excuse me for a moment."

As Lady Penelope swept from the room, Oscar tried hard to find something in the sway of her gown to enjoy as she left. Unfortunately, he found nothing. His future bride didn't stir his senses in the least, not the way Agatha Birkenstock did.

Oscar pushed away the image of Agatha forming in his mind. Wallowing in the memory of the physical joy they shared in each other's presence was hardly appropriate to the situation. He had to put those kinds of desires firmly in the past or else he'd run mad and spend the rest of his life in misery.

Resolve reaffirmed, his glance flickered to Lady Penelope's brother by marriage. Prewitt had followed her departure too and now stood at the front windows, brooding on the view. His arm gestured to the world outside the window. "I see you've brought the closed carriage again."

Oscar joined him and peered up at the darkening sky through the glass. "It seemed a wise decision, given the threat in those hovering clouds. I did not wish for Lady Penelope to suffer unduly if the elements proved disagreeable."

"Yes, that could be one explanation."

Oscar heard his implication—that he'd planned on the closed carriage's seclusion to take liberties with his future wife, as he was supposed to have done on the night they became engaged. But he had indeed only been thinking of her comfort. "Before her marriage, my sister always complained about gentlemen who didn't think ahead to consider the weather. She once came home soaked to the skin and had to lie abed for almost two weeks. The moaning drove us all mad. Are you acquainted with my sister?"

"No. I do not believe I've met her. Excuse me—I'll see what's keeping Penelope." Prewitt spun on his heel and left the room.

Prickly chap. No matter how hard Oscar tried, his future brother-in-law was not inclined to drop his reserve. Perhaps the move away from Town would be for the good. He wouldn't have to deal with disapproving scowls too often if they could reside more than a day's ride from London.

Cheered by that thought, Oscar would find out if Lady Penelope preferred the country or the coast. And really, he should begin to think of her as simply Penelope to help both of them grow more comfortable with each other.

When she swept down the main staircase resplendent in a high-collared, skirted pelisse, matching hat, and leather gloves, Oscar waited for his heart to leap in anticipation. The dark blue really suited her complexion and the high flush to her cheeks indicated she'd hurried for him. But his heart stayed stubbornly dormant. He offered what he hoped was a smitten expression as she joined him.

Penelope stared at him. "Lord Prewitt stepped in to speak with his wife before he took his leave."

Bully for him. Oscar could care less about Prewitt's whereabouts. Pleased that he had Penelope alone for a moment, Oscar drew closer. "Are you fond of the country, Penelope?"

Penelope's bland expression faltered, her lips turned down. "I don't like it at all."

"Ah, so you're fond of the coast." Oscar smiled. "So much activity in the ports to take in, don't you think? I'm partial to Portsmouth and Bristol myself." A little estate by the seaside was within his means, even without Penelope's dowry. They could be quite comfortable there, and still partake of short visits to London during the season.

"You misunderstand me, my lord. I care only for London."

The happy fantasy Oscar had conjured of life by the wild sea coast frayed before his eyes. Living only in London would be impossible.

Penelope glanced behind her.

Lord Prewitt hurried down the stairs, pulling his gloves swiftly into place. Oscar saw no sign of a maid for chaperone. "Ready when you are, Carrington."

Well, so much for quiet conversation with just a servant hovering. The brother-in-law followed Penelope everywhere, and that habit was getting on Oscar's nerves. That would stop once he and Penelope married. Prewitt could keep to his own wife's bedside.

Annoyed, Oscar decided to please himself about his future residence. He preferred the country. He preferred living closer to friends, so he would find a property either in Warwickshire or Northhamptonshire.

Penelope drew closer to her brother by marriage and took his outstretched arm. Oscar allowed them to precede him from the house and out to the street. His coachman sprang into action, dropped the steps, and held the door open as swiftly as he could.

It was Prewitt who handed Penelope into the carriage. Prewitt sat beside her, too. To Oscar's recollection, he'd only touched his betrothed a few fleeting times. Yet Prewitt always seemed to be touching her.

As they made their way to the park, he tried to engage Penelope in conversation. Although her responses were polite, there was little in her answers to encourage further discourse. Oscar tipped his hat to the occupants of a passing carriage as he ground his teeth. Her reserve rankled.

He was not by nature a man given to jealousy or anger, but couldn't help but speculate again on which previous suitor had mussed up her skirts, trapping him into this miserable misalliance. The thought of his stupidity turned his stomach. Just how far had she been swept away by her suitor? Like Agatha, she appeared to be free of some man's bastard. Although some women hid their condition extremely well. He would keep a better eye on her and the gentlemen paying her attention. He'd certainly not like to find himself raising another man's child as his own.

Another carriage drew up beside his, and when he focused on the occupants, his heart skipped a beat. Then pounded. Mr. Birkenstock was taking the air of the park with his granddaughter at his side. Agatha looked breathtaking in pale lemon muslin that flattered the smooth creaminess of her skin to perfection. His mouth watered, and his hands itched to leap carriages and take her into his arms for all to see. Agatha's lips stretched into a strained smile, and then they pulled ahead and out of sight. Disappointed that she was taken from him so soon, Oscar glumly returned his attention to his companions. Lord Prewitt watched him, one brow raised in amusement.

Penelope suddenly leaned against her brother-in-law's shoulder. "I see Mrs. Leyton, Prewie. May we stop?"

Prewitt smiled at Penelope, his gaze filled with so much warm affection that Oscar grew discomforted. "Of course. Carrington, stop the carriage. My sister sees a very good friend of ours."

Not on his life.

Oscar folded his arms across his chest. "Mrs. Leyton has a somewhat questionable reputation in society. I'm uncertain Penelope's father would wish me to further his daughter's acquaintance with such a woman without knowing his feelings on the matter. I wish to spend the afternoon with my betrothed, not create a scandal. You may see Mrs. Leyton on your own time."

Prewitt leaned forward toward Oscar, but Penelope caught his arm and rubbed it in what appeared to be a soothing manner. Oscar stared at the intimate gesture. Prewitt shook off Penelope's grip. "Mrs. Leyton is a close friend. You would do well not to interfere."

Surprised by Lord Prewitt's presumption to control their afternoon, Oscar tapped on his groom's shoulder with his cane. "The outing is over. Return to Brook Street," he called.

Damned if he'd have Prewitt manage his social acquaintances. He'd hold his ground on his view of Mrs. Leyton. A woman like that could do irreparable harm to Penelope's reputation, and Oscar would rather avoid any further blemishes on their marriage.

Yes, a house in the country would be essential. He'd send out inquiries today.

Seven

THE MAN ACROSS the room snorted, napping with his feet perched on the table edge, head lolling to the side. The sound covered the ominous creak of the floorboards beneath Oscar's feet as he moved further into the room. The shabby, untidy sprawl of the office conflicted with the neatness of the slumbering factor. There were papers strewn everywhere, books lying in untidy piles on the floor. Such disarray was simply unacceptable, and tidying this room would be the first task Oscar insisted upon.

Mr. Dickson of the Grafton Street Orphanage was supposed to be waiting for him. But Oscar was not so tardy that the factor should have wearied of the wait and fallen asleep. Perhaps it was foolish that he'd let the other trustees run the place up till now. He'd thought they knew what they were doing. He doubted they knew of Mr. Dickson's habit of sleeping his day away though.

Oscar cleared his throat, and the man before him bounced to his feet.

"Lord Carrington, I presume."

Oscar bobbed his head sharply rather than voice his displeasure.

"Please, won't you take a seat?"

He settled into a chair, wincing when it creaked as ominously as the floor. "I understood that you would have everything ready for me. Do you require more time?"

The factor blinked rapidly. "Everything about the running of the orphanage is within this room. What else do you require?"

How about a system of neatness? Of order for the accounts? Oscar pinched the bridge of his nose and expelled a frustrated breath. "I've been asked to review the accounts. I was assured everything was in order for my examination. This—" he swept his hand in an arc over the untidy heaps— "is not what I expected to see. I shall be here for weeks."

Dickson straightened a letter on his desk. "The board never quibbled about how I ran the place before."

"Well perhaps it's time they did."

Dickson rocked back in his chair as if Oscar had struck him, but Oscar had no time to settle the man's feathers. The quicker he could get this done and return home, the better. He did not want to bump into Agatha here. He'd promised her that he would keep a distance between them, both publicly and privately. The chances of running into her were very great indeed, given his mother's hints on how much time she spent at the orphanage these days.

"I'd like the ledger for this month's accounts, if you please. And if you could arrange a cup of tea, I would be most appreciative. I fear I shall be here for some time."

The factor blinked, then shoved his hand into the upper draw, retrieved a battered ledger, and then thrust it in his direction. "I'll go organize the tea, my lord."

The man hurried out.

When Oscar opened the ledger, he was pleasantly surprised to see the disorder only extended so far. The ledger was neat. Meticulous, in fact. A welcome relief, indeed, after the shock of his initial impression.

Pleased with this new development, Oscar stood, circled the desk, and sat himself in Dickson's place as he began his calculations. The quicker he started, the quicker he could be done and gone.

Sometime later, a giggle sounded at the door, but when he glanced up he couldn't see anyone about. Oscar drew out his pocket watch to check the time. He'd been here two hours and had yet to receive that requested cup of tea, or glimpse Mr. Dickson again. Annoyed and thirsty, he marked his place in the ledger with a scrap of parchment then stood, intent on finding the absent factor.

As he stretched his back, someone giggled nearby within the room he occupied. Curious, he looked about. But wherever the sound came from was a mystery. Perhaps the sound came from the floor above, not in the room with him.

Shrugging off the distraction, he took a step toward the door, but the sight of grey fabric disappearing under the desk caught his attention. Oscar crouched low.

A pair of solemn eyes peered at him from beneath the desk. The child was tiny. A drab, little girl whose eyes widened with surprise at being discovered.

Not wishing to frighten her, Oscar smiled before he held out his hand. "How do you do there, miss? Do you like it very much there beneath the table?"

"No one would think to find me here, would they?" she whispered so low that Oscar strained forward to hear.

"I'm afraid they could if they listened very hard. You seem to be in the habit of giggling. The others will hear that if they are searching."

Her hands clapped over her mouth. "So that's how they always find me so quickly," she mumbled. "Not one of them said a word."

Amused, Oscar chuckled and lifted his hand again. "I suspect they don't mention it so they might be assured of the win. Here, you must consider yourself found. Come out now. Let me take a look at you."

Obediently, the child crawled out, and then to his utter surprise she threw herself into his arms. "Are you my Papa? Have you come to take me home?"

Startled, Oscar set the girl from him and held up one hand. "No, child, I am not your father. I am Lord Carrington."

The girl's face fell at the news. "You don't look like a lord."

"What does a lord look like?"

The little girl scrunched up her face as she considered her answer. "A stuffy, overdressed turnip."

Oscar stood to his full height, displeased by her words. The little girl scurried back under the desk. After everything the charitable society had done to improve their lives, the expense and effort to take in orphans who'd been deserted by their parents, he was appalled that one so young could speak ill of the trustees. He dragged her out again and held her in place before him.

The little girl shook like a leaf and Oscar instantly calmed. Perhaps the child knew no better than to speak to him in that way, but she needed to be corrected. And now, before she blurted out those words to someone without his patience.

He sat in the rickety chair so he did not tower above her. "You must not say such things again." The little girl bobbed her head quickly in agreement, eyes glassy bright as tears threatened to spill. "What is your name?"

"It's Mabel."

"Well then, Mabel, I think you should not utter those words again. You should not say such mean things to another soul."

"But I heard someone else say them. Someone of the quality. I do want to be a lady when I grow up." Mabel bit her lip as a single tear flowed down her cheek.

Oscar felt like an utter monster. "I'm sure you will, but those are not the words a lady would speak."

"Is Lady Carrington not a lady? Everyone said she was. She said those things about Lord Carter." Mabel leaned close to his ear. "He pinches."

His mother! Heaven help him. "Then stay far away from Lord Carter, but what my mother said was wrong and I shall have a few words to her about it, too. Now, off you go before you are missed. And don't let me hear you talk like that again about your betters."

"Yes, sir." Mabel skipped toward the door, but stopped at the threshold and scowled at him. "You won't beat her too badly, will you, my lord? I couldn't sleep a wink if I got Lady Carrington into too much trouble. She's too nice to be unhappy."

"No! No, of course I won't beat her." Oscar rubbed his brow. Since he rarely spoke to children, he found the way this particular one spoke rather disconcerting. "Run along now, Mabel."

The little girl hurried back to him, pressed a kiss to his cheek, and then scurried from the room. Oscar shook his head. What a peculiar little creature.

With the girl gone from sight, Oscar rang the bell. After a lengthy delay, a maid eventually joined him. "Can I help you, my lord?"

"Yes, I'd like a tea tray brought up and Mr. Dickson reminded that I am impatient for his return. Whatever else he is doing can wait."

The maid bobbed a curtsey and then hurried away. While Oscar waited, he inspected the room. From what he'd seen so far, the property was in dire need of maintenance. The paper on the walls of this room needed repair or replacement, and the entrance hall had been decidedly shabby, too.

Drawing out a little journal from his pocket, he scratched down the details of the repairs required for this room. These matters should be noted to the trustees in his report. He would have to have Mr. Dickson give him a full tour of the place so he did a thorough job of it.

The maid returned with the tray. China rattled as she set it down awkwardly over the messy table surface. "Excuse me, my lord, but I've not been able to locate Mr. Dickson."

"Then look again. I'm not inclined to wait around all day for an employee."

The maid bobbed another curtsey before hurrying off.

Really, how hard could it be to locate one man in a building housing small children? He grimaced as he poured a cup of pale tea, obviously reused many times, and then settled in to wait.

He'd just finished his second cup when the butler hurried into the room. "Forgive me, my lord. I've only just heard that you were looking for Mr. Dickson. I am afraid he went out not long after your arrival."

"Went out? But the man knew I was waiting for him."

"I'm sorry, my lord. But he did not say when he would return." The butler stood rigidly in place, obviously unable to explain more about Dickson's sudden leave-taking.

"I will have to make do without. Do let me know immediately when he returns."

"Of course."

The butler disappeared, leaving Oscar alone with the disaster. Where in God's name to start? He had the ledger, but those papers really needed to be filed away properly. He grabbed a pile to shuffle them into date order, but one order stood out. Three barrels of rum. What in world did an orphanage need that much rum for? Or any at all.

Come to think of it, where had the entry for that purchase gone to? It wasn't in the ledger that he could recall.

Oscar skirted the desk and flipped the pages in the ledger. March fifth—nothing. He set the bill of sale down and glanced at the next. May twenty-first—fifteen yards of muslin. But no corresponding ledger entry. What madness was this?

When the ledger didn't match the purchases of five more items, Oscar grew angry. The place had been swindled of more than a few pennies. No wonder the trustees wanted the place held to account for its spending. Was that the reason for Mr. Dickson's unexplained departure?

The only way to be certain of what had transpired here was to find every scrap of paper Oscar could and reconstruct the whole damned ledger. It would take him an age. Much longer than he could hope to hide his activities from Agatha Birkenstock. What would she say if she found out her precious orphanage was under threat of closure?

~ * ~

So this was the tall lord who made little Mabel cry, was it? Agatha gritted her teeth and moved into the small cluttered office. "Just what do you think you're doing with those papers, Lord Carrington?"

Oscar heaved a dramatic sigh and dropped the papers to the desk. When he raked his fingers through his hair too, Agatha grew impatient. Damn him for his floundering. She wanted an honest answer, not a carefully worded lie. "I am waiting, my lord."

"I am sorting through the mess."

"That is Mr. Dickson's chore, if he should ever lower himself to straighten the place. What I don't understand is why you are here frightening the children."

"Do you mean the little girl, Mabel?"

Agatha set her reticule on the table. "Yes, I mean Mabel. She's just spent the last ten minutes confessing that you frightened her witless."

"Little girls are known to exaggerate. I caught her fair and square, hiding beneath the desk here." Oscar flashed his charming smile at her, but she was having none of his sly manipulations today, or any day from now on.

Agatha skirted the desk. "Then what are you doing snooping through the orphanage's papers?"

Standing this close to Oscar was perhaps a mistake. She could see how tired he was. The dark smudges beneath eyes that usually held laughter distracted her for a moment. She doubted their parting had affected him this much, and she wanted to know what was wrong with him. What had taken away his sparkle, his merriment in life? His appearance tugged at her heart in a way that couldn't be allowed.

"I have been asked by my fellow trustees to assess the orphanage. To see whether the place has a viable future."

His response took her breath away. She sagged, dropping her hand to the stacked desk to hold herself upright. This could not be. Why had she not heard a whisper about this before? Or from her grandfather, for that matter. He was a trustee too.

When Oscar settled a hand to her shoulder she pulled away. She could not let him get close again. Her heart couldn't take much more anguish. "And what are your findings?"

"Give me time, Agatha. I have only just begun, and given the state of this room I shall be here for some duration. I am very sorry, Agatha. You may have to see me everyday."

"Everyday." No, that was not to be borne. To see him so often would be a painful, unending torment. When he cast her an apologetic smile, Agatha snatched up her reticule, and hurried for the door. She'd been on the point of leaving when she'd spied Oscar, so she gave him no chance to speak again. The door slammed closed behind her and she rushed for home.

At home she could scream her frustration where no one could hear. At home she could throw something to rid herself of her need to throttle Oscar.

How could he invade her world? Her orphanage. Damn him—must he take every dream away from her?

In the square, she barely missed colliding with a gleaming curricle. At the last possible moment, a stranger caught her arm and prevented her from barreling straight into the side of a passing conveyance. She thanked whoever it was then glanced up at the occupants.

Of course. Oscar's future bride barely glanced her way as she concentrated on tooling down the street, but her brother-in-law, Lord Prewitt, looked her way, eyes widening with surprise. Agatha rocked back on her heels and dragged in a deep breath.

She'd not let her discomposure over Oscar take her life from her too. Damn him. Damn him to hell and back.

With more care for her surroundings, Agatha crossed the roads and park without further incident. She reached her house and the upper corridor with a semblance of decorum, secure in the knowledge that her grandfather was from home. But the minute her bedchamber door closed and she was assured of privacy, she screamed. Loud.

"Really, that was hardly ladylike."

Eight

AGATHA LOOKED UP as Oscar darted into her room through the open window. Despite his flushed appearance and the possibility he'd hurried home to speak with her again, she couldn't bear to have him here. "Get. Out."

"No. I'll not leave you when you're this angry. You could do yourself harm."

"The only person that stands to be harmed is you, Oscar. Get out of my room. Get out of my life."

Instead of complying, Oscar drew closer. "I don't want to leave you when you're angry with me."

"Angry with you? Why on earth would I be that?" She set her hands to her hips and glared at him. "You've had your fun with me, convinced me to let you under my skirts, all the while courting an earl's daughter. Congratulations. Now you can hold your head up in society around the bucks and bloods you envy. But you've invaded the one place I have left."

Agatha choked on a sob. She curled her hands into fists and pressed them against her belly. All her plans were in ruins. All her dreams in tatters. If she lost the orphanage...

"That's ridiculous, Agatha. You have your whole life ahead of you. One day you'll marry too and have children, your own children, to nurture. The orphans are simply a passing fancy."

Agatha swung her hand at him in anger, but he caught it and held her tight. "How big a fool are you, Oscar? I'm soiled goods. What manner of man should I foist myself upon? I won't be your mistress. I won't ever marry. You ruined me."

He swallowed, and the movement of his throat beneath his cravat distracted her. "You ruined me, too." He caught up her other hand and pulled her into his arms. "Of course, you'll marry. But don't think I'll care for the notion."

As she stared into his familiar face, fighting against the gentle pull that would settle her deeper into his arms, she grieved anew for the loss of her perfect future. This would be the last time they touched. It had to be.

"You should leave."

Oscar drew her wrist to his lips and pressed a kiss to the delicate skin. Agatha shuddered as desire skittered along her arm. His lips hovered above her flesh, and his next breath across the damp skin forced a whimper from her lips.

"I know."

His gripped loosened and she pressed her hand to his shoulder, but he tugged her hips closer until she could feel the heat of him. With his breath hot against her neck, Agatha gripped his broad shoulder to keep from falling against him. Moments were all it took to lead them astray. Brief moments of touch dissolved the world around them until all that mattered was each other.

Agatha captured Oscar's gaze. His eyes were wide and filled with longing, his breath a rapid pant across her skin. On impulse she kissed him, kissed him as she'd longed to do since their eyes had met across her bedchamber.

Oscar dragged her against him. He shuffled them across the room then tumbled them onto her bed. The rapid, burning pain of denial eased into a heady gentleness of sweet caresses. Agatha slid her fingertips across his scalp, loving the feel of his curled locks between her fingers.

On a groan, Oscar turned them until she lay on her back while he hovered above. Breath churning, they gazed at each other, neither willing to break the silence with words. Agatha reached for his cravat pin and gently tugged it free. She untied his cravat, let the fabric slide from his neck slowly, as his eyes closed. He was rigid with tension; the arms that caged her trembled.

With a few flicks of her fingers, his waistcoat buttons were open then his shirt. As she touched her fingers to the smooth expanse of his chest uncovered by her exploration, he gasped her name and trembled anew. With slow, determined tugs she pulled his shirt free of his trousers.

His arms failed and the heat of his body engulfed her. Agatha parted her legs to accommodate him. Snug and tightly pressed together, they kissed again. Deep consuming kisses which silenced the voices that shrieked for caution, demanding restraint. She'd never managed to deny how much she had desired Oscar in the past, so she didn't try to fight it now.

Oscar's skin burned her fingertips. She palmed the hard curve of his lower waist, digging into the deceptive strength of him, letting her eyes close and hide reality. Oscar nibbled at her neck. He planted soft kisses down the column of her throat and across her chest. His tongue flicked into her cleavage and she arched upward to his mouth, wanting more of his special torment, more of his pleasure.

He groaned and kissed her breast over the fabric then his hot, open mouth found her nipple and he suckled, gown and all. Agatha groaned and threaded her fingers into his hair, keeping him close where she liked him.

With her other hand, she found the buttons of his trousers and worked them free. Oscar lifted his hips so she could slide her hand beneath the restricting fabric. His hot breath hissed against her skin through the gown then he was kissing her, showing her beyond words how much he desired her.

Agatha slid her fingers around his length and gently stroked him. He flexed his hips, sliding his cock slowly across her palm, settling into a steady rhythm. Oscar settled his weight on one arm then played havoc with her senses with his free hand. Roughly, her gown was yanked from her shoulder, exposing her breasts to the air. His fingers plucked at her nipple, twisting the peak until she was gasping for breath.

Agatha opened her eyes to find Oscar watching her body, his face free of whatever doubts had plagued him earlier. Lips replaced fingers at her breast, but he wasn't finished with his torture. Cool air caressed her legs as Oscar raised her skirts higher and higher.

When his warm hand touched her thigh, she closed her eyes again, knowing that Oscar's special brand of torment was just beginning. She wanted him so badly that her whole body shook. Oscar would take his time toward the ultimate pleasure. He wouldn't rush to finish.

He grazed her inner thigh with his fingertips. The light touch tickled, so she bent one leg and opened to him.

Oscar chuckled. "So impatient, precious."

"Do you blame me?"

He kissed her again, gently, but the pads of his fingers moved closer to where she wanted them at a snail's pace. In frustration, Agatha pushed her tongue into his mouth with more insistence than usual, holding his head close to hers so he could not control everything.

Finally, his fingers touched her curls. Agatha flexed her hips into his hand, desperate for more. Now. He parted her lower lips, pressing into her body, sliding across her slick entrance.

Agatha tightened her grip on his length, moving her hand against the rhythm of his flexing hips. When he gasped, shuddering away from her touch, Agatha chuckled. Poor Oscar, he'd taught her his desires far too well. She knew every little devious trick to bring him pleasure too.

But the thought of never touching him again trickled into the back of her mind. She'd never experience a moment like his again. She didn't want anyone else. Agatha buried her head to his shoulder to hide her sadness from him.

"You don't want this, do you?" Oscar asked as he dropped his head to her chest, his breath a fast pant across her damp skin.

"Don't leave me like this, Oscar. I'll run mad."

His lips pressed against her skin. "Then I'd run mad with you."

Oscar shifted out of her grip. He hovered above, but then slowly fitted himself at her entrance. Agatha wriggled to make room for him and then he was sliding inside. The slow joining took her breath away.

When he was settled deep, she met his gaze. Grey eyes had brightened to an intense silver, holding her fascinated as he moved within her. Agatha captured his rear with one hand, his nipple with her other fingers, and squeezed. His slow coupling faltered, but soon resumed the steady possession.

She hitched her legs high around his waist, opening her body to him fully, tilting her hips at a better angle. A sweet flush of pleasure swept over her skin.

"That's it. Bring me deeper into you."

Agatha met his gaze as her hand slipped from his bottom to his thigh, tucking him tighter against her, allowing him little movement. His eyes widened with alarm, but his careful passion broke. He thrust harder, pounding against her body so hard she shuddered. The careful lover replaced by the wild one.

The less gentle man.

The one she loved.

Agatha left off her explorations of Oscar's body, clutched his shoulder with one hand, then slid her fingers down her own body to touch herself. Although she'd pushed Oscar's passions higher, she wanted to come with him, to feel her body peak as he did.

She inched her hand between them, slicking her fingers as Oscar's wet length entered and left her body. He groaned then bent his head to capture her lips. Joined with him in every way possible, Agatha let pleasure take her to the edge and beyond. She sobbed into his mouth as her pleasure spiked, shuddering around the rigid length embedded inside her body. Oscar pressed deep, holding still as she found her release. But then he jerked free and the hot moisture's sting of his release bathed her thigh. He'd never withdrawn before.

Humiliated, Agatha blinked back tears. The futile wish of a forever after with Oscar had been truly denied her. When he ceased groaning, she pulled him hard against her chest and held him until she regained control of her emotions.

Oscar turned his head and kissed her cheek. "I've missed you, so badly."

Instead of answering, Agatha pushed him away. "That is neither here nor there. We cannot and should not be alone again. Let that be the end of it."

He sat up with a groan. "I know. I don't trust myself either. Are you all right?"

Agatha swung her feet to the floor and stood shakily. "Of course." But her gown stuck to her leg and she hurried to the washbasin to cleanse herself.

Behind her, Oscar dressed swiftly. "I was mad to ever let things go so far with you. I'm truly sorry that we cannot remain as we were."

Agatha shrugged, saddened he thought their friendship a mistake too. Once, when she'd thought his betrothal a terrible injustice, she'd hoped he'd throw propriety aside and whisk her to Gretna Green for an anvil wedding. It wouldn't be exactly what she'd dreamed. She'd hoped to marry in St. George's Church. But at least they would have wed.

Oscar approached and, instead of pulling her into his embrace, he merely kissed her shoulder. "Promise me you will take more care on the streets. You almost died today."

Agatha turned slowly. "Did you follow on my heels?"

He cupped her face. "I caught you before you were run down. Were you so angry that you didn't hear me call out to you?"

Agatha looked away, discomforted that he'd been so close to her, that he'd touched her, and she'd not noticed. Even in a crowded ballroom, separated by half the *ton*, she'd been aware of his location. Agatha had always taken her awareness of him as one more reason they were meant to be. "You should go."

He pressed a kiss to her hair and turned for the window. Yet he hesitated, hovering with one leg raised in preparation for the final step through.

Footsteps rushed up the hall and halted outside her door. "Miss Birkenstock," her maid whispered. "Your grandfather wishes to see you. Now."

"I'll be there directly," Agatha called.

When she turned to say goodbye to Oscar, he'd already disappeared.

Nine

THE CHILDISH SCREAMS of happy pleasure lifted Oscar's head for the third time that morning. He was supposed to be sorting through the accounts before his next appointment, but the orphans' shrieks kept pulling him toward the window.

Agatha was outside playing with the unruly bunch. The first time he had dared look, he found her swamped by children. Two on her knee, the others hovering about. Agatha sat inside the circle of children, but it was the look upon her face that kept him by the window for more minutes than he should.

The children had her complete attention. An older boy was showing her something cupped in the palm of his hand. Agatha had examined it carefully, smiled, and then the boy had run to a corner of the garden. The other children had followed, but Agatha had remained seated with the baby bouncing on her knee.

It was the sight of Agatha's joy that demolished the little of his. Even through the dirty glass, he could see she loved the child she held. Her face was a mix of contentment and acute longing as the child patted her face and pressed, no doubt, wet kisses to her cheek.

From the start, Agatha's loneliness had tugged at him. The orphans seemed to fill a void in her that life couldn't fill. But as tempting as she was, he hadn't considered marrying her. He had to look higher for his bride. Love hadn't featured in his calculations. Yet he missed Agatha with a fierce ache.

He sighed. He couldn't look outside again. Agatha had caught him last time and scowled so fiercely he dreaded speaking to her again. Today his chest pained him, and it was from remembrances of yesterday. He hadn't wanted to leave. He had wanted to stay warm and cosseted in Agatha's arms, but when the maid invaded their private world, he had made his escape without a word of goodbye.

So it was over. Finally.

He should marry Penelope as soon as it could be arranged. Yet his heart sat like a lead weight, dragging his spirits lower. With time and luck, the sensations would dim until he could think of Agatha with only fondness. But today the thought of her was a thousand knives piercing his heart.

So he sat at the desk, straining to hear the world outside while futilely trying to add the same column of sums.

"Darling, why so serious a face?" His mother hovered at the door, her arm twined about Mr. Birkenstock's.

He threw his pen down with relief. "'Tis nothing, Mother. To what do I owe this unexpected pleasure?"

"Can a mother not enquire about her son if she chances to come upon him?" She slipped into a chair with a delicate huff, but Oscar wasn't fooled. Her eyes darted about the desk, no doubt trying to ascertain his progress.

"Of course."

Oscar nodded to Birkenstock. The older man's face had slacked of expression, but Oscar thought him quite weary. "Please, take a seat, sir. Shall I have your granddaughter called to you? She is out in the gardens, I believe."

"No, no." Birkenstock mopped his brow. "I shall search her out directly."

Disappointment thundered through Oscar, but he forced a smile to his lips. "Very well."

He shut the ledger, more certain than ever that he would never tally the page today. It wasn't as if he were in a rush to confirm his greatest fears that the orphanage was struggling to pay its way. He looked expectantly at his visitors. As always, there was a definite companionship between his mother and Agatha's grandfather. A subtle and unspoken ease which spoke of a deeper acquaintance than they let on to others. They had always been on friendly terms, even when his late father had lived, but quite frankly, Oscar was tired of pretending he didn't suspect they were closer than mere friends.

"Was there something you wished to say to me?"

His mother squirmed in her chair. "No. Nothing out of the ordinary. I just wanted to remind you that I'm bound for Chertsey soon."

"Ah, yes, your annual pilgrimage to see your old school friend. I do, indeed, remember. Please convey my regards to Miss Hill." He glanced between them. "Was that all?"

Mr. Birkenstock shuffled awkwardly upon his chair then let out a loud breath. "Lady Carrington was telling me her itinerary this morning, and since our travel plans coincided, I thought to take her up in my carriage for both journeys. I'm bound for Winchester tomorrow morning on business, but I'd happily delay my plans to deliver her safely to Chertsey, given the recent spate of attacks by brigands on the roads."

Oscar raked his fingers through his hair. "Yes, I remember reading about those again this morning at breakfast. Until I was roped into sorting through this mess, I was toying with the idea of accompanying Mother to Chertsey myself. But considering I was absent from Town all of the last month, I am hesitant to abandon my future wife so soon. It is very good of you to oblige me and take my place."

Oscar turned to his mother. Her eyes widened in shock at his easy acceptance of the lie. He gave her a weary smile. Far be it for him to quibble over her pursuit of happiness. If Birkenstock could make her happy, then he'd be the last man to stand in her way.

Birkenstock clambered to his feet. "Well then, my lady. We should be going. Lady Jamison will frown upon any delay. I'll just pop out to speak to my granddaughter and return momentarily."

When he was gone, Oscar's mother sighed. "You know the truth, don't you?"

Oscar nodded without meeting her gaze.

"Thank you for your understanding, Oscar. Although it is none of your affair who I see, Thomas has been worried how you might take the news of our association."

Oscar smiled, but inside an appalling thought had presented itself. What if his mother and Mr. Birkenstock married? He could become related to Agatha and not in a way he cared to entertain—to see her with family about them each holiday. Could he bear it?

Oscar shook his head to toss away the idea. His mother would never consider marriage again. He could not believe it. She was too fond of the social whirl to buckle under a man's rule again. He remembered the disagreements between his parents when he was a child. His father had been an extremely hard man to please. He'd been jealous of every petty compliment she received and had always claimed his mother encouraged flattery. No, Oscar couldn't believe the affair would come to marriage. But everything else he could be deaf and blind to.

A movement at the door caught his eye. Mr. Manning waited to see him.

Oscar waved him in then flipped open his pocket watch. "Mr. Manning, you are right on time. Please, take a seat."

Manning sank into the chair Thomas Birkenstock had just vacated and turned his gaze on Oscar's mother. She squirmed and refused to look in his direction. "Essy."

"Mr. Manning." She stood and Oscar stood too. The rector climbed to his feet leisurely, and when she made a move to pass his chair, Manning snagged the edge of her gown, letting it slip through his fingers as she passed.

He watched her depart then turned a rueful smile on Oscar. "Your mother is still such a lovely woman. She is little changed from my boyhood. She was quite a catch, even then, and believe me, I tried."

Oscar dropped to his chair in shock. Mother had *two* men chasing after her? And one of them the most moral vicar he'd ever met. Oscar coughed. "You knew my mother when she was a younger woman?"

"Since I was in short pants. Long before she married. We were ... friends."

Manning's words hinted at a great deal more than friendship. The smile that crossed his lips—a bittersweet remembrance? Oscar started to feel distinctly uncomfortable about his mother's love life. Just how many beaux did she dangle on her arm?

"Just friends, my lord. However, I do intend to change her mind and persuade her to a permanent change in her status."

Oscar passed a hand over his mouth to hide a grimace. His mother was headed for a week-long sojourn in the countryside with her lover, Thomas Birkenstock, and the Rector of St. George was telling him he planned to court her for marriage. This could only descend into social disaster for the family—something he'd been raised to take great pains to avoid.

Perhaps he should attempt to subtly discourage Manning. "That might prove more complicated than you believe," he murmured.

Manning merely smiled at his warning, a Cheshire smile that boded ill for his mother. But that smile triggered a memory he couldn't seem to place. It reminded him of someone he knew, but the name escaped him.

"You wished to see me, Mr. Manning?" Agatha stood poised at the doorway, keeping her gaze firmly on the rector, ignoring Oscar's existence completely.

Manning gestured for her to come closer. "Yes, child. I thought that since Lord Carrington has been little involved in the orphanage that he should be given a tour by the one person who knows the place so well. My lord, Miss Birkenstock has investigated every nook and cranny of the house and can give you a detailed history of the improvements made over the years."

Agatha's face flushed at the compliments. "Of course, I would be happy to." However, she looked anything but pleased.

Manning chuckled. "Well, now that is settled I shall leave you to the grand tour. Carrington. Miss Birkenstock."

Manning departed, leaving them alone. "Good morning, Miss Birkenstock. Please be assured that I had no idea Manning would do that to you. I assumed he was here to offer advice."

Agatha scowled. "Good morning, my lord. If you would please follow me."

Without waiting to see if he was ready now, Agatha disappeared beyond the door. Oscar rushed to follow and found her waiting upon the first landing above his head. She appeared, at first glance, impassive, yet her hostile gaze spoke volumes. Oscar interpreted her gaze to mean that he was to behave and to keep a distance.

He tucked his hands behind his back.

The tour was conducted with excruciatingly polite conversation. He saw the linen closets, the children's dreary, cold bedchamber, the schoolroom, and the servants' quarters in quick succession. He supposed he should have concentrated on every word Agatha uttered. However, the lingering scent of roses tickled his nose, reminding him that all but twelve hours had passed since he'd held her in his arms, their bodies fused together as passion took them to new heights.

Agatha turned. Sunlight pierced through the cloudy sky at that moment, falling through the window and striking her in brilliant light. She looked heavenly and without caution, Oscar approached until a bare inch separated them. Time stilled, and then Agatha stepped back and around him, pacing away to put a respectable distance between them again. "Did you wish to see the cellar, my lord?"

Oscar cursed under his breath at his foolishness. "Will there be rats?"

Agatha rolled her eyes then turned to begin her descent of the servant's stairs. "There are always rats, Lord Carrington. But if you find yourself about to faint, do give me warning so I might step aside. I have no wish to be crushed by a falling lord."

Oscar barked a laugh. "I was, in fact, worried about your delicate sensibilities, Miss Birkenstock. I would not like to have you confronted by the fearsome beasts in such close quarters. You might have sought comfort in my arms."

Agatha turned and pierced him with a scornful look. "You might wish for it, my lord, but such a circumstance will never occur again."

Oscar passed before her and took the lead down the stairs in case she fell. "I shall keep hope within my breast until eternity ends then. It's either that or haunt Berkley Square, remaining watchful for your next misadventure."

At the lower door, Oscar dug into his pocket. The comforting weight of gold chain slithered between his fingers. He caught up Agatha's hand and pressed the bauble into her palm. "A replacement. Your neck looks bare without your cross."

Agatha examined the jewelry in the weak light, her lips pressed together. Oscar had managed to find an almost identical replacement for her stolen necklace, but in all the excitement of yesterday, he'd forgotten to offer it up.

Watching her jiggle the chain between her hands unnerved him. Judging by her expression, she was debating whether to keep the piece or toss it back in his face. He hoped she kept possession of the chain. The gift wasn't much; it wasn't even truly expensive. But if Agatha kept it, he would know she had something to remember him by. She would remember that he cared for her.

With a sigh, Agatha tucked the chain into her pocket then pressed a handkerchief over it. "We should continue the tour."

Relieved, Oscar reached for the knob. But the door wouldn't open. It was jammed, stuck beyond his understanding.

Behind him, Agatha huffed. "What are you doing?"

"Trying to win a round with a hunk of wood and a bit of brass. The door is stuck."

Agatha pressed a hand to his shoulder and shoved. "A nice trick, my lord. Here let me try."

Amused, Oscar watched her shake the door handle repeatedly then take a pace backward to stare at it. A sliver of light seeped around the frame and the door, illuminating her squinting expression. Suddenly she stepped forward, placed her hands on the wood, and pushed upward.

"What are you doing?"

"Trying to adjust the door. It has dropped in the frame, I believe. It is not quite plumb anymore."

Oscar stood behind her so he could see what she was talking about. Less light filtered into the crack on the right than on the left. He moved behind Agatha, placed his hands higher up on the door, and dropped a kiss to her hair. "I'll lift the door. You turn the knob and pull when I tell you to."

God, she smelled heavenly. Oscar dragged in a deep breath but kept his hands on the wood. As much as he wanted, he'd not create scandal with her here. The walls would be paper-thin and gossiping servants would not hesitate to circulate rumors about their masters. He'd already taken enough risk with their brief conversation.

Her head nodded beneath his lips, and Oscar strained upward, watching the crack of light until it appeared even on both the right side and the left. "Now, Agatha."

The door shrieked and swung inward toward them until the stairwell blazed with light. Beyond the opening, voices rose in agitation and Oscar peered around Agatha.

A good many servants stood watching them.

"The door was stuck," he explained.

"Has been for a week, milord. Why'd ya use the servant's stairs for anyway?"

"Miss Birkenstock was kind enough to give me a tour. Clearly, she doesn't know everything about the orphanage or she would have known about this stuck door." He caught her gaze as her skin pinked with embarrassment.

She gathered her skirts and swept past him. "It wasn't me who made the claim, my lord. Could you make provision to have the door repaired?"

Back to the business of the orphanage before he could blink. "I think that could be arranged."

Agatha led him through the kitchens, down through the cellars, and back up without further incident. There were precious little goods in the cellar anyway. Certainly no sign of the rum the orphanage had paid for recently. "Is there a separate wine cellar in the place?"

"No . . ." Agatha staggered back a step. Alarmed, Oscar rushed forward, but discovered her to be pinned by a pair of childish arms.

"Mabel," Agatha exclaimed. "What are you doing in this part of the house? You should be with your brothers and sisters outside at this time."

Mabel glanced at Oscar and then shrank back. "They wanted me to hide again. I needed a better place."

"And not to giggle," Oscar chimed in.

The little sprite flashed a quick smile in his direction. "Do you know where I could hide so even Simon can't find me?"

Oscar considered it while Agatha tucked a stray curl behind the child's ear. Mabel was light, small. She'd fit easily atop a high piece of furniture. "Come with me, Mabel. Miss Birkenstock, if your tour is finished, I'll be heading back to the office."

Agatha frowned when Oscar held his hand out for Mabel to take. The little girl let him lead her toward the office, lift her up in his arms, and then place her atop a tall bureau. Her eyes widened a bit, but then her smile turned beatific. If she kept her giggles in check, she'd be very hard to find up there. For good measure, he collected a short stack of books and set them so Mabel's peeking head could hide behind them.

"Is that acceptable, my lady?"

"Oh, you are the best lord I have ever met. Will you marry me someday?"

Oscar choked. "No. Of all the ridiculous notions." But this girl had them by the dozen. She'd be easy pickings if she found herself in the street, should the orphanage close. The notion made him shudder but he ignored it, turned back to his papers to await the confused searchers looking for Mabel.

Ten

THE CREAM OF London society swirled about Estella as she stood with her friends on the boundary of the dance floor. She smiled at the happy faces about her and preened as more than one eye cast an envious glance toward her circle. Oscar stood with Lady Penelope's arm wrapped about his. He seemed in a good mood at long last, possessiveness clear as his hand covered Lady Penelope's. He looked down upon her with an air of satisfaction.

"They make an interesting pair," a deep voice murmured in her ear.

Estella turned. "Your Grace, such an honor." She dropped into a curtsey.

The Duke of Staines shook his finger at her. "Now, now, Essy. No need to take that tone with me. We've known each other far too long for you to ply me up with insipid affection and think I'll be satisfied."

Although Estella scowled, she did rise up on her toes and press her lips against the duke's clean-shaven cheek when he offered it. He smacked his lips against her cheek in return.

Estella blushed. "Beastly man. Now the tongues will wag again." And indeed, the rise in chatter around them seemed to confirm that all eyes and tongues had taken in their affectionate exchange.

When he straightened, his eyes had creased with mirth. "They like nothing better than a good gossip about nothing. Besides, it will make Lynton livid with jealousy."

Estella glanced away. The duke's habit of annoying his younger brother was none of her concern. What did it matter if Lynton knew of that kiss? The duke meant nothing by it, aside from stirring up attention for himself. Lynton Manning could go to the devil. "I thought you would have grown out of teasing your brother."

Staines threaded her arm through his and moved them away from her group. "You mean you'd thought I would finally grow up and behave like a real duke. Don't pretend you don't think it. It is the primary charge my brother levels at me during his weekly sermons. I must have some form of revenge for having a pious, church-bound brother. He used to have a fine sense of humor before he took orders."

Estella could remember that, although Lynton's smiles and laughter seemed a lifetime ago now. "And how do you like being preached at?"

He shrugged. "In one ear and out the other. But I have my man, Redding, pay attention and he nudges me should I fall asleep during any important bits."

Estella glanced behind them. Redding, the duke's long suffering footman, offered a courteous nod, but remained three paces behind. "That man must know a great deal of secrets about you," she laughed. "Do you think he could be bribed so your brother could trip you up on occasion?"

The duke's expression changed. He glanced at his footman, a slow smile tugging at his mouth. "You would have no chance with Redding. He is utterly incorruptible."

Estella shuddered. "No one is incorruptible."

"I take it you have learned that from experience." The duke waved his cane toward Oscar. "I see your boy has finally filled out from a stick. Thought he'd never sprout outward."

Thankful for the change of subject, Estella admired her son's face. He was a little more drawn than usual, but he'd be certainly larger than when the duke had last laid eyes on him. Staines usually kept to less polite circles and, to her knowledge, had little cause to know her son in recent years. "He eats nonstop," she confessed. "But where it all goes is beyond me."

The duke laughed. "A family trait. I swear I had to protect my interests from Lynton's incessant appetite when he was that age. To this day, I still believe he lightened my breakfast tray every morning while our valet's back was turned."

"Such habits didn't do him any lasting harm. He seems trim enough."

The duke chuckled again. "I'll be sure to mention your warm admiration for Lynton's figure the next time he comes to berate me for my sins. That should prove very amusing."

Estella's mouth fell open. She closed it swiftly. "You will do no such thing. I merely said he had not run to fat. There was nothing warm in my comment."

The duke stroked her hand where it had curled into a fist. "Settle your feathers, Essy. You are too much fun to tease. Might I convince you to dance with me? There's a waltz starting up, and I'm growing restless with this party."

Although annoyed, Estella nodded. It did her no ill to be on good terms with the Duke of Staines. For a while, there was even a rumor that she would receive a proposal from him after she'd observed her mourning. Staines had never proposed; he'd merely teased her about admiring Lynton. Nothing could be further from the truth. Lynton Manning was an annoying bee spoiling her contented life.

As Staines drew her into the waltz, Estella raised her chin. "I am surprised to see you here. I would have thought this much too tame for you."

"Well, I knew I should find you here, so where else would I be?"

Estella chuckled as they moved off. "Oh, don't talk nonsense. What on earth do you want with an old widow? I'm hardly your usual fare and we both know it."

The duke's nostril's flared. His hand tensed on her back. "And what exactly do you know of my usual fare, Lady Carrington?"

Startled by the abrupt change in his mode of address, Estella's heart raced. What had she said to upset him? The truth had always appealed to him in the past. She opted to keep to that very habit. "That you have two young mistresses in Conduit Street, and look upon many married women as your own. A widow would never do for you."

The hand at her back relaxed and she wondered what she'd missed in her accounting of his reputation that caused him to do so.

"You should never listen to gossips, you know. I could not lower myself to house a mistress in that part of Town. Too near my brother. He has such a fear of scandal, much as he is likely to cause one himself."

The duke twirled her about the floor in silence while Estella considered the change that had come over him. He was no stranger to scandal, but his lapse into serious conversation about scandal made her uneasy. When the dance ended, he bowed over her hand. "Are you not curious about my brother's indiscretion? It could affect the people you love most."

Estella swallowed, and then forced a carefree smile to her face. "There is nothing in your brother's life that could affect me or those I love."

"Is that so?" The duke scowled. "Then can you tell me why your son and my brother could use each other as shaving mirrors? I do wish to hear an explanation for that. Apparently, I have another relation I should have been informed of."

Estella's breath caught. "Don't be ridiculous."

The duke pulled her into an unoccupied window embrasure. Estella glanced over his shoulder as the duke's footman took position to give them privacy. "You, my girl, are on a very slippery slope. Do not lie to me again."

Estella licked her lips. "It is merely a coincidence."

"Bollocks."

Estella searched for an escape. She couldn't explain the similarity between her son and Lynton Manning. Despite the duke's assumption, she'd never betrayed her husband. The resemblance was an act of God. "I must return to my party."

The duke set his hand to her arm. "I do not like the connection he has made with Lord Thorne's daughter. She is not good for my nephew."

Estella glanced up into the Duke of Staines' face and saw determination in the set of his features. She shook herself out of his grip. "No matter what you claim, he is not your relation and you have no say in his life."

Staines set his hands to his hips. "You misunderstand me, quite deliberately, I think. He is family, and I will not accept this match for him. Is that understood?"

Despite her efforts to hide her feelings, Estella trembled. "Leave him be."

Staines shook his head slowly. "I will be watching, Essy. I should have been watching over the boy all along. Imagine my surprise to see my brother's replica parading as Carrington's boy. When I leave here I will be calling on my brother, and I will drag his pious arse from the very church altar if necessary to finally hear some truth. You have both lied to me. One by omission—for Lynton cannot be unknowing of the boy's origins—and you to my very face. It will take quite some time before we are ever on equal ground again, Lady Carrington. We will speak of this again. We will speak very soon."

Estella shook her head. He was wrong. He had to be wrong about Oscar. How could he be Lynton's son?

She stumbled two steps forward, but was caught by a firm hand beneath her elbow. When she glanced up, Redding, His Grace's footman, had moved to support her. He must have heard it all. Shame and uncertainty gripped her, and she glanced about wildly until her gaze settled on her son.

Oscar turned at that moment and rushed forward. "Mother? Whatever is the matter?"

Estella's mind raced. She couldn't tell him of her confrontation with the Duke of Staines. She couldn't allow him to doubt his place in the world. She glanced behind. The Duke of Staines watched from the shadows. Estella smiled quickly. "A spell of dizziness came over me. It's nothing, but I fear I should return home."

Oscar took her arm, thanked Redding for his assistance, and escorted her toward the door. "I'll come with you."

Estella stopped. "No, no. I should not like to ruin your evening, too. You must stay with your Lady Penelope."

Oscar looked behind them and snorted. "Lady Penelope has disappeared without a word the minute I released her arm." He smiled suddenly and tugged her onward. "Let's get you home and tucked up in bed. Perhaps I could convince Cook to whip up something sweet to give you pleasant dreams."

"Yes. Pleasant dreams would be wonderful." They would banish the fear of Staines' accusation.

As she settled into the carriage, Oscar tucked a blanket around her knees and caught up her hand. He was a sweet boy. A kind man.

He had very little of her husband about his manner, except impatience.

Could it be true?

Estella closed her eyes and cast her mind back to the time of Oscar's conception. Had she done the unthinkable and lain with a man not her husband? Carrington had rarely spoken as he'd bedded her. The candles were always blown. Darkness could have hidden a different lover, but how had she not recognized the difference?

Estella curled her free hand over her belly. Why would Lynton steal into her bed and dishonor her this way?

Eleven

IN THE PAST, the climb up the front steps of the Earl of Daventry's residence would signal a woman's complete fall from grace. Today, a month after the scandalous earl's marriage to Miss Lillian Winter, her oldest friend, Agatha's call would be viewed with considerable envy.

Everyone was talking about the earl's unexpected marriage, but since Agatha had a past acquaintance with the lady in question, she was filled with foreboding. The last time she had laid eyes on Lillian, Agatha had cried for a week. Lilly had been in agony, writhing upon the bed, whimpering as leaches were removed from her arms. The remembrance chilled her still.

How would Lillian survive marriage and all it entailed?

The broad doors clicked shut behind her back, dimming the sounds of the world outside. She handed off her bonnet, cloak, and gloves then stepped after the butler. Ahead of them, Agatha could hear giggling and deep, rumbling laughter. The butler knocked on a door and waited, flicking a complex glance over his shoulder, one that conveyed amusement and resignation. The sounds of rushed movement ceased behind the door, and after a moment Lord Daventry bade them enter.

"Miss Birkenstock!" Daventry exclaimed. "Thank you for agreeing to visit on such short notice."

"It is my pleasure, my lord." Agatha's gaze drifted to her friend. Gone was the writhing, tormented body. The blonde before her was still familiar, her features a little changed with the passage into womanhood. The pretty, smiling woman was held in place by her husband, however, and she couldn't move an inch from his arms. Agatha had never seen the earl behave with such familiarity.

"Lady Daventry, a pleasure to see you in such good health." Uncertain of what to do next, Agatha dropped a curtsey.

Lilly burst into laughter. "Oh, how could you know Agatha would do that? You are a beast, Giles. Go off and leave us in peace." She swatted at her husband's clutching arms, and he released her.

Daventry smiled and set his hands to his hips. "Already displaced by old friends. Whatever shall I do without you?"

The little blonde scowled after him until he fled the room. "Agatha don't you dare do that again. Giles said you would curtsey, but I just couldn't believe him."

Agatha grinned. "Things change. You're a countess now. Certain courtesies are due to you."

Lilly moved forward. "Between us, my dear, such courtesy is evil. I've missed you so much." The little woman caught Agatha in a hug and held her close for an age. When Lilly released her, they both had tears in their eyes.

Agatha cupped her friend's face gently. "I was so astounded to receive your letter last month. What is to account for your swift recovery?"

Lilly's grin grew broad. "My husband, actually. Apparently there was quite a lot of benefit to be found in the debauched life Giles led prior to our marriage. His hands cured me of my ills. But he must reapply his treatments frequently. Marriage seemed necessary to fit his schedule."

Agatha's face flamed with heat. "I think perhaps this is more information than the earl would care for me to know."

"Nonsense." Daventry reappeared and then a tea tray-bearing maid followed. "The art should have been tried before to save my wife so much pain and suffering, but I can selfishly say I am glad no one else touched her." Daventry smiled impishly at his wife and Agatha glanced between them.

They were speaking in riddles and behaving improperly again. The earl drew Lilly into a embrace, pressing kisses to her brow. Agatha looked away, hoping Daventry would remember they had company sooner rather than later.

"Forgive me, Miss Birkenstock. My wife has quite changed me."

Agatha looked at him, saw the same wicked glint in his eye that she had glimpsed during previous encounters with him in society, and doubted the change was very significant.

The earl's eyes sparkled with amusement and his hands stroked over his wife's exposed skin. "You may be completely honest, Miss Birkenstock."

"You seem the same, my lord."

His expression sobered. "Ah, but the difference is that my eye, and every other part of me, is firmly fixed on my wife's happiness. There is not another woman like her."

Lilly turned in his arms, swiping at her cheeks. "You are about to get ridiculously sentimental, aren't you?" At the earl's nod, she pressed a quick kiss to his lips and pushed him away. "Go and check the value of your investments again, Giles. I'd rather not spend Agatha's visit weeping at your declarations."

The earl grinned again and ducked out the doorway.

"I take it back," Agatha murmured.

Lilly laughed heartily. "He is the most devoted man. So patient with me when I don't understand the significance of the commonest of news." Lilly caught up her fingers and led her to the couch. "He has been such a dear friend to me."

Curiosity ate at Agatha. "What did he do to cure you?"

Lilly passed over a teacup. "Have you any understanding of treatments applied to horse limbs after exertion?"

Agatha nodded. Her grandfather was always berating the grooms for inattention to his horses in the cold.

"Giles said my limbs were stiff with tension so he tried to soften them. It worked startlingly well, but I need regular treatments to remain pain-free."

"That was terribly clever of him. Had no one ever tried that before? I thought your father had taken you to every medical man he could find."

Lilly leaned back in her chair. "No one even suggested it, as far as he could remember. Anyway, I wouldn't care to have a complete stranger touch me."

"And Lord Daventry determined this treatment after you married?"

Lilly bit her lip over a smile. "Between us? Before."

Agatha pressed her hand over her face. She should have known there might be some wickedness involved, but Lord Daventry was famous for his rules. No virgins or married women. It was a shock to discover that he'd broken them.

"I was always his, you know."

Agatha forced a smile to her lips, remembering Lilly's aborted betrothal. "That's right. I had forgotten all about that. So he offered to honor it?"

"Yes, he did eventually." Lilly admitted. "But I did my best to refuse him. I thought he shouldn't have to deal with my troubles for the rest of his life. He disagreed."

Moved, Agatha caught up her friend's hand. "Well, however it happened I am very glad to see you well and happy."

"I have been more fortunate than I know. He loves me, Agatha. How is that possible?"

"Because you are you?" Agatha caught her friend in a gentle hug and squeezed carefully. "He had no chance of escaping you."

"Indeed I didn't." Lord Daventry laughed as he approached. "I am going to step out, my dear. Is there anything you need?"

"You have spoiled me enough as it is. Have a nice time."

Lord Daventry swooped to capture his wife and pressed a long, possessive kiss to her lips. Eventually, he let her come up for air. "I won't be long."

Lord Daventry hurried out again.

"Goodness."

Lilly fanned herself. "Exactly."

They burst into giggles and spent a very pleasant hour discussing the change in Lilly's life.

"Now, what about you?" Lilly asked as she stretched out on a couch.

"Me?"

"Yes, you. What wonders fill Agatha Birkenstock's days?"

Agatha smiled. "The children from the Grafton Street Orphanage occupy most of my time."

Lilly frowned, and shuffled around to get comfortable. "Is that all?"

"Yes, that is all. I spend my days there, and I manage my grandfather's house for him."

Lilly frowned. "You've never married? But you are so pretty."

Agatha laid a light blanket over her friend's legs, fighting a blush at the compliment. "No, I've never been asked."

Lilly caught her fingers and squeezed. "I'm so sorry. I remember you were looking forward to managing your own house."

Agatha forced a smile to her lips. Such days seemed so long ago now. "Perhaps it is for the best. I manage my grandfather's home and do not have to please a husband's demands."

A secretive smile flitted over Lilly's face. "Sometimes the demands are very pleasant."

Agatha sank into her chair, attempting to hide her understanding of Lilly's words. She did know the joy a lover could bring a woman, but for all Oscar's skills he was quite undependable. When she glanced at Lilly, there was a question hovering in her gaze. One she didn't want asked because she would never answer it honestly.

Lilly fussed with her blanket. "Giles is determined to show me off soon, and I was wondering if you would accompany me as my companion. I am anxious that Giles not be forced to stay by my side all night."

Agatha was not keen to rejoin the earl's circle of acquaintances. She didn't feel comfortable there. "Judging by his behavior today, you might have trouble getting him to leave you. Besides, his friends will not desert you when they return to Town."

"Do you mean Lady Ettington and Lady Hallam?" Lilly's fingers brushed harder over the blanket. "I haven't met them yet."

Sensing Lilly's unease, she reached forward to still her hands. "They are both wonderful women, very kind, and without a hint of coldness about them. You will be in good company with them. With all the earl's friends, for that matter."

Lilly sat up. "I've already met Lord Carrington. He tells me you are acquainted."

Agatha's heart stopped for a full minute. In all her pleasure at hearing of Lilly's return to good health, she had forgotten the connections Lilly would now make due to her marriage. Had Oscar been indiscreet about their association? She hoped not. If he had, Agatha would have to deny it and lie to her friend. "His London residence is next door to my grandfather's," she answered carefully. "We have had some conversation over the years." Very little really. Conversation didn't feature heavily in their recent interactions, only mind-numbing scandalous pleasure.

"He visited with Giles recently." Lilly laughed. "Can you imagine we didn't get along at first?"

"No, not really. He appears to be a universal favorite with the ladies." Agatha quashed the bitter jealously filling her mouth with bile. Countless *tonnish* ladies threw themselves at Oscar. He had never been without his admirers.

"He came to Cottingstone Manor while I was there. He saved my life."

Lilly's words echoed around the room. Saved her life?

Agatha swallowed. "What?"

Lilly's lips twisted with distaste. "I shall say this in a rush because the memory is still vastly unpleasant. My cousin, Bartholomew Barrette, was quite mad and meant to kill me, as he had tried to do many years before. To cut the story very short, Carrington saved me when I thought Barrette would either shoot me or shoot Giles. Lord Carrington's accuracy with a pistol was quite deadly. One shot, and Barrette was gone."

"He killed someone?" Agatha held a hand to her chest and pressed her fingers into her skin. "I don't believe you."

Lilly nodded. "Giles tells me we should keep it quiet, but since you are my friend, I cannot see the harm. You do hold some regard for the viscount, don't you? I wouldn't have the story gossiped about. The viscount and I, as you can imagine, have become friends."

Agatha shook her head in confusion, then quickly nodded as Lilly's expression turned grim. "Of course I will keep the secret."

Oscar had shot someone dead. Could that explain the haunted look in his eyes, the sadness that lingered just below the surface? And the sleepless nights he'd mentioned. Agatha pressed her hand to her face, horrified that Oscar had been placed in a situation where a killing had been the only solution.

"This must come as a shock to be living next door to a man capable of such an act, but you can understand that I am forever in his debt. I fear I must warn you that he will be here directly. Giles went personally to invite him to luncheon with us. We have much to be thankful to him for."

Agatha surged to her feet. "Then I should go."

Lilly swung her legs out from under the blanket and stood too. "Are you certain? I am now considered a suitable chaperone. You may stay with no risk to your reputation, and besides, he is an engaged man."

Agatha's heart beat fast in her chest. "It is not that," she lied. "I have duties at home that I have neglected. Thank you for the wonderful visit. I'd like to call again another day, if I may."

Lilly came forward to embrace her. "Of course, I hope to see a lot of you too. We've missed so much time."

Agatha turned away, collected her bonnet and gloves, then hurried out the door, ignoring the butler's protests that her conveyance wasn't ready. She'd not wait for a carriage. The walk would cool her mind from its panic.

Oscar had killed to protect Lilly and had become her friend.

There would be no doubt that she'd be forever stumbling into him now. What to do? She couldn't very well break off her connection to Lilly without explaining her dilemma and hurting her feelings. Yet their friendship had survived Lilly's illness. Agatha would just have to try harder to ignore Oscar, should their paths cross while she was visiting with her friend.

Twelve

THE FLOOR BOARDS creaked behind Agatha's back, and she turned to find her grandfather hovering at the door. Garbed in expensive superfine and crisp, white linen, he intimidated her without even trying. Immediately, she closed her book and stood. "Can I help you, sir?"

"No, no." He moved into the room, peering around him, frowning at her scattered possessions. "I just thought I'd enquire how your visit with Lady Daventry went. I imagine her drawing room was quite full."

Agatha smoothed her slightly wrinkled skirts. "Lady Daventry chose to entertain in a limited fashion yesterday."

His dark eyes narrowed. "How limited?"

She took a cautious pace to the side, under the pretext of more fussing, but she was afraid he would be very unhappy after she spoke. "I only saw Lord and Lady Daventry, sir. As far as I am aware, there were no other guests invited."

Her grandfather's jaw clenched over the news. As she had feared, he had expected the drawing room to be filled with the cream of London society, all clamoring for a glimpse of the new bride. And filled with potential candidates for her to marry, no doubt. Agatha braced herself for the lecture to come, but instead of puffing out his chest and blustering, he sank into a deep chair.

"I had expected Lord Daventry to show off his wife now that he's stirred himself to marry and work on getting his heir. Is she an embarrassment to him?"

Agatha gasped, affronted on Lilly's behalf. "Of course not. He was very attentive to his wife." Almost too much so, Agatha thought. Daventry was besotted.

"Hmm, well give the man a wide berth anyway, child. He'll soon go back to his scandalous ways, once the shine of his marriage dims. Most men are the same."

While Agatha struggled to hide her surprise at his candid confession, her mind shrieked. How could he sit there condemning—no, not even condemning—his own sex and expect her to marry one of them?

His fingers tapped his knee. "When I come back from my business trip, we shall have to widen our circle of acquaintances. I had hoped that my extended dealings with the Marquess of Ettington and his circle would prove beneficial to you. Never mind. I think a few new dresses and an increase in your social engagements should do the trick."

Agatha nodded, keeping her face clear of expression. A dozen new gowns would hardly matter to the gentlemen he introduced her to if she never gave them the slightest encouragement, a habit she'd managed to hide from her grandfather for the last few seasons. "How long will you be gone this time, sir?"

A brief smile flickered across his face then just as quickly disappeared. "I will return on Wednesday, late in the day perhaps. The negotiations should be easily dealt with."

Agatha sank into a chair, relieved that he'd dropped the discussion of their association with Lord and Lady Daventry. "Well, that is all to the good. Wouldn't it be wonderful if a simple letter could deal with the situation instead of dragging you from London so frequently? You must become quite vexed with Mr. Carney's incompetence."

"Tis not incompetence, but my affairs do require a firm hand and the personal touch to keep them running smoothly." Her grandfather chuckled. "You will remember that George is to accompany you when you leave the townhouse in my absence. I could not bear it if something was to happen to you while I was away."

Agatha forced her lips to curl into a smile. "Of course I will take George. I agreed, didn't I?"

Grandfather clambered to his feet, crossed the room, and cupped his hand around her jaw. "Always the dutiful granddaughter. But I see resentment bubbling beneath the surface of your eyes. What troubles you?"

Agatha shrugged, attempting to dislodge his fingers. "I do not like to be followed about."

His fingers slipped from her skin. "It is for your own protection. A woman's virtue, once lost, is irreplaceable. I am only thinking of your future. The man who marries you expects a certain kind of female. One untouched by the sordid traps women often fall prey to by the rogues of society. Suffer George's company so that I may be at peace."

Agatha lowered her head. Again, despair trickled through her over how he would react to the news she had no virtue to protect. "Yes, Grandfather."

His large palm pressed upon her head briefly then his heavy footsteps crossed to the window. She lifted her head and watched him watching the view. His presence in the chamber made her feel decidedly untidy.

After a moment, he turned to face her again. "I will be leaving in a moment. So you are not unduly surprised should anyone relate the news, I am escorting Lady Carrington part of the way, to Chertsey. She's visiting with a friend there. Given the demands of her son's engagement, he isn't free to accompany her. I thought it prudent to offer my protection from brigands on the road for the trip there and back. There has been much made of their activities in the press."

"Yes, I had heard something of that. Are you really expecting trouble?"

Grandfather tugged on his waistcoat, smoothing the already precise material. For all of his advancing years, he still kept a trim figure, still retained a vital physique that was much admired by the ladies. Agatha had heard more than one salacious whisper about him, and from surprising directions.

"I am always prepared for trouble, but I have made arrangements to stop overnight along the road so as not to travel through that troubled part of the countryside late at night. I'll keep the good lady safe."

Agatha smiled. "I'm sure she appreciates your efforts."

Another fleeting smile crossed his lips as he bent to kiss her cheek. "Be a good girl, Agatha. I will see you on Wednesday."

With a spring to his step, her grandfather hurried from the room and began shouting orders to George. Within a quarter hour, his carriage had drawn up to the door and he was on his way after briefly returning Agatha's happy wave.

No lectures, no precise routines to follow.

She had five whole mornings of complete bliss ahead of her. Agatha twirled about the entrance hall, determined to make the most of her temporary freedom.

She would spend all day with the orphans.

~ * ~

"Can you make my hair as pretty as yours?" Mabel asked as Agatha ran her brush over the girl's gleaming locks. They were settled in the nursery, Agatha sitting on one of the lumpy beds while she twisted and tied Mabel's hair into a neat braid.

She leaned close to the child and kissed her cheek. "I might. But I think your hair will be much lovelier. I quite admire your dark curls."

Mabel clutched her hands together. "Really?"

Agatha turned the girl around and touched her nose. "Really." She looked past Mabel to the last girl waiting. "Come along, Kitty. Your turn."

Kitty had fine, straight hair, and Agatha twisted the pale strands into braids quite quickly. When the pair was done, she stood and held out both hands. The girls bounced on the spot and they slowly descended to the rear gardens. Agatha crinkled her nose. The grim yard was hardly a pretty space, but the children knew no better. It was good enough for their imaginations, and she wondered what fantasy place she would be transported to today. A pirate ship, or one of the King's vessels. With the boys outnumbering the girls, their play tended to be much more rough-and-tumble than her own childhood had been.

"Avast. Who be comin alongside?" Simon demanded of the trio.

Kitty, the eldest, snapped to attention. "Miss Kitty to the quarter deck, Captain."

Mabel tugged her sleeve. "I wanted to be a fine lady today."

Agatha crouched down. Poor girl. They hardly ever got to play at being ladies. "Perhaps you could be a sea-faring lady, chasing down adventure on the high seas."

Mabel cast her a puzzled frown, shrugged, then ran off to play with her brothers and sisters without a backward glance. Agatha turned to join the nurse where she sat on a sunlit bench by the wall with the infant, Betty, playing at her feet. With a happy wail, little Betty crawled off her blanket, caught Agatha's gown, and pulled on the material until Agatha relented and picked her up.

She hugged her close. "Oh, you are an angel, sweetheart."

"More like a devil in disguise," the nurse muttered. "She's biting something fierce today."

Agatha peered at Betty's wet mouth. "Thank you for the warning."

The nurse stood. "It's your fingers."

She hastily pulled her hands away from Betty's eager mouth. "Naughty girl. I need those to play the pianoforte with." She reached for Betty's doll and turned the child so she could nibble while she watched her siblings play. "Do run along, Bates. I'll mind the children for a while on my own."

The nurse nodded. "Your ears."

Once the nurse disappeared, the children mobbed her. They had all kinds of questions and indeed, Agatha's ears did cause her some pain after twenty minutes of solid chatter. Suddenly, Simon pulled at her sleeve. "Who's that over there watching us?"

Agatha peered around the children and spotted a man's hat at the garden's boundary fence. "I don't know. Kitty, will you play with Betty for me on her blanket?"

Kitty clapped her hands and Betty happily went to her. Simon's hand crept into hers. "You should call one of the servants," he whispered.

"Nonsense. It will surely amount to nothing."

"Then I'm coming with you." He squeezed her hand.

Agatha ruffled his hair. "If you must. I should enjoy your escort, young man."

Arm-in-arm, they approached the stranger. When they were within a few yards of the rear gate, they stopped. Better to be cautious. She didn't know what type of fellow would peer over a fence into a yard filled with children.

"Good afternoon, Miss Birkenstock."

As she shaded her eyes to peer at the stranger, Simon's grip tightened over Agatha's hand. "Good afternoon. Can I help you?"

The gentleman removed his hat and Agatha relaxed. It was only Lord Prewitt, Oscar's future brother-in-law. "Lord Prewitt."

"Ah, good. You know me. Run along, boy, while I speak with this lovely lady."

Simon didn't budge.

Prewitt frowned at him then smiled smoothly. "My dear, you look lovely among those thorns. You'd do much better on a gentleman's arm."

All of Agatha's senses came alert. "I am content where I am, my lord."

He hung his arms over the fence, and a pretty necklace slipped through his fingers to dazzle in the sunlight. "A pretty girl requires something pretty about her neck to show she is appreciated. Something more costly that a two penny bauble."

Agatha resisted the urge to place her fingers over her necklace. The gift from Oscar was a mere trifle beside the finery Lord Prewitt dangled. But she knew its worth. What Prewitt offered was payment for services she must render to him. Distasteful service, judging by the way he stared at her. What Oscar had offered came solely from friendship.

Beside her, Simon fidgeted. He drew her hand toward the others across the garden, silently urging her to come away from Lord Prewitt.

Agatha squeezed Simon's hand. "Forgive me, my lord, but I must get back to my charges. Good day to you."

Unease prickled Agatha's back until Simon whispered that Lord Prewitt had gone.

~ * ~

The sleepy village of Staines was a place of great comfort for Estella Carrington even if they didn't know who she truly was. To her servants and neighbors she was Mrs. B—Thomas' second wife. After so many years, she was used to the lie. As she pushed open the front gate, she drew in the clean scents of her garden—so missed and longed-for throughout the season.

"Welcome home, Mrs. B. We are so pleased to see you return safely."

"Thank you, William." Estella glanced back at her weary companion. "I'll see to any mail in the morning, but please send up a light supper for my husband."

"Of course." The butler backed away, returning to the depths of the house.

Thomas Birkenstock slipped her arm through his. "I do like to hear you address me that way, even if it's not true."

Thomas drew her through the front entrance and upward to their bedchamber without a glance left or right. There would be time enough to enjoy the house tomorrow. Once secure in their room, he let her go and poured himself a brandy.

"Do you think they suspect us of subterfuge?"

He set his glass down and let out a sigh. "I imagine so."

That thought wasn't pleasant. She'd been playing at being Thomas' wife for the past few years, maintaining the fiction that they traveled extensively, but always returning to this house for brief interludes. It was an imperfect arrangement, but it was the best compromise they could reach.

Estella slipped her arm around Thomas' back and held him tightly. He turned his head and smiled down at her, but a little frown tugged at the corner of his mouth. "You do understand that I couldn't let you marry beneath your rank."

She squeezed him tighter. "And I never wanted to marry again. There is no discord between us, is there?"

Thomas slipped out of her grip and sank into a chair. "You know as well as I that any marriage between us would have embarrassed your son. But we do not get to choose who we love. I would have been content with just your smile."

"And you shall always have it."

A knock sounded on the door and their punctual servants settled a heaped supper tray before Thomas. Once they departed, Estella slipped off her shoes, sat with her legs curled beneath her on the bed, and nibbled at some bread.

Thomas picked at his food.

"Were you not hungry?"

He pushed the plate away. "It seems not. Perhaps I'll eat more later tonight."

Estella climbed to her feet again and approached him. He seemed more worn down by his concerns tonight than usual, so she pulled him to his feet with the intention of undressing him.

Amusement arched his brow as she unpinned his cravat and slowly tugged it from his neck. She removed his coat, waistcoat, and shirt then bent to undress the rest of him. As she stood, she let her hands slide up his sides until she could meet his eyes. Instead of the desire she expected to see, there was an unguarded weariness to his features. Without a word, she led him to the bed and tucked him between the sheets.

Thomas didn't protest at her mothering, so she left him to remove her own gown, thankful she'd chosen one where she'd not require his assistance. When she was bare, she slipped into bed only to find Thomas was already fast asleep.

Estella watched him for a long time, concerned by his fatigue. His light snore reverberated around the room.

She tucked her arm beneath her head and listened. He was growing older—so much more quickly than she realized. At nearly four and sixty, Thomas Birkenstock was still a powerfully built man, still strong enough to lift her into his arms for a night of lovemaking. But not tonight, apparently.

Estella rolled to her back and stared up at the shadows flickering around the ceiling. He had bought the house because she liked to garden, but couldn't do it in London. He'd also purchased the house so they could pretend, for just a short while, that the differences in their class, their stations in life, didn't matter. Estella had never thought much about it before she met him all those years ago. But over time she had come to see integrity and strength of will were not confined to the aristocracy. Such characteristics belonged to the man.

Her husband had not been a good man. She did not miss him.

Despite his ardent pursuit prior to marriage, and infrequent visits to her bed to get her with child, he'd preferred his actress mistress for his pleasure and more often than not ignored her needs. But it was not until Carrington had died that she'd pursued an affair with Thomas. The older man had taught her much about meeting her desires.

Estella blew out the candle, but sleep was a long time coming. In her mind, she kept remembering how Lynton Manning had kissed her with such urgency, such eager hunger for her lips. Was it wrong to lie beside a sleeping lover and think about the effect another man had on her senses?

She'd almost begged Lynton to come back. Estella rolled away from Thomas and punched the pillow. Damn Lynton for stirring up such a conflict within her. His stolen kisses and hints of faithfulness were highly disturbing. But she could ignore him and the wild accusations about Oscar's parentage.

Thomas rolled in his sleep and pulled Estella into his arms. Growing drowsy and content, she closed her eyes.

When morning came, she was alone.

Estella slipped from the warm bed and dragged her wrapper over her bare skin. She looked about. Thomas had a habit of early rising even when immersed in the country with nothing to do, and he appeared long gone. As she pulled the bell for assistance with her early morning toilette, she heard men speaking outside. Curious, she pulled back the thick drapes and spied Thomas seated in the garden, talking with earnest concentration. The man he was speaking to was dark-haired, like Thomas had been, tall but with none of his physical strength. With the stranger's back to her, she couldn't tell who it was and curiosity bit deep. He never discussed business here, and the man resembled none of their closest neighbors.

By the time she'd bathed and dressed for the day, the men were nowhere in sight. She could still hear them though, within the house now, and on instinct she kept her steps light.

"Sign here and here. William, you will witness and sign the other paper with your mark, too."

Estella leaned against the door, trying to hear more of the conversation, but deeply puzzled by the need for witnesses. What was Thomas up to?

"I am happy to oblige, Thomas. I've no need for another house as London doesn't agree with my disposition. I'm much happier in Winchester, and it's closer to the port. Please give my regards to my cousin. It has been much too long a time since we've met."

"That I will, Robert. You may draw on my bank as soon as you care to."

Estella backed away quietly and hurried into the morning room. Voices grew louder in the hall and then Thomas' heavy tread approached. "Did we wake you?"

She looked behind him, but he was alone. "No, of course not. Who was it that came to call so early?"

Thomas heaped a plate with food and sat down beside her. "My brother's grandson, Robert Birkenstock. We had a bit of business to discuss."

"He works for you?"

Thomas chewed slowly. The delay in answering sent a prickle of unease up her spine.

"He's been learning the ropes, as it were, as an employee over the past few months. I think he will carry on my concerns quite well."

"Carry on your concerns? Are you handing over the business to him?"

Thomas reached over and squeezed her hand. "He will have it, in time. He's my heir. I cannot live forever, and I have quite a number of people depending on the business continuing for their survival. Robert has a level head on his shoulders and is eager to take the reins."

Estella couldn't think of what to say. Thomas was setting his affairs in order. The thought, coming so soon on her concerns of the night before, sent a chill to her heart. She clutched at his hand.

He patted hers in return. "Now, my dear, there is no need to fret. A man with my responsibilities must make certain his commitments will be met. Robert will do well by the business, and by Agatha too."

"By Agatha? Thomas, what is going on?"

He took a deep breath and let it out slowly. "Given her recent moods, and the difficulty of finding a suitable husband, I have come to the conclusion Agatha may never marry. I thought to forewarn Robert of the possibility. With his agreement, we have drawn up papers to allow her to live out her days in the London townhouse, if she so chooses, and to receive a regular allowance from a trust. Since Robert's wife is increasing again. He has no wish to add possible contention with another female in her domain." Thomas pushed his unfinished plate away. "Agatha should be pleased. She will have a limited independence."

Not *want* to marry? Estella had never received that impression from his granddaughter. She'd always thought it a shame Agatha hadn't already found a deserving husband. She had such pretty manners and such a good way with children.

Thomas cleared his throat. "I would like to ask, should you have the time and inclination, to keep an eye on Agatha's wellbeing if something should happen to me. Only at first, mind. I'm sure she won't require much of your attention. But the girl is too fiercely independent for my taste, and I fear she will do something foolish once I'm gone."

"Of course I will. I had no idea she was set against marriage. How extraordinary!" Estella swallowed down the pain in her chest. She didn't like this morbid turn of conversation at all. Thomas was a strong man. He just needed to relax more to get over his current lethargy. He couldn't die. With that thought in mind, Estella vowed to see the next few days were as undemanding as possible.

"She hides it well, mostly to save me from embarrassment, I think." Thomas sank back in his chair with a softly uttered groan. "Now, what shall we do today? Your garden is looking a little lonely, out there."

Estella forced a smile to her lips. "Perhaps we could have the lounge carried out and you could read to me while I garden?"

His warm smile settled her anxious heart. "With pleasure, my dear."

Thirteen

OSCAR FORCED ONE foot before the other as he climbed the front steps of St. George's Church, following the cream of London society as they came for Sunday worship. Given that the building didn't collapse upon him as he crossed the threshold, he took his usual seat, but kept his gaze forward rather than lingering on those around him. Attending church hadn't ever been high in his priorities. It was an event that many of his peers avoided, yet he was in sore need of guidance.

As the cool chamber filled with the purer elements of society, he let his mind drift back to that terrible night and the dreadful days that had followed. He'd killed a man. Shot him with his pistol from ten feet away without hesitation. A fatal shot that had extinguished a life in seconds. The image of how easy it had been wouldn't leave Oscar's mind.

It didn't matter that the magistrate had absolved him, had in fact applauded his quick thinking in saving the Earl of Daventry and his betrothed, Lillian Winter, from her cousin's murderous intentions.

At the time, and in the few days that had followed, he'd lived in a dream state, accepting the profuse thanks of his friends, unable to comprehend the full importance of what he'd done. Yet the temporary state of calm had thinned when he was alone, and at night he relived the moment in excruciating detail. Images now were becoming twisted into a nightmare he couldn't shake even in daylight.

Oscar stood for the first hymn, his mind still picturing the slow trail of blood running down Mr. Bartholomew Barrette's temple. He sang with the congregation, but the words were muted, dimmed by the vast horror in his mind. When the time came to sit, he sat, noticing for the first time that a few eyes had turned in his direction. Their curious regard brought him back to the present, to the calm sanity of the church. Mr. Manning stood at the pulpit, quoting from the scriptures with such burning conviction that Oscar soon forgot his troubles and focused on the here and now.

Manning was a passionate orator. He focused so clearly on his congregation and the meaning of his words. Oscar bowed his head and prayed. Prayed to one day find a way to banish the nightmares from his mind. Banish lustful, wicked thoughts of Agatha too. He had to. He couldn't continue as he was and retain a sound mind.

As the service ended, he stood and looked about him. God clearly hadn't heard his plea to forget lust. At the back of the church, Agatha Birkenstock ushered the orphanage children from a pew toward the rear door. Sunlight bounced off her golden head, teasing him with countless secret memories of the past. He turned away and moved toward the vicar.

"Lord Carrington! Wait."

Oscar spun and found his legs trapped by a pair of tiny arms belonging to the irrepressible orphan, Mabel. She was alone. He quickly disentangled her and searched for Agatha in the crowd. Unfortunately, he couldn't see her anywhere close.

He glanced down at the fidgeting girl. "You shouldn't have left Miss Birkenstock's company, Mabel. She will worry where you've gone."

Mabel bounced on the balls of her feet. "But I wanted to invite you to tea this afternoon, my lord. Miss Birkenstock said we are to have tea and crumpets out on the lawn. Please come."

Oscar stared at the girl in astonishment, unsure how to answer. As much as the invitation appeared harmless, Agatha wouldn't be pleased. He hated to spoil the little girl's enjoyment, but he had to decline.

"As much as I would love to attend, I unfortunately have a prior engagement this afternoon."

The little girls eyes grew glassy, her pink lips pressed together. Just when he feared she was about to cry, a hand clapped over his shoulder. Oscar jumped, but it was only the Rector of St. George's smiling at him and then at Mabel.

"Hello there, Miss Mabel. You're looking remarkably pretty today."

The little girl's expression changed from supreme disappointment to a wide smile. "Thank you, sir." She hurried to bob an off-kilter curtsey. "Will you come to take tea with us today?"

The rector lifted her chin with his finger. "I would be very happy to, child. Now run back to Miss Birkenstock's side. You don't want to worry her, do you?"

"No, sir." Mabel turned and skipped down the aisle.

The little girl reached Agatha and was drawn into a hug. Agatha bent down to listen to Mabel's news and then she ushered the children outside.

"I've not seen you in church in quite some time, my lord. Welcome."

"Thank you. I..." Oscar shuffled his feet. "Well, you see..." He didn't want to blurt out his troubles for all to hear. He just wanted to find peace again. But there were far too many ears around them to unburden his soul here.

Manning slapped his shoulder again. "So very much like your mother. She never could come straight to the point of a problem either. And judging by your hesitation, you are not quite ready to unburden yourself. But come see me later. My door is always open for you, son. Excuse me."

Manning turned away to say goodbye to his parishioners, leaving Oscar with the uncomfortable feeling that the vicar knew his sin. Thou Shalt Not Kill.

His unease returned.

Turning for the doors, he fell in behind the chattering mass of decent society and stepped out into bright sunshine. Momentarily blinded, he blinked away the stunning effect and descended the stairs. The August morning was clear of rain for a change, so he declined the services of a waiting hack and set off for home on foot.

Perhaps the long walk would be good for his spirits. But ahead of him Agatha and two ineffective servants were shepherding the orphanage children across the street through traffic. He had the worst luck at keeping his promise to maintain a distance from Agatha.

Once they made the sidewalk, he let out the breath he'd held. Their attempts to control the children were being met with considerable resistance. The boys wanted to run ahead; the girls wanted to linger and admire every pretty sight to be seen. They were threading their way down the street at a snail's pace. Oscar would overtake them easily if he wished, or he could divert from the path and take the longer way home. But then the children's voices rose in disagreement over something on the ground, and Agatha stopped to speak sharply to them. Even from a distance of several yards away, he could hear how vexed she'd become. He hurried after her. Agatha shouldn't have to deal with this rabble alone.

"Lord Carrington," Mabel squealed, breaking ranks with the other children to reach his side.

Oscar scowled, imitating how his own father had behaved when forced to walk with him as a boy. "Mabel, that's no way to behave. Return to your spot beside the other girl and walk quietly now."

Mabel blushed pink. "That's Kitty."

He crossed his arms, and glanced up the line of staring children. "Then return to Kitty. She looks to be waiting for you."

Mabel rushed back to her former place and took up Kitty's hand again. The other children were also very quick to resume their places in the line too. As he suspected, all they needed was a father figure to make them behave themselves. Children learned early not to listen to any suggestions made by a mere servant, and

Agatha was too soft-hearted for her own good. She might be a good influence on them singularly, but en masse . . . she hadn't a hope.

Oscar let his gaze travel further up the line and caught her frowning expression. He tipped his hat, but made no move to join her. She'd been adamant they keep a distance. Well, for today, the distance would be seven restless children, one maid, and one groom. There should be enough propriety in that to keep her happy, at least for now.

With a quick flick of her hands to encourage the children, they resumed their fast walk. Oscar followed along, keeping a watchful eye on the children's behavior, but his thoughts were grim, turned inward to his own troubles. Should he confide his terrors to the morally upright vicar or keep his own counsel?

The Earl of Daventry hadn't understood. Not really. Oh, he had tried, but then the man had been too preoccupied with his own happy change of circumstances to grasp the extent of Oscar's distress. Would anyone understand? Would Agatha?

He would very much like to talk to her. When they were together, he felt such intense peace, such perfect symmetry with the world. These days he was beginning to forget what it was to be happy.

On Grafton Street, the children hurried up the front stairs of the orphanage and noisily entered the building. Agatha gave him an odd look as he turned to follow her inside. He had no intention of talking with her, staring at her, or thinking about her soft curves sliding through his hands. But the work he had to do to assess the orphanage would distract him from his morbid thoughts for perhaps an hour. He handed off his hat and cane then turned for the study. He shut the door behind him. The work, however short lived, should distract him enough to let him get through another day.

At least that was the plan until the music started.

Oscar dropped the pen to the desk, listening with every nerve as Agatha's music filtered through the house from the parlor opposite his door. She played a slow melody—one he wasn't familiar with, but one that instantly calmed his racing heart. Sitting back, he imagined her playing in the little sitting room opposite his office, her back to the door, the smooth line of her neck bent to the instrument.

His imagination removed her clothes so she was naked at the pianoforte.

Such thoughts were not helping. He had to forget her, but the delicate playing, music that stirred him body and soul, would drive him insane. Oscar closed the book and gathered together some papers. This was not the place to forget the past. Not when the past seemed determined to keep him firmly in its clutches. Taking the receipts and journal with him, he quietly stepped out into the hall, not wanting to draw attention to his leaving. Just across the way, Agatha sat, tapping out the tune for the children. The previously unruly orphans appeared spellbound, their upturned faces enraptured by Agatha's skill. This was how she'd charmed the children so thoroughly. She'd found the perfect use of her talents.

The butler approached.

"My hat and cane, if you please," Oscar whispered.

"Yes, my lord."

At the instrument, Agatha's head turned as if she'd heard him. He took a step closer and her head turned to an almost painful angle. That she would still acknowledge his presence raced along his clamoring nerves. He couldn't stay. He wanted more of Agatha Birkenstock than he was allowed.

The butler let him out, ushering him into bright sunshine, but he felt none of the warmth. His soul was chilled to the core.

Partway down the road, a gruff voice hailed him by name.

Oscar turned and found an unfamiliar gentleman approaching.

"Lord Carrington, isn't it?"

"Yes. May I help you?"

The other man was weathered, expensively dressed, but a complete stranger to him. "My name is Leopold Randall, a silk merchant from India. I was wondering if you might spare me a few moments of your time. I'm looking for information."

That explained the dark, weathered complexion, but what the man could want with him escaped him. Randall appeared harmless, so Oscar gestured him closer. "I'll help if I can. I'm headed to Berkley Square. Why don't you tell me what you're seeking while we walk?"

Randall glanced behind him toward the orphanage. His lips compressed, but then he nodded and fell into step. He did not, however, immediately launch into his tale.

Oscar grew impatient. "How may I be of service?"

The other man heaved a heavy sigh. "I've been away from England for some years now, in India for business, and I've lost track of my family. I was hoping to search the orphanage's records for any information they might contain concerning their whereabouts."

Oscar stopped, frowning. "The orphanage is a relatively new venture. When was the last you heard of them?"

"Ten years ago, now. The youngest pair, my brother and sister, would be four-and-twenty and six-and-twenty by now."

Oscar smiled apologetically. "Then I'm very much afraid I cannot be of help to you. The place was established just last year, and the children are all aged under eleven years, I believe."

Beside him, the other man swore. The colorful oaths that burst from Randall's mouth surprised Oscar for their complexity and venom. Although he was sure none were directed at him, he started walking again. Randall hurried to catch up but held his tongue. He was no doubt deeply disappointed by Oscar's news. Poor fellow. It must be dreadful to lose one's whole family.

As they reached the center of the square, Oscar stopped. "Randall?"

The other man looked up.

"You aren't by chance one of the Romsey Randall's?"

The other man's gaze grew wary. "I am a cousin to the current duke," he admitted slowly.

Oscar smiled. "Well, that is a spot of good news. I had heard there was some vigorous debate about the duchy's succession. Lord Carmichael, at one time, petitioned for guardianship of the duke, but met with resistance. You should present yourself to him forthwith so he may be easy again. I know there will be great relief when word spreads that another Randall has been found." Oscar looked about him to see if he could spot another peer nearby to pass along the good news.

Leopold Randall took a step back. "If I might ask you not to inform anyone of my whereabouts at this time, I would be grateful beyond belief."

"Why the hell would I do that?"

Randall glanced about nervously. "Because I believe the former Dukes of Romsey were responsible for the disappearance of my siblings. I want to find my family first, well before I make my existence known to the current duke and anyone else closely associated with the duchy."

Fourteen

ASTONISHED, OSCAR SCRUBBED his hand across his chin. "He's just a child. A drooling infant, if I remember correctly."

Randall still glanced around them nervously. "Still, it pays to be cautious."

A memory of a whispered conversation at his club flitted through Oscar's mind. It had been well known that the old Duke of Romsey had not been a man to cross. Randall's statement, and the fact that the succession for the duchy was unclear due to the disappearance of all other Randall relations, made Oscar inclined to believe him. "Yet you approached me. Why?"

The other man met his gaze directly. "While I might have little faith in the benevolence of the aristocracy, I have had some dealings with one Mr. Thomas Birkenstock, a fellow businessman living here in London, in this very square. Over the course of our dealings, he's mentioned some of his connections, and you by name once or twice. I called on him earlier, but was informed that he was away from home. I was invited to contact him as soon as I returned from India."

Ah, so Birkenstock was the reason for this approach. If Birkenstock admitted this man was a friend, then Oscar would have some faith that Randall spoke the truth about his identity. "I believe he's attending to his business interests in Winchester."

The other man nodded. "Thank you for that. I shall have to assume that he will not return to Town for some time." Randall squared his shoulders. "I should be going. Thank you, my lord, for your trouble."

Randall tipped his hat and made to leave.

"Wait," Oscar called.

Randall turned and Oscar approached him. "I would like to help you. If you would care to join me for luncheon, you could provide me with more particulars. I have friends I can approach, decent men of particular discretion, who have a wide range of interests across society." When Randall shook his head, Oscar rushed to add, "It cannot hurt to try. You do not need to confide your directions to me."

After a long moment, Randall nodded. "That is very good of you, my lord. But I should not like to put you out."

Oscar smiled, feeling his spirits lift as a surge of anticipation filled him. "Nonsense. I am happy to help in any way I can to see your family returned to you." It would be good to be useful. Oscar could engage runners on Randall's behalf and keep his whereabouts secret. Feeling the nightmare of the past months dim, Oscar led Randall inside his home and through to his bookroom. He slid the orphanage accounts to the side of his table.

Randall looked about him with an amused grin. "I hadn't realized you lived next door to Birkenstock. No wonder he mentioned you with such fondness."

Oscar smiled, but didn't elaborate on why Birkenstock might think fondly of him. "Would you care for a brandy?"

Randall nodded and set himself down before Oscar's tidy desk.

Unused to such silence in his companions, Oscar poured drinks and settled behind his desk, drawing out his little pocket book and pen to make notes. "When did you see your siblings last?"

"Christmas eighteen-three." Randall sipped another mouthful of brandy, but his face had darkened with emotion. "I had returned home from school to spend the holiday season with my family at Romsey."

"The ducal estate?'

"No, the village. My father was already out of favor with the duke, for having the bad form of producing too many healthy children, I believe. The ducal line produced few offspring that survived infancy, whereas mine produced many more. We lived in a small house on the edge of the estate."

Oscar stood and pulled his Burke's Peerage from his bookshelf. The Duke of Romsey's entry was easy to find without Randall's assistance. What he said was true. The current duke had no uncles remaining. The only distant relations were of Leopold Ramsey's line.

"My younger brother and I had been returned to school a full month before we heard of our parents' deaths. A carriage accident, I was told. My youngest brother and sister were not mentioned at the time, but my parents were uncommonly doting parents and always traveled with their children. I've not heard of their whereabouts since the Christmas of '03. Then, a few weeks later after our parents' deaths, Oliver, my younger brother by two years, ran away from school during the night."

Oscar frowned. The tale was quite fantastical, but if the brother had run away of his own accord there was no mystery there at all. "Was your brother unhappy at school?"

Randall's expression grew darker, if that were possible. "No, Oliver was happiest when surrounded by his books. We were to meet that morning before class. He said he had a secret to tell. He never arrived at the appointed time, and then I was called into the headmaster's office and informed he'd run off."

Quite fantastical. Oscar didn't know whether to believe him or not.

"I can see how you doubt," Randall said quietly.

Oscar decided to be blunt. "I'm not sure what to believe, but it is clear you fear the worst. Why do you think they were disappeared?"

"Because the Duke of Romsey had the gall to promise them harm if I flinched at doing any of his dirty work to keep me in line several years ago. To keep me in my proper place. He gave me no cause to disbelieve. My family had never wanted more from the duchy. We were no real danger to his power, or to Edwin, his heir, but he wouldn't loosen his control over me. I was his son's heir until the current duchess gave birth to a son."

"I'm surprised he left you alone after that."

Randall laughed, a bitter sound that chilled him through to his toes. "I am no threat to the child. The old bastard made sure of that."

Oscar wanted to ask how, but by the fierce expression on the face of the man before him, Randall wouldn't confide what obviously was an unpleasant memory. He scratched down the date of the accident and the interval till Oliver's disappearance. "Do you remember what your siblings look like?"

Randall reached into his inner coat pocket and threw a pile of drawings across the table. "These are a fair likeness, but they are over ten years old and may not be of much use now."

Oscar flicked through three sketches. The images were of children, but he could see a strong resemblance to Leopold Randall. Oliver, Rose, and Tobias Randall. An experienced runner should be able to make use of them. "They are a start. May I keep these?"

Randall sank back into his chair, weariness dragging the animation from his face. "Of course. I have made other copies."

Randall's flat tones brought Oscar's own fears rushing back. While Randall had talked, he'd quite forgotten his own problems. If he kept his mind focused on investigations for Leopold Randall, maybe his own concerns would disappear. He tucked the drawings into his inner pocket along with his notebook just as luncheon was announced.

Once Randall was on his way back to wherever he was staying, Oscar would visit with Lord Daventry and the Rector of St. George. The holy man and the former sinner might be able to shed some light on the fate and potential location of three children the Duke of Romsey had deemed expendable.

~ * ~

Agatha inched the window in her bedroom open, a light breeze wafted across her thighs through her thick nightgown. She shouldn't open the window, but her day had been haunted by images of Oscar's distress. Despite the knowledge that he was forever beyond her reach, she needed to talk to him.

She'd caught a glimpse of his expression as he'd sat in church that morning. The strain was so clear her heart had raced, raced so badly she had almost run to him, despite the numerous members of society sitting between them. But that very action would have ruined the rest of her life.

Then he had followed them home, casting a stern eye on the children so they behaved properly for a change. The fact that Oscar had a calming effect on the children had surprised her. He was, quite simply, the most casual of men. But not anymore, it seemed. His silent disapproval of their high spirits had quieted them faster than any words she'd uttered that morning.

Once returned to the orphanage, the boys had peppered her with questions about the viscount. They wanted to know everything: who his tailor was, did he ride a great hunter, drive a phaeton, and was he Whig or Tory? Agatha had tried her best to appear less knowledgeable than she actually was. She wasn't quite sure she achieved it because her maid, mending the children's clothes by the window, kept casting her odd looks. Agatha was very glad when Manning had arrived to distract them all and they'd gone outside for tea.

Agatha popped her head out her bedroom window and let her gaze rest on the adjacent balcony. Oscar wasn't there. Not yet. She let her head fall, disappointed, and noticed a bag of sweets waiting. The sign of his constancy made her heart ache. She had thought he would stop leaving her little gifts.

She hefted the bag, and tossed it between her hands. By rights she should not accept such small pleasures. She should return them and hope he stopped being so kind. His continuing kindness was a sharp pain that never truly left her. The rattle of a door handle reached her ears. Agatha drew back, knowing the sound came from Oscar's door. The sharp rap of boots rang on the tile, then a slither of sound and a heavy thump.

When she peeked out the window again, Oscar sat with his back to her. Glass clinked to the tile and she heard his heavy sigh. She laid her head on her arms, staring at the back of Oscar's head and willing him to turn.

He stubbornly stayed facing the other way, drinking slowly from his glass. When the glass was empty, he stood and brushed off his clothes. His head turned fractionally, finally acknowledging her presence. "I miss you."

Then he disappeared inside his townhouse.

Agatha lifted her hands to the window frame, slid it shut, and then wiped the tears from her eyes.

Fifteen

"SO WHAT YOU'RE saying is the orphanage cannot pay its way," Lord Carter summarized, quite incorrectly, to Oscar's annoyance.

Oscar scowled across his bookroom, where the gathered Grafton Street Orphanage trustees were crammed into the tiny space. His opinion of Lord Carter decreased every time he spoke. "No. I am not saying that at all. I need more time. It appears the industrious Mr. Dickson has cause to explain his overuse of Orphanage funds. There are a vast number of discrepancies between his accounting and the facts as I find them. God knows where all his purchases have gone, but they are not at the orphanage and I can see no evidence that they ever arrived there."

"Gentlemen, this is an alarming development," Mr. Manning conceded. "But it is not the worst it can be. As Carrington has promised us, the orphanage's expenses are well within the boundaries of the combined annual contributions made to the fund. If only Mr. Dickson hadn't squandered them, we might be much better off. And so would the children."

The other trustees muttered between themselves. They'd taken the news surprisingly well. But the thefts by Mr. Dickson, gone unnoticed for the last year, had ruled out the expense of attempting any repairs to the premises, at least for this year. There was so much to be done and no ready funds to accomplish the task. There was just enough to feed, clothe, and warm the children and the few servants for the coming winter.

As the opposing arguments between the trustees rose to a loud roar, Oscar met Mr. Manning's gaze. There was something quite familiar about the man's face. Oscar felt he should know him better and be happy to spend more time with him. But they moved in different circles, their only connection being the Grafton Street orphanage and his occasional church attendance.

Manning smiled and closed the gap between them. "They will be like this for hours, I assure you. I envy you your earlier reticence to involve yourself in the orphanage's affairs. I might have saved myself considerable vexation should I have followed your example."

"The charity is my mother's pet project. I only continued my contributions to please her."

"I'm sure she appreciates it. She is quite passionate about the children's welfare," Manning murmured with approval. "When does she return from visiting with her friend?"

"Not till Wednesday."

"Ah." Manning glanced around the room and didn't elaborate. Was he aware of his mother's affair with Birkenstock? That could prove uncomfortable, should he discover the truth of her trip.

Yet curiosity ate at Oscar. There was something about the flush of color to Manning's features that hinted he was much more concerned than he dared let on. "Was there something I can help you with in her absence?"

"No, not really." Manning chewed his lip. "However, I am curious to know if your mother appeared in good spirits before she left?" He sighed. "I ask because the Duke of Staines can be a trifle meddling, and I understand they had some few words recently at a ball. Now there appears to be some salacious gossip circulating about the pair."

Oscar remembered the night he had spotted her speaking with the duke quite well. It had not appeared a friendly conversation by the end. "Mother did appear upset that night. But she did not choose to confide in me. Given her melancholy on the journey home, I put little faith in the rumors of any kind of affair between them. If anything, they seemed to have had a falling out."

Manning's gaze fell to the floor and he rocked a little from one foot to another. "My brother likes to flirt and stir up society. There is nothing between them now, nor has there ever been in the past, I'm sure."

Oscar had forgotten the connection between the Duke of Staines and Mr. Manning. He knew Staines by reputation only, but surely a brother would know the truth of any affair. "Then I am happy to hear it, but what do you think they disagreed on?"

Manning rocked again on the balls of his feet.

"I say, Manning. What do you think of this notion?" Lord Carter called and drew Mr. Manning away. But Oscar was now rather intrigued as to what Manning's answer might have been. What business could his mother and the duke have in common?

Oscar rejoined the conversation while the debate about pursuing Mr. Dickson was discussed at length.

"I refuse to allow myself to be cheated in this," Lord Carter fumed.

"We were all cheated," several grumbled.

"The orphanage was the one swindled," Manning reminded them gently.

"Yes, well, that is really beside the point. One does not swindle the nobility. It shall not be endured," Lord Carter asserted with force.

Manning offered a tight smile in return.

The conversation moved in circles.

When Oscar caught his eye, Manning rolled his but just as quickly hid the gesture. The sight of Manning's fleeting expression reminded Oscar that he had always liked the man. He had found him quite intelligent—with a duke for a brother, he certainly should have been—and in his own way, quite amusing. In a vicar, his attitudes were unique.

It seemed a shame that his mother should so disregard the man's attentions. Mother enjoyed a good laugh and always scolded Oscar when he rolled his eyes as Manning had done. It seemed that they shared a sense of humor. Society wouldn't turn a hair if his mother chose to take up with Manning. His relationship to a duke would smooth any ruffled feathers while Manning persuaded Oscar's stubborn mother to marry again.

With shock, Oscar settled against his heavy desk and considered his line of thinking. He could easily accept the change, if Manning could convince his mother to marry. But he couldn't say that about any other man. What was it about Manning that soothed him?

He looked Manning over critically. Tall, as tall, if not an inch higher, than Oscar. Pale, his neat hair was peppered through with grey. He was lean too. Just like Oscar, Manning had not an ounce of spare flesh about him. Blue eyes, a shade paler than Oscar's mother's. In his youth, he must have been much admired. So why hadn't he succeeded in winning over Oscar's mother now?

Perhaps Manning reminded her too much of her own son. There were some similarities between them—like height and build and complexion. Then there was Manning's damaged hand. Oscar couldn't believe his mother would be so squeamish as to discount a man because of an impairment. Honestly, he'd be more inclined to state nothing much could be wrong with Manning at all. He was a duke's brother, one that appeared quietly devoted to living a good life. He was by no means poor himself, if the gossip were anything to go by. And he did seem a nice, gentlemanly-like fellow.

Oscar would be proud to have him as a second father.

"The Duke of Staines, my lords."

Oscar looked up with shock as his butler stood aside to allow the Duke of Staines to stalk into the room.

What the devil?

"Ah, Lynton. What the devil are you doing bickering with this bunch of old goats?"

Several of the trustees blushed. A few snarled, "Nothing that concerns you."

The duke, however, laughed. "Lynton, I'm bored. Amuse me." With a quick glance about the chamber, he settled himself behind Oscar's desk and propped his feet up on the desk.

"Your Grace," Manning said around his clenched jaw. "Perhaps I could call on you at home when I finish here?"

The duke ignored his brother and looked at Oscar instead. "Any chance for a spot of brandy? I'm parched."

The plaintive question brought a smile to Oscar's face. He poured a glass and passed it over without comment. Damn funny fellow to be dropping in here for amusement. There was nothing entertaining about the trustees at all.

Manning turned his back on the duke. "So are we decided to leave things as they are for now?" Several of the trustees glanced toward the duke and nodded, then, within a few minutes, they were all on their way, except for Manning and the Duke of Staines.

Staines cleared his throat. "Good to see I haven't lost my touch at clearing a room of quarrelsome creatures. At least now the annoying rabble is gone, we can get down to serious business. My nephew's townhouse is too small."

Oscar's mouth fell open, startled by the quick change of subject. He shut it swiftly.

"Where he chooses to live is of no concern to you," Manning growled. "Why must you meddle?"

"Because that is what family is for." Staines drained his glass and held it out. "More please."

Really, what on earth was the Duke of Staines doing in Oscar's bookroom? How did one subtly suggest a duke leave? He had things to do for the orphanage, and he'd like to discuss his findings further with Manning before he left today. His Grace was in the way.

He poured the brandy and passed it over.

"There's a good fellow. Don't mind me, I'm always this way. Just ask Lynton here how annoying I can be when I want something."

Manning pursed his lips as if he'd bitten sour lemons.

"Now, where is that delightful woman? Essy and I have a few more matters to discuss."

Manning set his hands to his hips. "She isn't here, Ambrose, and you'd better leave her be or I shall knock you on your arse and leave you there."

"Just look at that. It only takes one potential scandal for him to lose his preachy reserve," Staines said to Oscar. He turned to his brother. "Remember Lynton, it wasn't me who misbehaved. I expected better from you than to keep something of this importance from me."

Manning cast an apologetic glance toward Oscar. "I wasn't certain before. It's something of a shock after so long of not thinking about it."

"Careless of you," Staines murmured. "Carrington must have been supremely put out."

Oscar stepped forward. "Manning and I are not on unfriendly terms, Your Grace."

Staines smiled suddenly. "Good to know. Hopefully that won't change anytime soon." He stood and approached Oscar. "You have your mother about the eyes, but the rest of you is all your father," he laughed. When Staines held out his hand, Oscar took it and returned the firm handshake. Then the duke hurried out.

Oscar turned to Manning. "What the devil was all that about?"

Manning wiped his hand across his jaw. "Congratulations. The Duke of Staines has decided he likes the look of you. You have not seen the last of him, I'm afraid."

"Ah." Could that be a good or bad thing for his position in society? The way Manning phrased it, he sounded doubtful it could be good. He would keep his distance from the duke until he was sure. Although, he could end up with an invitation to Staines' private gaming hell, the Hunt Club, if he continued to like Oscar.

Manning's stare pierced him. "Don't even think about applying to him for admittance to his club. Your mother will throttle you if you end up there."

"How did you—?"

A wry grin crossed Manning's face. "I wasn't always committed to the church. Ambrose opened the club before I took orders. I'm well aware of what goes on there. Which is why he imposed a rule that family be excluded.

His own son cannot cross the threshold. Given his fondness for Essy, he won't let you even breathe the air from the street front."

"It's that bad?"

"Worse, and certainly no place for you."

Although vexed that one, Manning could read his mind and two, that Manning didn't hesitate to offer an opinion about his unlikely admittance to the Hunt Club, Oscar let the matter drop. He had other concerns that took precedence. "I wondered if I might apply to you for advice. I had a visit today from a fellow who's looking for his lost siblings. They disappeared some ten years ago. Do you have any contacts at the Foundling Hospital I could apply to for information?"

Manning mulled it over. "Perhaps. Who are you looking for?"

"I. Ah. I'd rather not say at this time."

Manning raised a brow at his hesitation. "Makes it rather difficult to help."

"I know. But I am honor bound to keep quiet for the time being."

"If he's a common man, he might apply directly to them, but it could be some time before they attend the matter." Manning arched a brow. "If he is someone altogether more important, as I'm sensing might be true in this case, given your hesitation to speak his name, then I'd be happy to act as intermediary."

Oscar nodded. He didn't know whether to confide or not. He'd have to discuss the matter with Randall first. "I'd appreciate you're efforts, but I'll need to apply for permission."

"Of course. Was there anything else?"

"No, no."

"Then if you will excuse me, my lord, I must return to St. George's. Good evening to you."

As Manning left the room, Oscar followed. "I say, Manning, what will happen to the children should the orphanage close?"

Manning set his hat in place, but his expression turned sad. "I expect they will go where every unwanted child goes. Back onto the streets, unless someone else is prepared to step forward to see to their care. It is a matter that lingers in my mind. I should not like to see them gone away for good. I've grown particularly fond of the little ones."

Sixteen

OSCAR PRESSED HIS fist to his mouth to cover his reaction to the stench of the crowds inside the lobby of the Theatre Royal. London's most popular theatre might be *the* place to be seen, but it thrummed with the vast unwashed and over-scented, threatening to overwhelm his senses. He craned his neck, glancing over the dark head of his betrothed, hoping to catch sight of his friend and his wife before the cloying scents caused him to gag. The Earl and Countess of Daventry had refused callers today, but Daventry had later sent a note promising to be at the theatre tonight. He couldn't see them yet. Damn it.

Lord and Lady Prewitt, along with Penelope, moved through the crowds without waiting for him. Oscar hurried to catch up, eyeing his party with growing frustration. Lord Prewitt had his wife on one arm and Penelope on the other. Given Prewitt's refusal to give up either one on the way to their seats, he commanded a wide path through the throng.

The upper corridor was thick with the *ton,* and Oscar was stopped one time too many to have any say in the seating arrangements for his box. Both Penelope and Lady Prewitt took the front seats. Prewitt sat behind Penelope, leaving Oscar to take a place behind Lady Prewitt, diagonally opposed to his betrothed, and unable to even whisper privately to her during the performance.

In fact, it seemed the chances of pleasant conversation were suspended for the evening. Neither Lord nor Lady Prewitt appeared keen to speak, and Penelope ignored everything but the empty stage.

Oscar settled in the chair and withheld a grimace. Quite frankly, he was shot of this whole getting married business. The chance of any intimacy with his future wife before they married was apparently not open to discussion. He was very firmly being held at a respectable distance. Anyone could think they were not to marry at all.

The theatre was abuzz with activity. Oscar scanned the other boxes, searching and tipping his head to acquaintances but hoping to find Lord Daventry in the crowd. His regular box was still empty, but Oscar couldn't see him paying his respects to any other party. Perhaps Daventry had had a change of plan and decided to stay at home with his lovely wife. But then, punctuality might not be high on a newly married man's priorities. And Lilly was often ill. While the short carriage ride shouldn't harm her, the earl might travel London's streets with more caution now.

As angry voices rose from the pit, Oscar glanced down. The mob was unruly tonight, pushing and shoving without much thought to propriety. He'd never wanted to venture below. He'd always had a box from which to view the drama of the night. A woman shrieked and then the crowd laughed. Oscar caught a glimpse of a woman thrown over a man's shoulder as he marched out the opposite door.

His lips quirked. At least someone was fortunate tonight.

Oscar turned his head to the left as Leopold Randall's dark form prowling the crowds below. His seemingly random path suggested to Oscar that he was searching the rough crowd for the familiar faces of his family. Had Randall mentioned that any of them had a fondness for the theatre? Oscar tried to remember, but didn't think they'd touched on the siblings' talents or proclivities. That could be useful information too.

Thinking of Randall's searching below, Oscar turned his attention back to the upper boxes, peering intently at every woman present tonight and particularly at the ladies he didn't know well. It was not beyond the realm of impossibility to imagine that the old duke had married Randall's sister to another peer. He could have bought the loyalty of the man by arranging such a distinguished connection, with a hefty dowry thrown in for good measure. The thought sickened him. But none of the ladies he spotted bore a strong resemblance to the female sibling of Leopold Randall. For a minute, Oscar couldn't remember her name. Rose. Now he remembered. All sweet smiles and a thorny disposition when crossed, according to Randall. If the chit had maintained her fractious temperament, she'd be so much easier to identify.

Unless her fiery spirit had been crushed by her situation.

Oscar shook himself. It didn't do him any good to harbor such morbid thoughts. The siblings would be found, alive, well, and everything would be right with the world again. Well, right for everyone except him.

As the house lights dimmed, Oscar spotted movement in the Earl of Daventry's box. They had arrived just as the opera was to begin. Daventry settled his wife, dressed in a revealing, dark claret gown, into her seat with such focus that he never noticed the crowd loudly acknowledge his tardy arrival.

Oscar leaned forward, closer to Lady Prewitt, so he might whisper into her ear and be heard clearly. "Forgive me, Lady Prewitt, but I must leave our party for a few minutes. I have an urgent matter to discuss with the Earl of Daventry."

Lady Prewitt nodded, her head turned fractionally, and then her lips moved lightly against his cheek. "I will inform my sister."

Nonplussed by the intimate contact, Oscar snapped his head back an inch. "Thank you."

Instead of embarrassment, triumph tugged Lady Prewitt's lips into a pleased smile. Oscar rushed to leave the box, appalled that he might have unwittingly offered encouragement somewhere along the way. He could not and would not act so shamefully toward his future sister by marriage.

He hurried along the deserted corridor, dragging the purer air deep into his lungs. Here the noise of the crowd was muted, most patrons having found their seats already, and he reached his friend's box without interruption.

"You wasted no time," Daventry exclaimed as they shook hands.

"Of course, how could I miss paying my respects promptly when Lilly attends the theatre?"

Smiling, as always, Lilly turned so Oscar could take her hand and squeeze. Marriage agreed with her. Or more precisely, marriage to the Earl of Daventry agreed with her. She looked radiant in red. Lilly returned the pressure, but her eyes swerved back to the crowds after a bare moment.

"I see I'm not an interesting enough companion tonight?" Oscar noted wryly to Daventry. He was hardly offended by Lilly's preoccupation. He liked Lilly. Until recently, she'd had very little to do with the world, being confined to bed for much of her recent life. Her transparent fascination with the theatre brought a smile to his lips. She was refreshingly natural and deeply in love with her husband. A fact that he'd long since grown used to, but he still couldn't quite help being amazed that Daventry loved her so deeply in return.

Daventry laughed. "Go easy on her. She's never been to the theatre before. My butler mentioned you appeared quite disappointed we were unavailable this morning. What can I do for you?"

Daventry sat in silence while Oscar related his conversation with Leopold Randall, revealing his identity to the only man he trusted not to repeat it. His eyebrows quirked a few times, but other than that, he didn't interrupt. Knowing his friend never rushed to offer advice, Oscar waited, keeping his eyes on the crowd and stage, ignoring how his friends hand moved restlessly on his wife's leg. Clearly, marriage hadn't interfered with his fascination with the opposite sex.

Oscar envied Daventry his happiness.

Across the theatre, Oscar's future wife sat as remote as marble, staring at the stage and languidly fanning herself. At her side, Lady Prewitt appeared less sedate. Her posture was one of tense disapproval. Oscar wondered if his quick exit from the box had offended her or if her mood was triggered by something else entirely. Lady Prewitt caught his eye and a slow smile replaced her displeasure. Oscar looked away. He didn't want to encourage her.

He had to find something to admire in Penelope before the wedding day. She sat with an elegant poise, a far greater degree of decorum for one so young. At nineteen, she outshone many of the debutants coming out in society, but she'd never rival Agatha's pull on his senses, and he feared she'd never match Agatha's claim on his heart.

A brief smile flitted across Penelope's face, an expression he was quite unfamiliar with. What could possibly provoke such a reaction? Oscar glanced at the stage. The heroine was dying, lying at her assailant's feet and pleading for mercy. The play tonight was a tragedy, yet when he glanced at Penelope again, his future bride was grinning with an almost giddy delight. Oscar scrubbed a hand across his jaw, confused by the sight.

"I'd be inclined to believe the man if he thinks his life, and those of his siblings, are in danger," Lord Daventry acknowledged. "The Romsey's are a dark breed of men, despite the fair complexion. There's years of unsubstantiated rumors floating about them. Randall is right to distrust."

"Hmm, I was convinced of his sincerity too, but I've not much idea of how to go about an investigation without alerting the entire House of Lords that a Romsey spare has been located. Randall was very adamant to keep his whereabouts secret. Luckily, he never mentioned where he's staying so I've not the worry of lying to contend with."

"Smart of him." The earl rubbed his hand along his wife's leg again and she turned, a smile pulling her lips into a delighted expression. Devotion, adoration, love.

Daventry was a lucky man. The earl's fingers slipped to his wife's chin and stroked along her jaw. "Come and see me tomorrow. We can go over it all again and discuss where to begin your enquiries. Make it later in the day, around one."

Oscar nodded. "One more thing. I've a mind to purchase an estate in the country." He glanced at his betrothed and found her head bent to hear whatever witty repartee Lord Prewitt refused to share with his wife. Frustration welled in him again. "Something greater than a day's carriage ride from Town. Would you be aware of anything suitable, by any chance?"

The earl glanced across the theatre where Penelope sat listening to every word her brother-in-law uttered. A frown turned Daventry's mouth down as if he'd tasted something bitter. "That should annoy Lord Thorne nicely. Unfortunately, nothing springs to mind this very instant. But we can discuss what you want in a property tomorrow, too. Come for luncheon. I believe Lilly has invited Agatha for the afternoon."

It was on the tip of his tongue to refuse. Agatha would want him to keep away, but with the earl and countess as chaperones, they might be sociable without any scandal attaching to the event. He'd have to keep his hands, and other parts of his anatomy, to himself, but he would be able to hear Agatha speak.

"I'll see you both at one o'clock. Lady Daventry, a pleasure to see you again."

Lilly beamed, but her eyes soon turned back to her husband. Oscar slipped out of their box before things got too heated between the earl and his new wife. They made love at the drop of a hat, a handkerchief, or her pretty grey eyes. Daventry couldn't have made a better choice in marrying Lilly.

The corridor was deserted. Oscar ambled back to his box, in no hurry to return to his guests. Outside he paused, drawing a deep breath of scented air into his lungs before rejoining his party. What he wanted to do was turn around, return home, and climb in through the window of Agatha's house. He wanted her in his arms with a powerful ache.

Last night her heavy breathing and quiet, watchful presence, safely tucked inside her bedchamber, had soothed him. But he'd been moments away from leaping the railing. If she'd spoken up, offered him any encouragement whatsoever, he'd have done his best to climb into her bed again.

Oscar parted the curtain and let his gaze fall on Penelope. Her whole attention was focused on the stage, but then he noted her arm hanging awkwardly down beside her chair. Puzzled by the odd posture, he inched into the box. Thanks to Prewitt's broad shoulders, he couldn't see what she was doing. Prewitt was watching her though. He was sure of that. Oscar took another step, letting the curtains close behind him, encasing him in the dark shadows of the box. But he must have made some sound for Prewitt turned, a dark flush upon his skin. Penelope's shoulders squared, and she lifted her hand to fan herself with the same languid ease of earlier.

Prewitt said nothing, but he shuffled in his chair as Oscar sat, his face fixed upon the stage once more. The feeling of intruding surfaced again and he wondered just what he was getting himself into. Although he did his best to quell the increasingly bitter taste in his mouth, he decided it might be in his best interests to keep an eye on his betrothed and her brother by marriage. There was an odd connection between them, one he'd never noticed between other siblings. It was almost as if ...

Oscar shoved the thought aside and forced his eyes away. He was simply looking for excuses to get out of this marriage. Surely his mind was playing tricks on him. His gaze settled on Penelope and Lady Prewitt again. For all Penelope's languid fanning, Lady Prewitt was a stark contrast. She appeared blindingly happy at his return. He returned her smile and shuffled to get comfortable in his chair for the endless night that was the theatre. Given that the chairs were drawn uncomfortably close together for his long legs, he stretched one out in front of him and kept his attention to the stage.

Something touched his leg. He glanced down at his limb, peering into the shadows. Another touch and then he realized that Lady Prewitt was strumming her fingers along his leg. Shocked, Oscar withdrew his leg. The lady returned her hand to her lap. How odd!

How bizarre.

How utterly disgusting!

What the hell kind of family was he marrying into?

Seventeen

OSCAR STOOD AS the ladies entered Lord Daventry's drawing room. He held his breath as his gaze settled on Agatha's stiff-backed posture. Today she looked elegant in plum muslin, no insipid prints for her, but her eyes flashed with anger at his being here. She might be put out with him, but it was far too late to plead another engagement.

Lillian swept past him in a rustle of green silk and let Daventry gather her in his arms. "Did you have a pleasant morning, sweetheart?" he whispered to his wife as his hands roved over her back and dipped lower.

Oscar looked away, giving them privacy. Unfortunately, his gaze settled on Agatha. His former lover was looking anywhere but at the newly married couple too. Oscar crossed the room, keeping the kissing couple hidden behind his back, to stand before her. More than anything he wanted to take her into his arms. She must have read his intentions because her body swayed back a little.

Rather than embrace her, he glanced over his shoulders at the married couple. "They can be a little inconsiderate in displaying their affections at times, but I do think passion in a marriage must make for a comfortable life."

"They are happy," Agatha whispered back.

Their eyes met and held. "That they are. But I've never met a couple so prone to forget they have company." Oscar spoke the last words with greater strength, hoping the kissing couple would hear them and end their embrace.

Lilly giggled. "My apologies again, Lord Carrington. Giles brings out the worst in me."

Oscar turned and smiled. "From what I've seen, you are quite the matched pair. And please, it's Oscar."

Lilly quirked her eye at Agatha. "Perhaps we could be informal, today. I do find it quite agreeable. Do you mind, Miss Birkenstock?"

"Whatever the countess commands is perfectly agreeable to me." Agatha laughed as Lilly rushed her, stepping away from the countess' mock fury. "All right, all right, Lilly it is."

The two women embraced quickly, but then Lilly linked their arms. "Gentlemen, we are to eat informally today. Luncheon will be served in the rose room in less than half an hour."

"Of course," Oscar murmured.

Lilly's pain returned more quickly if forced to dine formally for every meal. To compensate, and keep her happy, Daventry dined very informally. Society would be shocked if they knew the earl and his wife forced their guests to eat while reclining upon the pillow-strewn floor.

With a saucy wink for her husband, Lilly dragged Agatha from the room.

"They get along well," Oscar murmured, missing Agatha the minute she disappeared from sight. Their steps disappeared along the hall and then all grew quiet again.

Daventry clapped a stunning blow to his shoulder. "They are the best of friends. I am happy Lilly has some feminine company from time to time."

Oscar turned, catching an odd expression on his friends face. "I should have thought you'd want her all to yourself. I've often felt in the way."

Daventry grimaced. "Believe me, I'm grateful for any distraction."

"You are? Why? Are you not as happily married as you seem?"

Daventry raked his fingers through his hair. "My wife is impossible to resist."

Oscar couldn't help the laugh that escaped him. The most debauched rake in London, tamed by a mere slip of a girl. The idea would be absolutely absurd if he wasn't certain it was true. The Earl of Daventry was a smitten man—deeply devoted to his wife and faithful to a fault.

"Don't laugh. Lilly wants a child."

Oscar sank onto the arm of a chair, nonplussed. "And you don't?"

The earl didn't answer at first. He seemed hesitant to confirm or deny Oscar's question. He turned away and his hands raked through his hair again. He gave the ginger locks a harsh tug and then turned. "I do want children," the earl whispered. "It's just that Lilly is . . . "

"Delicate." Oscar finished for him when he couldn't seem to end his sentence. Of course that was a worry for any man. But in Daventry's case, his fears for Lilly might have some validity. From what he understood, Lilly's condition had altered drastically once the earl had got his hands on her, quite literally the same night. His skill at seduction had reduced her pain significantly, but a birth—he didn't know how that would go, either.

"Have you spoken to Lilly about this?"

Daventry dropped into a chair and pressed his head into the seat back. "No. I don't want to say anything that might disappoint her. She's had enough of that already."

At some point close to when Lilly and the earl had become reacquainted, Lilly's family had given up on her recovering her health. That she was well enough for rational conversation and not deeply drugged by laudanum was entirely thanks to Daventry's inappropriate and scandalous behavior. Oscar drew in a deep breath. What Daventry needed was advice: advice from females who would forgive any blunt and indelicate questions, but not gossip about him later. He needed his family. But his mother was dead these past years and his sister a veritable shrew who'd make a fuss.

"I doubt anything you do would disappoint that woman, but you should talk to her about your fears." Daventry didn't look convinced. "At least, consider it. In the interim, should I approach my mother for advice for you? She's always nattering on about women's complaints. She's from Town at present, but she returns tomorrow."

Daventry bowed his head. "She's invited to tomorrow night's dinner. Did you know?"

"Actually, no. If I catch her as she arrives home, you might be able to have a quick word to her in private without Lilly realizing. Who else is coming?"

Daventry, if it were possible, looked decidedly uncomfortable as he rattled off the acceptances.

Oscar pushed to his feet, quite prepared to bolt from the house. "My God. What were you thinking?" Both his former lover and future wife were to dine together in the same house, on the same night, at his best friend's table. It would be a catastrophe. It was his worst nightmare come to life.

Although, when he thought about it properly, his current life was as much a nightmare as it could possibly be. Daventry grasped his arm in a tight grip. "I couldn't convince Lilly of the problems, and I forbid you to make the evening more difficult for her. She's a bundle of nerves as it is."

"Was Agatha informed of the guest list?"

"Agatha has helped Lilly plan the dinner party, right down to the seating arrangements. She knows exactly who's coming and didn't say a word."

Daventry gave his arm a rough shake then set him free. "We'll muddle through. Somehow."

Oscar settled to a chair. Agatha was in for an uncomfortable night. Didn't Lilly care about her at all?

The luncheon bell rang out and Oscar's stomach fell with the last bell. No wonder Agatha had been angry, but if he'd known, if he'd understood what Lilly intended, he might have had better luck convincing her of the harm her plan could bring.

Daventry hurried from the room, no doubt heading for their informal luncheon. But Oscar lingered, trying desperately to work out what he could do or say to make tomorrow night less of a trial for Agatha. Unfortunately, his mind had completely blanked of witty, clever, or even desperate suggestions.

Maybe he should have stepped between Bartholomew and Lilly and let him pull the trigger. The pain of death might have been brief, but it would have been far preferable to the hell he had to live. Anything would be better than his current life.

A timid tap at the door snapped his head up. Agatha stood waiting, fingers curled around the door frame. "You left me alone with them." Her face was grave, but her eyes sparkled in amusement.

"Sorry." Oscar dragged himself to his feet and walked the few short steps until they stood side by side.

Her blue eyes widened. "You really are unwell."

When her hand rose to cup his jaw, he closed his eyes. He couldn't help it. He had the sudden urge to confess every single fear he possessed, to tell her about the endless nightmare of his dreams. But he couldn't do that here. He didn't want his friends to realize how badly he was affected. Agatha's thumb brushed across his lower lip. He drew in a ragged breath, tears causing a sting to his eyes at the tenderness of her touch. He didn't try to deny her accusations, didn't try to reassure Agatha that he was well, because he had an inkling he'd started down this path the moment he'd let her go.

Agatha's hand pressed to his chest and he stepped back, eyes still closed. He couldn't help but react physically to Agatha even if he wanted to. His prick thickened, straining from just her light touch. Tomorrow night's dinner would be awkward in the extreme if he couldn't control his desire for her.

The sound of the door closing and the lock snapping shut opened his eyes. Agatha had locked them in. She stood with her head turned slightly to the side, eyeing him with concern. He tried to pull himself together, but regaining his composure was beyond him. Agatha's arms slipped around his waist and she hugged him against her. He folded, adjusting his height a little so they rested more comfortably together, her legs wedged between his widespread ones, his lips inches from her skin.

Agatha's hands skimmed his waist, thumbs sliding over his waistcoat, fingertips burrowing under the band of his trousers. The warmth of her touch set his body aflame. He fought it, striving to keep his wits about him in a sea of desire. Agatha breathed deep and then lifted her face to his.

Their lips touched without effort. Warmth pressing them together, desire making their bodies as restless as the wind. Agatha slipped her tongue past his lips. He let her be the aggressor. As much as he wanted her, he could never force her to act so recklessly in her best friends' house.

He should stop her.

But Agatha's fingers were digging beneath his clothes restlessly, tugging at his clothing with impatient hands. His shirt came free of his trousers and Agatha's hands scorched his flesh.

"Agatha, no."

Her fingers squeezed his flesh tight, her head burrowed to his shoulder. "You'll be married soon?"

Oscar pressed his lips to her hair. "Yes."

"You'll be a faithful husband. This is our last chance." Agatha's impatient fingers snapped the buttons of his trousers open.

"Daventry will come looking for us. We cannot act out our desires here."

Her hand burrowed and closed upon his shaft. Oscar groaned.

"Lilly has plans for the earl. She wishes some extended time alone with him. I am to distract you while they talk."

"It's working," he whispered. Privacy and a willing accomplice to their rendezvous. What more could a desperate man ask for?

Oscar crushed Agatha against his chest, trapping her hand between his legs as she worked to arouse him. She didn't have to work too hard. It would take very little to push him to the peak. He slipped a hand over her hip, enjoying the firmness of her body. As his fingers found the limit of his reach, she bent her knee, curling her hips

into his thigh. He rocked her against him as she
shuddered and work harder at arousing him. Her hand
squeezed and pulled in a delicious rhythm, disintegrating
his resistance completely.

They turned, and Oscar pressed Agatha against the
book case. His fingers wandered down her leg and then
slowly, very deliberately, raised her gown past her knees.

"Stop me."

Agatha's free hand cupped his face. "Never."

Her lips settled on his again, searching and destroying
his ability to think. She was, quite simply, voracious for
him. Given that Oscar felt the same way, he dragged her
gown the remaining distance until his fingers curled
around her warm thighs. She was restless, hungry, and
when his fingers brushed her curls, he found her wet for
him.

He couldn't stop.

Agatha widened her legs.

A knock sounded on the closed door. Oscar's eyes
opened and he glanced around them guiltily. They were
still alone. He pressed his brow hard against Agatha's.
"Almost."

Her fingers slipped from his cheek, her body left him
slowly, a tender parting that threatened to undo him
once more. Her breath panted rapidly over his throat.
"Perhaps next time we'll be luckier. I suppose we should
rejoin our hosts."

Despite the disappointment, Oscar chuckled. "Must
we?"

Agatha nipped at his jaw. "Lilly would be disappointed
if we never came out."

"And Daventry would be offended if that happened."

"Damn right," Lord Daventry growled from the other
side of the door. "Join us as soon as you're both decent
again."

The earl's footsteps hurried away.

Agatha grinned at Oscar. "We have no choice? For
now."

Desire still gripped Oscar. His prick ached. He shook
his head sadly. "None at all."

Agatha kissed him fiercely. When she pushed against his chest, he staggered. "Until later tonight, then?"

Oscar's heart raced. His body, his blood, demanded action. His hands needed nothing but the sweet softness of Agatha Birkenstock in his arms one more time. Judging by Agatha's high color, their desires were in perfect alignment once more.

Eighteen

DARKNESS HID DESIRE well, but Agatha could sense Oscar's presence by the swirl of the fog obscuring his house. She walked forward, her body humming already with the hope that he'd been waiting for her all night as she had been. The hours since they kissed in Lady Daventry's townhouse had seemed far too long ago. How she had made it through the afternoon while Lord Daventry smirked at her, she didn't know. She hadn't expected him to be amused or even aware of their secret liaison, but it seemed Oscar had told one person about them.

At least the person he'd told abhorred gossip. Yet it pained her that Lilly must remain in ignorance. She'd likely be as disappointed with Oscar as Agatha had been when she'd learned of his lies. But Oscar was to marry another. There was nothing she could do to change his path to include her. She could only have him like this. In secret and fleeting meetings she'd never get enough of.

Oscar appeared out of the mist. Silent. Body taunt with tension. Agatha held out her arms and he swept her over the railings, tucked her against his body and hurried into his house.

Agatha curled her hand about his head and brought his lips to hers as they traversed the dark hall. The light pressure soon blurred into possession and compliance.

Each of them giving and taking what they needed from the exchange. Darkness faded as Oscar swept her into his candlelit bedchamber and locked the door to keep the world away.

Slowly, he dropped her to her feet, but Agatha wouldn't let go. Not yet. Not completely. She needed him too much to lose his touch so soon.

She wriggled her hips against him and his breath hissed through his teeth. She silenced him with more kisses. He need not say a word. They both wanted and they both could have. She'd share this last night with him, and she intended to burn the memory of their passion deep into his soul.

But that wouldn't happen if he controlled their pleasure. His habit of seeing to her needs first went against her plans for the night. He had his own needs he'd rarely asked her to fulfill and by night's end, she'd do her best to meet every one. Gently, Agatha pushed against him until a foot of air stood between them.

Oscar's face had flushed a hot color and his chest rose and fell in a harsh rhythm.

"Sit on the bed, my love," she whispered.

His brow rose, an amused smile tugged his lips, yet he did as she asked, dangling his long legs over the side. She admired his legs as she raised her hands to her hair. Oscar liked to play with the long strands over his chest, so she slowly removed the pins. As the pale mass fell, Oscar moaned.

Agatha smiled and drew the locks forward to cover her breasts then slowly worked the knot at her waist free. The dark material of her robe pooled at her feet, and Oscar bit his lip. She loosened her nightgown and inched the material down a bit at a time.

Oscar met her gaze. "Resorting to torture, are we?"

"I'm hoping to seduce you."

He smiled. "You have me, precious. You have always had me."

As her nightgown slid down her legs, she smiled. His gaze roamed up and down her body hungrily, his robe tented by his hidden erection. She had him for one last night and if one night was all she could have then she would make it count. She took a step forward and played with the ends of her long hair, conscious that when she did her nipple would appear to him then disappear. She took another step until she stood before him.

Agatha gestured to his robe. "Take that off."

Still smiling, he shucked the robe and sat before her in all his naked glory.

"Beautiful," she whispered, running her fingers over his exposed thighs and upward to brush his cock lightly with her fingertips. He shuddered.

Agatha widened his legs so she could get closer. Her gaze rose to his. As she leaned in to kiss him she also gathered the strands of her hair and swiped the ends over his erection. A rough pant passed his lips. She smiled at how simple their lust could be. A touch, a brush of warm breath and they were both gasping to find release.

Oscar cupped her face in his hands and kissed her. She knew she should resist just a little longer, but the pleasure of being completely naked with him left her body too restless to protest. She climbed onto the bed until she straddled him and thrust her tongue into his mouth time and again. Oscar's fingers dipped into her body. She arched as a hard shudder rocked her. He knew exactly how to tease her in return. Although she'd like nothing better than to let him into her body, she wriggled her hips away from his fingers until she could touch his cock with her lips.

She swiped her tongue over the head then pressed little kisses to the soft skin. Above her head, Oscar moaned her name. She smiled and wrapped her hand about him.

A drop of fluid beaded on the head and she lapped it up eagerly. Opening her mouth wide, she struggled to take him in. He grunted as his head settled on her tongue, and she licked the shaft to help his progress. She rose and fell again, taking more, slicking him with her saliva and did her best to ignore the ache between her legs. Her nipples hardened to points as his fingers stroked over them and pinched. Agatha sank lower, and then bobbed up and down, tightening and relaxing her grip on him until he moaned again.

Oscar twisted, one hand smoothing over her bottom, the other penetrating her from beneath. Agatha moaned around the cock in her mouth, but didn't stop, despite the distraction. She slipped a hand to his bollocks and rolled them.

He pulled her hand away. "You do that and I'll come too soon."

His cock popped from her mouth and she twitched her bottom to dislodge his fingers. "Then you have to promise not to make me come too soon either."

He grunted and tossed her onto her back. "Can I help it if I'm irresistible?" He covered her breast with his hand and kneaded. "Or that you love everything we do together?"

He drew the peak into his mouth and sucked hard, then lapped the nipple tip quickly. Agatha threaded her fingers through his hair and kept him there, but her body quivered, her pulse raced. She curled her leg around his hip, opening herself to him again. "I do love you. I couldn't do this with anyone else."

Oscar buried his face in her neck, his breath harsh and hot against her skin. "And you won't. I'll see to it tomorrow. You're mine now and forever."

A few tears stung her eyes. Her final fall. His mistress. The die was cast, the deed done. Why fight the inevitable anymore? Agatha sought his lips again and plunged into her new life. She'd tease and please him so he never considered casting her aside for another.

Oscar appeared very ready for her change of heart. His hands curled over her bottom and squeezed, pulling her against his erection. She tilted her hips and he slid in a little. When she rocked against the intrusion, he claimed her a little more. She was desperate for his pleasure to take over hers. She closed her eyes and pinched his nipples. Oscar rose up above her and his strokes grew in strength, forcing her to grip him tight with her legs to keep them connected.

Suddenly he stopped. Agatha opened her eyes and stared up at him. His face held a foolish grin and she smiled back, content to share this small moment of perfection with him. He glanced down to where they joined and then back at her face.

"Marry me, precious." He smiled again. "I'd like to do this with you for the rest of my life."

"Marriage?"

"Yes. Marriage." He slid his finger over her cheek, wiping away her happy tears. "I should have done the honorable thing from the start. Forgive me."

He began to move again, and Agatha's heart soared. Marriage. But how? Oscar widened her legs, glancing between her face and where he invaded her body. She shuddered at the fierce look on his face.

"Touch yourself, Aggie, love. Let me see you do it."

Agatha ran her hand over her belly and into her folds. The hard nub tingled at the increased attention and she curled up to see them make love. Although her fingers strummed over her nub with increasing speed, she watched Oscar's thick length enter and leave her body. Knowing Oscar was watching too, his head pressed hard to hers, added to her pleasure and the precipice approached too swiftly. She removed her hand.

"No, don't stop, precious. I'm waiting for you. Waiting."

She met his gaze as her hand returned, then wailed as her body clenched around Oscar and he groaned in tandem. He pumped his hips hard again and again. They collapsed in a sprawling heap, limbs sticky with the sweat of their exertions. Yet he wouldn't let them rest like that. He scooped her up against him and flipped a quilt over her cooling skin.

"One of these days, precious, you're going to break me with that control of yours."

Agatha nudged him to gain a little space. She kissed his cheek. "Nonsense. It's you who breaks me every time."

He grinned foolishly. "So we are equals. I like that."

Agatha frowned. "Do you really?"

"Oh, yes." He stood suddenly, whipped the covers back properly and settled them both into his bed. "You keep me in line very well. I am a better man when I'm with you."

He drew her back against his chest, his grip loose but comforting just the same. Constant.

"You are a good man even without me, Oscar." She clutched his hands. "I know what you did for Lilly, my love."

Oscar stilled, and she wondered if she shouldn't have brought it up. But secrets were bad between them. He needed to know she knew everything. Otherwise he might never find peace.

"He haunts me," he said.

She rubbed her hands over his briskly. "You wouldn't be a good man if you did not question your actions, Oscar. He was dangerous and you had a clear shot, I'm told. If someone else had had a better idea, they would have acted long before you did."

Oscar remained silent behind her.

"Lilly lives and is happy. Daventry worships her and is content. Don't torture yourself with what ifs and deny yourself a chance for a happy life. Live for now and never look back."

"It is just..." His breath rushed out. "I don't sleep anymore. I find it impossible to relax. I have terrible nightmares."

Agatha frowned. That did not sound good at all. "No sleep at all?"

"Not enough."

Agatha squeezed his hands where they'd curled over her breasts. "Then think about what you do have instead of what you don't. Close your eyes, my love, and sleep. I'll keep your demons at bay."

Oscar snuggled closer. "I never do think of him around you. Don't leave before I wake. Please."

Such a sweet, confused man. The perfect lover, but so very unsure of himself because of the past. She looked over her shoulder. "Don't hog the blankets tonight like last time." But he'd already fallen asleep and didn't stir till early morning.

He stretched. "You're awake?"

Agatha smoothed his hair from his eyes as he blinked up at her. "I haven't slept. I was watching over you."

Oscar drew her close again. "No dreams. It seems you are exactly what I need in my life. I'll speak to your grandfather as soon as I can, and then we can be on our way."

Agatha sat up and hugged the sheet to her breasts. "On our way where?"

"To Gretna, of course. Lord Thorpe will be vexed about it all, but I'll deal with him when we return."

Agatha chewed her lip. "He'll sue for breach of promise, won't he?"

"More than likely, but we'll manage somehow. I want to marry you and only you. Mother will be able to smooth things over with the *ton* eventually."

"Oh, dear. Not a very good beginning." Agatha chewed her lip again. There was no telling how her grandfather would view the scandal. Would he still pay her dowry to Oscar under such scandalous circumstances? "Will Thorpe ruin you?"

"I have no idea." Oscar smiled wickedly. "Now, enough of the Thorpe's and problems. Come here. A very wise woman I know suggested I live in the past no more and hold on to the present. Right now I'd like to hold on to you."

As Agatha crawled across the bed to perch on his lap again, she noted the absence of dark circles beneath his eyes and the ready smile that lightened them. He was content again. Had her presence caused that?

Oscar drew her down upon him and she did her best to kiss his remaining cares away.

Nineteen

"HOME, SWEET HOME," Estella murmured as she looked about her entrance hall with complete satisfaction, admiring all the things she loved best in her life. Her possessions gave her comfort as they winked back at her in the sunlight streaming in from a high window. Every time she went away, she was always glad to return home.

"Good to have you back, milady," her butler said as he saw to the dispersal of her possessions into the upper reaches of the house.

Hellishly good to be home, in fact. Estella tugged her gloves from her fingers with relief. Her brief interlude with Thomas hadn't been the calm affair she'd anticipated. Thomas had been difficult. He had not liked her mothering one bit. Oh, she hadn't really attempted to mother him in truth, but he'd been tired and Estella had attempted to encourage him to slower pursuits.

They hadn't even made love—the first time they had traveled together and not done so.

Estella took her bonnet from her head. What had changed to set his hackles up so strongly? Had he tired of their affair?

Estella brushed the thought aside. If Thomas was done, he would certainly tell her so. He was a direct man in all his dealings and would not lead her on without a full explanation if he had withdrawn his affections. Perhaps the fault lay within him. He had struggled from bed most mornings and by their journey's end, dark circles had graced his eyes.

Perhaps he was frustrated by getting old. Heaven knew Estella sometimes peered into her looking glass, lamenting over the arrival of one more line to her face.

"Would you care for tea, milady?"

"Yes, I think I would. Send it upstairs to my chambers, along with some butter biscuits, too."

Estella climbed the stairs. She looked forward to the solitude of the afternoon before Lord Daventry's dinner party tonight. She quite thought she might lie down and rest for a good hour. Her maid could wake her when she needed to get up and dressed. Yes, a bit of solitude would be wonderful, indeed.

Yet as Estella crossed her bedchamber threshold, a loud knock sounded on the front door. Not the knocker, either, because it had not been put up. A man's heavy fist. She turned around and peered over the railing to spy on whom it might be.

"Lord Lynton to see Lady Carrington."

Estella drew back for two reasons. One, shock that Lynton had come to call on her the minute she'd returned home and two, shocked that he used his title in an attempt to intimidate her staff.

"Her ladyship is not receiving visitors, milord," Graves intoned.

"She'll see me."

"How dare you," Graves growled as Lynton pounded up the staircase ahead of the butler.

Estella stepped closer to the rail and looked down. "It is all right, Graves. I was expecting Lord Lynton."

Although the butler frowned at the news, he went away. Estella fixed her gaze on her unexpected visitor. Lynton was better dressed than his usual sober self. He reminded her of the young lord he used to be, except he moved without a self-assured swagger to his step. Right now, he seemed uneasy. "How may I help you?"

"We need to talk, Essy, in private."

Although she didn't particularly care for the idea, she retreated to her bedchamber, leaving Lynton to follow if he dared. He'd likely caused enough gossip already by demanding to see her this way. What was one scandal more to cap off the day?

He shut the door behind him and leaned against the wood. "I'm sorry about my brother."

Estella shrugged. "Your brother has some strange notions in his head. They'll soon disappear, as all his wild flights of fancy tend to do."

"I think not this time." Lynton grimaced. "He paid an unexpected call on your son while the boy was engaged with orphanage business. Staines made no bones about wishing the trustees all gone from Carrington's house."

Estella's heart fluttered. "He hasn't lost his touch at clearing a room. What did he talk about?"

Lynton set his hands to his hips, his gaze troubled. "Nothing specific, but he hasn't lost his habit of meddling. I foresee him continuing his new association with your son. It will be remarked upon and society will take notice. The current rumor is that you and Staines had a lover's quarrel and his coming to your son's house, when you were obviously from Town, will be fuel for speculation. If they consider the boy and Staines too closely, they might imagine a resemblance to the duke."

Estella closed her eyes, willing herself not to remember the resemblance between her son and this man. But it was there, despite her not knowing how it could possibly be true. Oscar had worn that same look of contrition on his face when he'd been scolded as a boy, when he was in the wrong and knew it. She opened her eyes.

Lynton hadn't moved. He stood still as a statue—an older version of her son. Very similar. Too similar for chance to have had a hand in Oscar's creation. How could she not have known? How could she have shared a bed with Lynton Manning and not realized it?

Estella spun about, pressing her hands together over her churning stomach.

"You were expecting your husband that night. I knew it. Saw it. Carrington had whispered in your ear all afternoon, and I had to sit through that interminable dinner while he smiled at you and brought a bright blush to your cheeks."

Manning drew closer. He stopped behind her back, but didn't touch.

"I had gone outside to cool my temper after you had retired to bed. I was jealous and heartsick all over again, as I had been when you'd married that slimy bastard. While I was venting my fury to the dark night, he left the house. He walked right by me with Lady Whitcombe and Lady Realford on each arm. He didn't see me. The women were laughing about you."

Estella's heart raced in anger over a dead man and his faithlessness, and over Lynton taking advantage of her that night. "So you decided to take his place."

Lynton's hands settled on her shoulders lightly, and then went away. "That was not my intention. I don't know what I was thinking. I suppose I went to tell you where he was. I wanted to point out his flaws so you would leave him."

Estella hugged herself. "But you said not one word. Not one."

"I couldn't. By the time I entered your bedchamber, I realized you wouldn't leave him. That you would avoid any scandal and stay with him to preserve your good name." His hands settled on her shoulders again.

"I don't know what I would have done if you'd told me the truth. It would have at least prepared me for the rest of my marriage." Estella forced a deep breath into her lungs. "Why did you take his place?"

Behind her, Lynton's head pressed against the back of hers. "You touched me."

Estella frowned. "That's hardly an encouragement to share another man's wife's bed."

His rough breathing behind her caused her heart to race. "With you, it's like fire on grass after a long, dry spell. I have loved you all my life. I desire you still."

Lynton didn't move, but his rough pant of breath over her neck sent her pulse racing. Again, she reacted to him with astonishing ease. And she had too, the night he'd taken her husband's place, if memory served. He had been . . . thorough. Gentle. And wonderful.

Estella covered her face with both hands. She trembled and fought the urge to turn around. But to see his face would make everything real. It would make this conversation utterly impossible to deny.

Lynton rubbed his hands up and down her arms. "Your son looks at my face and frowns, love. It is only a matter of time before he pieces together the puzzle."

A sob tore from Estella's throat. Dear God, what would Oscar do when he discovered the truth? What would he think of her then?

"I think, perhaps, we should tell the boy the truth before Staines gifts his new nephew with a larger townhouse. My brother has threatened to do so already."

Estella dropped her hands. "I'm sure your brother will enjoy himself at my expense."

When Lynton drew her into his arms, Estella didn't fight the feeling of comfort that swept her. She clung to him and wiped away her tears on his coat.

"He is excited to discover he has new family to dote upon. You know how he is, forever spoiling those he can." Lynton pressed a kiss to her brow. "He means well. He's just vexed at me for keeping secrets. He always wanted you in the family, and he hates that I took orders. Perhaps he will be happier now that I'm leaving the church."

Estella pushed away. "You're not leaving because of this?"

He smiled and brushed his knuckles across her cheek. "No, not entirely. But I very much fear for the children of the orphanage. Carter wants to pull out, and you know if he does the rest will go too. I cannot bear the thought of the children homeless again. Princeton Park is being opened again in readiness for the small arrivals."

Estella turned around. "You're taking them home?"

"They will enjoy the fresh air and greater opportunities for mischief and exercise. I know I did as a boy. Princeton will suit them all very well." He stepped close again and caught up her fingers. "There is ample room for visitors too. I should be pleased to have you, Birkenstock, and

Miss Birkenstock under my roof anytime you care to come."

"I couldn't do that," Estella whispered.

He squeezed her fingers. "The offer stands, regardless. I love you too much to care about Birkenstock. The children would want to see you again, and so do I."

Although her mouth no doubt hung open, Estella couldn't find the wits to close it. Lynton kissed her cheek and departed, leaving the door open in his wake. She stared at it. How had her world become so confused? She liked order and a scandal-less life. When had everything changed?

She took a deep breath and walked to the door, intending to close it and attempt to sleep off her anxiety. Yet before she could, Oscar appeared in the doorway, his expression unreadable, his gaze searching. "Oscar? I didn't know you had arrived."

"Yes, I've been here for some time."

"Oh." Estella licked her lips, and then cursed the nervous gesture. "How have you been, my dear?"

"Much better. I am content again." He looked behind him and Estella guessed that he had been outside her door while Lynton had been here, professing his love. But had he overheard the first part of the conversation?

She couldn't tell.

He cleared his throat. "I come on a commission from Lord Daventry. He desires to speak with you in private about birthing matters. He has concerns about Lilly becoming with child."

"Is she already increasing?"

"No. Not that he's aware of." Oscar shook his head. "But without a female acquaintance to reassure him, he's become a bundle of nerves. You know how he is with her. Would you attempt to speak with him tonight before or during the party? I thought you might be able to advise him, or at least set his mind at ease."

Estella nodded. "I will do my best."

"Thank you, Mother. They mean the world to me and I would not like to see them unhappy."

"You are a good friend, Oscar."

A sudden smile crossed his face. "Not always, but I mean to be from now on. Were you very content with your position in society, Mother? I ask because I have a feeling things will change very soon, and perhaps we shall not be as well liked in the future."

Tears pricked her eyes. He had heard it all. "Oscar, I can explain."

"A propensity for scandal seems to run in the family, doesn't it?" He took a step back. "Try not to be vexed with me and I'll do the same for you."

Estella frowned and held out her hand to Oscar. "What else is there that you are not telling me?" He took it and she gripped it, staring up into his face and hoping to find the answers that had eluded her all these weeks.

"You'll know soon enough." Oscar bent and kissed her cheek, too, and hurried out.

Twenty

AGATHA SWEPT INTO the room on her grandfather's arm and every nerve in Oscar's body tingled. She was here for Lilly, not him, and the knowledge twisted his gut into a crushing band. She should be on his arm and by his side. He still had to speak with her grandfather and gain his permission for marriage before he could attempt to obtain a special license or else run off to Gretna Green. If he could get a license, perhaps he could persuade Mr. Manning to marry them, too.

His father. His real father.

Oscar took a drink. Perhaps he wasn't quite as shocked as he probably should be with his mother over cuckolding her husband. But knowing the truth would take some getting used to. He had overheard the whole of the conversation and Manning's feeble excuse for sharing her bed. He could hardly begrudge the man who gave him life. But he did wish he could confide in Agatha about it. He couldn't keep secrets from her.

Oscar moved closer as Lord and Lady Daventry greeted her. Her simple gown of burgundy silk with fine lace edging accentuated the long, smooth curve of her throat and the tightly bound blonde hair on her head.

She looked enchanting.

She looked nervous.

Her gaze darted about the room and settled briefly on a far corner where Lady Penelope stood with her father, sister, and her ever-present brother-in-law, Lord Prewitt. It would be expected that Oscar should be conversing with their party, not delaying his return with meaningless chatter to another of Daventry's friends. But he wanted Agatha.

As he drained the last of his drink, a necessary fortification for the long dinner ahead, he noticed how often Penelope's eyes turned toward her brother by marriage. She was clearly fond of him, though there was never anything in Prewitt's manner to suggest he was similarly affected. Her sister gazed adoringly at Prewitt too, but in the manner acceptable in polite circles for a wife—a saucy smile, a gentle touch.

He looked forward to the day when Agatha might be that easy with him in society. He longed for the moment when he might introduce her as his wife.

He accepted another glass, swallowed a mouthful, and then considered his fresh glass. He wasn't foxed. The drink had had little effect on him so far, but he was well on the way to feeling more himself than he had in months. A man who was sure of one thing.

The woman he loved beyond anything else in life had stepped into the room.

Within moments, he was at her side. "Miss Birkenstock, may I say you look enchanting tonight."

Agatha blinked at his sudden arrival and then quickly dropped a curtsey. "You are too kind, my lord."

So formal, so proper. He caught her hand and kissed the air above it. Her lowered position gave Oscar a glimpse of heaven down the front of her gown. He let a little of his delight show in his grin, but only so much that Agatha would notice. He turned to her grandfather. "Mr. Birkenstock, sir. It is good to see you returned to Town. Was your trip a pleasant one?"

"Yes, yes. No trouble at all," Birkenstock puffed. "Although I did not like being absent from my granddaughter."

"I'm sure that being at any distance from Miss Birkenstock is quite unsettling."

Oscar spoke the truth. The minute Agatha was near, all his troubles vanished. His heart no longer raced, except with anticipation. But there would be very little touching tonight. He had to be on his best behavior or else risk spoiling Lilly's evening.

A little bell rang out in the hall and they turned for the splendor of the Earl of Daventry's dining table. The room was perfect, glowing with golden light with fine china and crystal. The servants waited patiently to ensure Lady Daventry's first dinner was a success, each determined to make the night perfect.

Oscar skirted the table until he found a servant holding his chair. When Agatha moved to sit in the space beside him, he was momentarily startled. By rights, Lady Daventry could place her guests anywhere, of course, but her choice tonight was interesting. He had expected to sit next to Lady Penelope. In fact, he'd dreaded that very event. But Penelope was seated far from him, and when the ladies all sat in unison he wasn't disappointed in the least.

But Agatha fidgeted, clearly uncomfortable with her location at his side. A glance across the table showed that more than one eye turned their way, considering the odd seating placement. Lady Daventry met his gaze and winked—actually winked across the long expanse of mahogany. If he didn't know her heart was firmly captured by her possessive husband, he'd be uncomfortable with the gesture. But knowing Lilly's nature, he concluded that Daventry had told her of his attachment to Agatha and she'd taken steps to place them together.

His mother, ever one to deflect attention from any faux pas made by new hostesses, began an animated, and very timely, conversation with their hosts as a distraction. But her glances in his direction hinted that she was going to question him later. He hadn't satisfied her curiosity earlier in the day, and he wouldn't be doing it tonight either.

Once all attention had been diverted by the delivery of the first course and further conversation, Oscar cleared his throat. "I understand you've been quite a help to our mutual friend. Daventry tells me you assisted Lilly a great deal with the planning for this evening. Everything looks wonderful."

"I did assist her with some things, but this, the seating arrangement, was entirely her doing. For all her delicate looks, she is quite the most willful creature."

He chuckled and signaled for Agatha's glass to be refilled as well as his own. "I must remember to thank Lilly properly later. She is a woman determined to secure my heart."

"Your heart? Is your heart so easily captured then by a saucy wink?"

Oscar pressed his napkin to his lips to hide his smile. "Affection and loyalty seems far too tame when offered such a great service. She has seated me beside my heart's desire, and a few paltry words cannot properly express my joy. You see, I may talk to you all evening without causing any great scandal simply because I *must* be attentive. Most hostesses have not been quite so nice to me in the past."

Agatha's lips lifted in amusement while she directed her attention to her fish.

Beneath the table, Oscar pressed his leg to hers. "You see now why I must love her as I would perhaps a sibling. But a nice sibling, not like my own sister, Mirelle. She would never be so good to me."

Agatha turned her head and caught his gaze. He'd told her of Mirelle's bitterness—a more disappointed lady in unrequited love as there ever was to be. Agatha's hand dropped to her lap and then, as she fidgeted with her napkin, her fingers slipped sideways to brush his encroaching thigh. A small tingle of awareness shot to his groin and then when she did it again, he had the devil of a time not returning the caress.

Thankfully, the meal was barely half over. He would have plenty of time to regain control of himself before he was forced to stand as the ladies left the table. "I see the Ettington's and Hallam's are not in attendance."

Agatha's hands returned to her utensils. "No. Unfortunately, or fortunately from their perspective, the ladies are in a somewhat delicate condition, and their husbands prefer them not to travel. Lilly looks forward to seeing them at Christmas."

Oscar sipped his wine. "As should you."

Agatha's gaze shot sideways. "My grandfather has made no decision, as yet, of whether to accept Ettington's invitation. I hope to go."

Oscar took a bite of lamb and looked about the table as he chewed. Most couples were either in deep conversation or devouring the earl's repast with great enthusiasm. No one was paying attention to them. He offered Agatha a quick, reassuring smile. "Depend upon it. You will be at Hazelmere for the house party. We are going."

Agatha's eyes widened.

"I'll call on him tomorrow." He nodded toward her grandfather. "I promise."

She quickly returned her attention to her plate, and Oscar relaxed. It would be nice to take Agatha away from London. He didn't think she'd left since she'd come to stay with her grandfather all those years ago. Wonderful years, where they'd grown to become friends.

They passed the next course in silence, but holding his tongue proved impossible. "I was unable to visit with the children at the orphanage today. How is little Betty coming along?"

"Very well," Agatha replied, after a footman had taken her plate. "She is full of health and liveliness again. And the other children are the same, as always."

Oscar laughed. "Full of beans and ready for adventure?"

"The very thing."

"Most boys are like that, and girls too, at a young age, before they are taught to imitate only their mothers." A smile flittered across Agatha's face at his words. "What?"

"The boys were quite curious about you the other day. They peppered me with all manner of questions. You've become quite the novelty. But I think boys learn a great deal from their fathers, too, without ever realizing it. It is such a pity they will be forever without one."

"I won't always be a novelty for them." Oscar took a hasty swallow of his claret. "With luck they will get quite sick of me."

Agatha grinned. "It won't happen. It is good that the boys have your influence at this stage of their life. I have noticed an increased attention to their appearance by the older ones, but I must arrange a tailor for some of them. They have quite outgrown their things. Simon's arms are very long now."

"How did Simon come to be in the orphanage?" Oscar adjusted his chair so they were an inch closer together. "There is very little noted about him in the records."

"We know little more. He was found waiting on the front steps one morning, a sack of clothes at his side and a handful of coins clutched in his fist. There was a note— a piece of much folded parchment with our address and my grandfather's name."

"Did your grandfather recognize him?"

She shook her head sadly. "Not at all. And since Simon will never speak about the past, we have little else to go on. He's a good influence on the younger boys though."

"How so?"

Agatha's smile returned. "He can read. His penmanship is quite superior to what was first expected. He's even started helping the little ones learn their letters."

Now that was surprising. "Well, perhaps his skills will set him up for a career when he grows older. I'll be sure to visit with him tomorrow."

Agatha's smiled dimmed. "That may prove difficult. He's not fond of gentlemen, by and large, and does his best to remain unseen. It's quite vexing to be always searching for him."

"He obviously does not take after Miss Mabel then," Oscar laughed loudly and all eyes turned toward them again. He forced his attention to the delicacies being placed before him with considerable reluctance. He liked discussing the children's needs with Agatha. And he was incredibly curious about this Simon boy. Reading and writing so well as to impress at the age of ten was quite an achievement for an orphan. Perhaps his circumstances now were far removed from where they had begun. He'd question the boy carefully so as not to frighten him and then see what might be done for his future.

At the end of the meal, once the ladies had departed for the drawing room, Oscar sprawled untidily in his chair. He had no wish to converse much at all; his thoughts lingered with the orphans, and with making Agatha his wife.

"You've got a fine handful there."

Oscar glanced at Lord Prewitt and frowned. "I beg your pardon?"

"Don't deny it. You practically made love to her over the table."

Oscar got to his feet. "Miss Birkenstock and I were speaking of the orphanage, actually. I suggest you keep your base accusations to yourself."

"Just remember, you're to marry Lady Penelope this month. She'll not tolerate you publicly embarrassing her by flirting with your light-skirt before her very eyes again."

Oscar ignored the revelation that the date he would marry Penelope was set for this month. He wouldn't stand for Prewitt's slander of Agatha. "Tomorrow . . ."

Daventry set his hand to Oscar's shoulder and nudged him back. "Here now. If there is a disparaging word to be said against my wife's closest friend, then I shall be the one calling him out. After all, this is my house and if a guest has imbibed too freely of spirits and ceases to speak as a gentleman should, then I shall be more than happy to take him to task."

Prewitt glanced between them, weighing up Daventry's threat. Eventually, he offered a lopsided smile. "Perhaps you are right. You do set a fine table, my lord. I should call it a night."

Daventry's smile was cold. "Perhaps you should."

Lord Prewitt collected his father-in-law and, with one last smirk, departed the room.

Daventry pulled Oscar away from his guests. "Have you lost your mind?"

"He insulted Aggie."

"And now he will be more curious about her place in your affections, given that you were about to threaten him with a duel. You could have handled that better."

Oscar shrugged. "Hardly matters now."

"Why? What's going on?"

Oscar clapped his friend on the shoulder. "Change is good for the soul, they say. I'm sick of playing by society's rules."

Daventry set his hands to his hip. "If you're about to elope, then for God's sake keep your voice down."

Oscar grinned. "Not eloping. Not yet at any rate."

"Good." Daventry raked his fingers through his hair. "Lilly is planning to host your wedding breakfast. Don't disappoint her."

"I wouldn't dream of it. Did you speak to my mother?"

"Yes, thank you. She was a great comfort." Daventry stirred restlessly. "We should rejoin the ladies. My wife will be wondering where we've gotten ourselves to."

Daventry moved off with the other men, but Oscar dawdled. He fell into step with Thomas Birkenstock. Birkenstock gave him an odd look then quickly crossed to his granddaughter's side, spoiling his chance to flirt with Agatha again that night.

Twenty-One

AGATHA POURED THE very last cup of tea for herself then sank into the nearest chair. Keeping her emotions under control tonight was proving more than a little difficult. She'd thought she could stand the strain of socializing with Oscar's betrothed, but quite honestly her thoughts were becoming a touch violent. The elegant, dark beauty and her equally admired elder sister were holding court a little to the side of Lilly.

They both seemed determined, by accident or design, to make Lilly appear a visitor to their social whirl. Not that Lilly, sweet but slightly naive Lilly, had the remotest inkling of their contempt. But Lady Carrington *had* noticed. The viscountess had taken up a post beside the new bride and was steering the conversation back into calmer waters where Lilly would feel at ease.

The main doors creaked open, and the gentlemen joined them not a moment too soon. Both Lady Prewitt and Penelope descended on Lord Prewitt, ignoring the rest of the male company as they returned. Agatha couldn't understand their fascination with Lord Prewitt. He wasn't even that handsome to look at. Perhaps he had hidden qualities that lent to his appeal.

"Ah, there you are, child," her grandfather gasped as he sat.

Agatha studied his face. He seemed more tired than when he'd first returned home. "Are you unwell?"

"No, no," her grandfather replied as he mopped his brow. "Just a spot of indigestion. Lord Daventry sets a fine table. I'll be right in a moment."

Relieved, Agatha patted his arm. "That he does. Lilly claims all his teeth are sweet, not just one."

Her grandfather gave her a shrewd look and nodded his head. "You are very much enamored of Lady Daventry, aren't you?"

"Yes, sir. She is my very good friend."

"And the seating arrangement tonight?" Her grandfather raised his eyes to the doorway and caught Oscar staring at them.

"I don't know what you mean, sir."

Beside her, her grandfather slumped a little. "I had an inkling once upon a time, but when nothing came of it I dismissed the notion. I was quite wrong to do so, wasn't I?"

Agatha's cheeks heated. Dash it. She had tried so hard to seem indifferent, but Oscar's attentive conversation tonight had ruined it all. Now she had to lie. "The viscount is an engaging man as a dinner companion. It would have been rude of me to ignore his conversation."

"Was he in any way forward with his speech? If he was, I'll have his head."

Agatha placed a restraining hand on her grandfather's arm, alarmed by the high color in his cheeks. "He was very proper in his speech, sir. There is no cause for concern."

Her grandfather subsided, but his high color remained. It wouldn't do him any good to become vexed over a simple seating arrangement. She hoped he wouldn't become equally distressed, should Oscar come to call tomorrow. Given Oscar was already engaged to be married, Agatha wondered how distressed her grandfather could become over the potential scandal. But if Oscar could convince him that they were in love, wouldn't that smooth things over with him?

To her relief, the Prewitt's and Lady Penelope departed early.

Good riddance. Now they could all be easy again.

"Agatha, would you mind finding a servant to fetch me a drink. They're not looking in this direction," her grandfather huffed, mopping his brow once more.

Agatha rose. "Of course, sir. I shall be back directly."

As she crossed the room, Agatha had to pass directly beside Oscar. He caught the trailing ribbons on her gown and tugged. Agatha ignored him. What else could she do? But she did hope her grandfather had not noticed. He was worrying her enough as it was, without getting into a temper over Oscar. He would understand everything tomorrow, once Oscar had spoken with him.

She accepted a glass of champagne and started back toward her grandfather. But the crowd had shifted and Agatha became trapped with Oscar in her way. He grinned down impishly at her and set his hand to her arm.

"Excuse me, my lord. May I pass?"

"Not just yet. I need to tell you something."

Agatha shook off his grip, afraid of how much she wanted to step into his arms and be held. "Now?"

"It can wait till tomorrow, but it is very important."

His face held a serious cast and Agatha was suddenly afraid he'd changed his mind about flouting convention and marrying her. Panicked, she glanced around him, but her grandfather had moved from his seat. "Do you see Mr. Birkenstock, my lord?"

"No." Oscar acquired her fingers to ease her through the cluster of gentlemen. "But we shall find him together if you like."

Lord Daventry approached. "Forgive me, Miss Birkenstock, I was just coming to find you. Your grandfather wishes to leave and requests your presence in the front hall."

With another squeeze, Oscar released her fingers. Agatha made her way to Lilly, wished her a good night then turned to find Lord Daventry waiting patiently. He held out his arm to lead her across the crowded room.

"Thank you, my lord."

Lord Daventry leaned close. "I wondered if I might have a word before we rejoin your grandfather. I didn't think he looked particularly well just now. Do not hesitate to send word if he sickens."

Agatha's heart began to thump wildly. So it was not just her imagination. She'd thought he had begun to seem older, weaker of late. Yet she'd stubbornly refused to consider the implications fully. He couldn't leave her. But he was nearing four and sixty. He wouldn't live forever, no matter how much she wished otherwise.

Agatha forced a reassuring smile to her lips, but inside she quaked. "I'm sure it is nothing serious. Good night, my lord. Thank you for a wonderful evening."

The earl frowned again, but then signaled for the footmen to open the doors without another word. She looked about her, but couldn't see her grandfather. The butler stood at the door ready with her wrap then escorted her outside and helped her embark. Inside, her grandfather appeared to be resting with his eyes closed. The carriage lurched and for a brief moment his eyes flickered open, but quickly shut again.

Unsure what to make of his reticence, Agatha watched the steady rise and fall of his chest. He was just tired. Tomorrow she would force him to remain in the house until he regained his stamina.

As the carriage rattled through the dark London streets, Agatha mulled over her evening. Until the later part, she had enjoyed herself. Dining at Oscar's side was a feat she'd never managed before. He was an engaging conversationalist. But for the first time, she appreciated being in his orbit. Although he had barely touched her all night, he had made her feel treasured and special. Would it be the same when she was his wife?

Or would he stray, as so many men did?

Although the future still held many unknown problems, she would set her worries aside for tonight. Tomorrow, she would send Lilly the largest bag of sweets she could find as a thank you for seating them together.

The carriage rumbled to a stop before her house. Her grandfather roused himself and exited the carriage. Eventually, just when she had begun to suspect he'd left her already, his hand extended to help her from the carriage. Agatha slipped her hand into his, the clamminess of her grandfather's grip was noticeable immediately.

"Sir?"

He slipped his arm about her shoulders and she almost buckled under his weight. Their butler, George, hurried forward to assist and looped his arm around her grandfather's back, taking most of his weight. Together they climbed the endless stairs and got her grandfather into the foyer. With the greater light, the shine of his sweat-soaked skin and the unnaturally light color of his eyes worried her.

"Wallace!" George shouted, struggling to take more of her grandfather's weight from her shoulders. The footman hurried to them and helped George support their master up the long flight of stairs. At the bottom, Agatha watched their unsteady progress, dread rising in a steady wave. Her grandfather's head lolled forward, his gaze fixed on moving his feet. But his movements were clumsy, and when they reached the top, both servants hefted him between them to carry him into his room.

A hand touched her arm. Nell watched the proceedings with tears in her eyes. Agatha's maid expected the worst. But it couldn't be. He was still too young, too vital for the cold of the earth to swallow him up. Agatha rushed up the stairs and turned for her grandfather's room. The servants had maneuvered him onto the bed and were removing his shoes and untying his cravat. Her grandfather lay silent, allowing the servants to fuss without comment. She glanced at his chest. It still rose and fell in a steady rhythm, but then she heard the loud rasp of his breath as the room fell silent.

Everyone turned toward the bed, perhaps counting the labored breathing. Agatha moved forward and clutched her grandfather's arm, then slipped her fingers over his broad hand. His hand was slack of strength and unnaturally cold.

George moved a chair close behind her and she lowered herself blindly. He was dying before her very eyes.

Agatha drew in great gasping breaths as her heart raced in fear. "Fetch a doctor. Now."

Twenty-Two

"I'M AFRAID THERE is nothing to be done, Miss Birkenstock."

Those words kept bouncing around inside Agatha's head until she thought it might explode from the anguish. Nothing. Not one single thing. Agatha stroked her fingers over her grandfather's unresponsive hand, feeling a chill seep into her bones. It might not be long, it might take all night, but either way this would be her last moments with family.

After that—vast loneliness awaited her.

No family, no husband yet, and no children.

No one to give a damn if she lived or died.

A rustle at the door alerted Agatha to her midnight visitor. After the doctor had made his pronouncement an hour earlier, Agatha had sent two letters: one to her cousin in Winchester and one to Lady Estella Carrington here in Town. It was far too soon for Arthur to arrive, but not too soon for her grandfather's closest friend. Although she shouldn't know of the affair between them, Agatha was observant and had made the connection long ago.

Despite any possible awkwardness, sending the letter was a kindness.

Estella Carrington rushed to the bedside and cupped her hands around her grandfather's face. Her expression, so full of anguish and worry, convinced Agatha she'd made the right decision to inform the viscountess, even at the risk a deathbed vigil could bring scandal upon the Carrington name.

Agatha dropped her gaze to her hands, waiting for the lady to absorb the change to come, to compose herself for the end. She ignored the sniffing tears Lady Carrington couldn't contain and tried to think of what she would have to do. Her cousin Arthur would own the house. Foolishly, she had never discussed what would become of her if her grandfather died before she married. And he'd been so adamant she marry soon. Yet he'd never live to meet with Oscar, if he should still want to marry her.

The cold hand beneath hers twitched and she glanced at her grandfather's face. His eyes were open. Agatha climbed to her feet to stand closer to his head.

"My angels."

Agatha hastily swiped a falling tear from her cheek and clutched his hand tightly. She couldn't think of what to say, but feared these moments would be her last. A glance at Lady Carrington showed she wasn't alone in her grief. Tears ran thick down the older woman's cheeks, casting her face in palpable grief.

"Oh, my Thomas. Don't leave us."

But there was no response to her words. His eyes widened as he drew breath and never let it out again.

The sudden silence was stifling.

Estella Carrington threw herself across Agatha's grandfather's unmoving chest and wept bitter tears of loss. Agatha watched, numb, unable to comprehend why he would allow such a display of emotion in his presence. And then she remembered. He was gone. He wouldn't tell anyone to leave him be again.

The hand in her grip slipped away. She stared at it, waiting for a movement that would prove this night was but a nightmare dredged from her deepest dreams. Yet it didn't move the slightest inch.

A sniff at the door caught her attention. She moved, turning to see who was crying.

Nell stood at the door, tears pouring down her cheeks, grieving for her employer with more emotion than Agatha felt. He couldn't be gone. Any moment now, he would rise up and tell them all to end their feminine wailing. He'd claim it hurt his ears and head for his study to bury himself in his papers. But when she noticed the butler's pained attempts not to shed a tear himself, Agatha had to face the future.

Alone.

With no one ever to lecture her again.

Agatha put her hand to the bed post to steady herself, pain and loss finally forcing her body to react. She didn't want this, but she had exactly what she thought she wanted all along. Freedom. Her view blurred as tears fell. Walls disappeared as strong hands pushed her down into a chair then pressed soft linen into her palm. A handkerchief. A man's handkerchief.

That simple gesture broke her last ounce of self possession, and she gave in to her tears until she thought her heart might break.

Oh, God, it hurt so badly.

Agatha wrapped her arms about her chest in a vain attempt at control.

Another hand pulled at her. The warm, delicate scent of lavender offered comfort. Agatha buried her head in Estella's shoulder and let her heartbreak flow. The viscountess held her, stoked her back, and rocked her gently while she cried.

Agatha ignored how odd it was to be comforted by the woman, and a tearful woman at that. She was Oscar's mother, a necessarily distant figure. But how strange to be held by her grandfather's lover.

Agatha pushed away and fumbled with the handkerchief in her hands. She had to regain some control; there were so many things to be done. She couldn't sit about wailing when her grandfather was gone. She wiped her eyes and dragged in a deep breath, trying to steady herself to face the future.

When she raised her face, she was startled to see Lady Carrington kneeling at her feet. She rushed to help her stand.

"Please, Lady Carrington, you will wrinkle your gown."

"Estella, please." She returned a weak smile and sank into her chair. "The gown hardly matters at this hour, child. Do not concern yourself with me."

George, standing patiently at the door, cleared his throat. "Forgive me for intruding, miss, but on behalf of all the staff we wanted to extend our condolences. He was a fine man, a fine employer, and shall be very much missed."

George's words made her eyes fill with more tears, but she couldn't let them fall now. Later, when her duties were complete, she would grieve again. For now, she had to make her grandfather's parting a tribute.

Agatha turned for the large bed and the empty shell of her grandfather. With George's help, she straightened his limbs, neatened the bedding, and, with a final glance at his immobile face, she laid her hand across his eyes to close the lids. George was prepared with coins already and slipped them onto his eyes.

"Thank you, George."

There was nothing else to do now but keep vigil. "Can you bring another chair please, and then you can retire for the night."

"Of course," George murmured, but he tended to the fire first, a task Agatha hadn't thought of, positioned another chair beside Estella, then ushered the servants hovering outside away from the door and back to their beds.

Agatha settled into the chair and pressed her head to the back of it. Nothing to be done. Those words bounced around her head once more, taunting her with the uncertainty of the future. She had nothing. Soon no home. And no one to care when that happened. Would Oscar still want to marry her now she was in mourning? He'd never said what had been so important before.

Tears pricked her eyes again and she clutched the chair arm to keep the growing dread at bay. She had to be strong and prepare herself for this uncertain future. Tears had never helped her in the past. They would be next to useless in the future.

Estella's warm fingers wrapped around her tense hand and squeezed. Not so alone tonight. For now, she had the consolation of Estella's company as she kept vigil. Agatha wondered how long the older woman would remain.

She turned her head and found the other woman's eyes filled with concern.

"I know this is an unfortunate time. You may think me heartless to bring up such a delicate subject, but you need not fear, not at a moment so close to his parting. Thomas has made arrangements for you. Let your mind be easy on that score," Estella whispered.

Peace lasted only a moment though. "What arrangements?"

Had grandfather arranged for her to live with her cousin and his growing brood? She hoped not—she'd never be happy playing second fiddle to Arthur's wife. She'd run her grandfather's household as if it were her own. Following another's orders would be unbearable.

"I do not know them all precisely, but Thomas spoke to your cousin recently and obtained his agreement that you shan't be cast out from this house upon his death. I have the papers in my possession should it become necessary to remind your cousin of the agreement. It seems your grandfather had more than a slight inkling that his time was coming fast upon him."

Agatha began to shake, distraught that she's missed the signs that he was unwell. "Did you know he was ailing?"

Estella raised Agatha's trembling hand and kissed the back of it. "No, child. He never spoke of his health. I thought him merely weary of his business dealings. They were a great burden upon him."

At least she wasn't the only one caught unawares. Lulled by the soft stroking of Estella's fingertips across the back of her hand, Agatha relaxed. Neither of them was to blame, but both of them would miss him.

A loud pounding on the front door dragged Agatha from sleep. She rubbed her tired eyes and for a moment wondered what she was doing in her grandfather's chamber. The dark room was silent but for her own breathing. Estella was gone.

Quiet conversation drifted up from the hall. A man's deep voice rumbled through the house. Astonished that her cousin could already be here, she climbed to her feet. Although unsteady, she cast a glance at her grandfather's still form then stepped out onto the landing. Below stairs, Estella was whispering to Mr. Manning, the Rector of St. George's. The viscountess must have sent him word while Agatha had been asleep. She must remember to thank her for that later.

Slowly, Agatha descended the stairs.

Manning hurried to escort her down. "My child, how great this tragedy. Please accept my condolences. Is there anything I can do for you?"

Agatha managed a weak smile as he stared at her. His pale eyes were etched with genuine concern and she knew she could depend on him to see her grandfather buried with respect. She gestured toward her grandfather's study. "Thank you for coming."

When they were all settled before her grandfather's desk, she fought to get her emotions under control. The scent of cigar was strong in the room and remembrances made her eyes sting with tears again. "I am uncertain how to proceed with the arrangements, sir. My grandfather never mentioned any concerns with his health or his wishes for burial."

The vicar cleared his throat and gave her a brief description of her choices. His choice was for a tasteful burial without the pomp and ceremony Estella kept suggesting.

When the tension between them grew unbearable Agatha raised both hands to silence them. "Please. I do not wish to listen to arguments today."

Manning had the grace to look chagrined. "Forgive us, Miss Birkenstock. We have an old dispute between us that, of course, should be dealt with another time."

That was surprising. Agatha had thought Manning and Estella were on the best of terms. "It is of no matter, sir. I expect we are both raw from grieving someone we loved very much."

Agatha caught Estella's pained gaze. Estella's grief was proof that her grandfather had been blessed by the love of two women—her grandmother and Estella.

Manning shifted in his chair as if uncomfortable. "He was a fine man, but we both loved Essy as much as she'd allow us. That kind of situation makes close friendship impossible between men. While I did not care for the nature of their relationship, I found nothing else in his character to dislike. Your happiness and welfare are my first concerns."

Agatha pressed her cold hands flat upon the table. The bloodless appearance reminded her of her grandfather, and she quickly buried them in her lap. She took a deep breath. "I believe my grandfather would have preferred a simpler service, in keeping with our position in society. I do not wish to give any offence, Lady Carrington, but what you suggest, while offered with the greatest proof of your attachment to him, is an elegant affair best suited to those of your elevated rank. My grandfather was merely a gentleman in trade, and I know our place in the world." She turned to the vicar. "It would please me if you could act on this matter on my behalf. I should like the simpler service you outlined, with the burial to be at the church burial ground."

Agatha rubbed her temple. The strain of last night was catching up with her. She was so weary, so ready for this nightmare to be over. Yet she could not rest until all was set in motion. "However, I do recall one conversation with my grandfather some time ago, but it was such a distressing subject, I am loath to bring it up."

The vicar moved to the edge of his seat. "Of course, but if the discussion would set your mind at rest, please, you must unburden yourself."

Agatha swallowed. "My grandfather had a fear of grave robbers. I should not like anything to happen to his remains once he has been laid to rest."

The vicar nodded, a grim frown twisting his expression. "The thievery practiced by Resurrectionist's is always a concern among our parishioners, but there are ways to thwart such despicable acts. A mortsafe has proved to be most effective. It is a cage of iron placed over the coffin that thwarts any attempt to remove the body. But we can also employ servants to watch over your grandfather as well. I shall make those arrangements too."

"Thank you for your assistance."

The vicar climbed to his feet. "If you will excuse me, I shall be off to make the arrangements. Miss Birkenstock. Essy. I will return later this afternoon with news."

The silence left behind in his wake was deafening. Estella held Agatha's gaze without flinching, but her lips were pressed tightly together.

"What troubles you, my lady?"

"I'm so sorry."

Agatha frowned. "For what?"

"For involving you in a discussion that was inappropriate for you to hear. I had thought we, your grandfather and I, had been discreet."

Agatha dipped her head. "I've not heard a whisper about it, but then again, I do live—did live—in the same house as my grandfather. I have always been alert to his changing moods. He was happier after seeing you."

Estella regarded her sadly. "He loved you so much. One of our last conversations was about your future. It vexed him to no end that you'd not married."

Could she share the news that Oscar had proposed? Of course she couldn't. She would have to wait to see if he still wanted her. "I'd rather not discuss marriage."

Agatha stood and turned her back to the viscountess. She could not have this discussion with Oscar's mother. She couldn't confide her reasons for discouraging previous suitors either. To answer truthfully, as she'd prefer to do, would cause unnecessary tension between them.

Better to be silent and wait and see. After all, there was nothing to be done.

She squeezed her eyes shut.

"I had a feeling he'd been somewhat of an ogre about a marriage. In my experience, most parents are. I have goaded my children to secure influential matches, but I sometimes wonder if their lives will be happier than mine."

Estella's words sent a chill through her. "You were unhappy in your marriage?" As soon as the words were out, she regretted the blunt question. She couldn't expect a woman of Estella's higher social standing to divulge such personal details.

"My husband was something of a bully. Luckily neither of my children take after him. Oh, I know that my daughter has a reputation for being a trifle shrill, but my son is calmer, possessed of a fine and open mind about matters of the heart."

Oh, this conversation really had to end. "I'm sure he is."

Luckily George chose the perfect moment to interrupt. "I've taken the liberty of laying on breakfast in the morning room for both you and Lady Carrington. Is that acceptable?"

What would she do without George? "Thank you."

Estella drew her toward the hall, away from her morbid thoughts, and to a waiting breakfast. Although her stomach revolted at the idea of consuming food, it was best she eat something. She had to stay strong to survive the coming burial and keep her mind sharp as she made plans for her future. At least she still had the orphans to love.

With that thought in mind, she filled a plate and sipped a cup of hot chocolate, all the while watching the viscountess pick at her food.

Twenty-Three

TWIN POINTS OF pain lanced through Oscar's skull when a shaft of morning sunlight hit his face as he crossed the bustling street. Whatever had possessed him to drink so much that he'd been grateful when Daventry offered a guestroom?

Desperation, most likely. He'd just begun to imagine climbing in through Agatha's bedroom window again when Daventry suggested it. But he'd never manage the climb without detection. Not while Birkenstock was in residence. So he'd spent the night away from home, endured Lilly's amused giggles at his condition this morning, avoided eating any breakfast whatsoever because his stomach was in revolt, and headed out into the London morning in his hastily pressed suit of clothes from last night.

He needed a bath, a shave, and several more hours of sleep in order to feel like a gentleman again and be fit for company. He needed to face Birkenstock this morning and get his agreement for them to marry. He couldn't do that until he could walk in a straight line without effort.

Oscar grunted as he collided with a dark figure. The man grasped his arm to steady him, and Oscar was incredibly grateful. "Watch yourself there, my lord."

Kindly pale eyes pierced through Oscar's thoughts. Mr. Manning. His papa. What rotten timing. He'd be sure to smell the sour whiskey on his breath and notice his rumpled state. Would he be subjected to fatherly scolding now?

"Good morning to you, sir."

Manning's serious expression cut into his misery. "No, it is not that. Not a good morning at all. Most distressing start to the day. But everyone's time comes when it will. We are but servants to God's purpose."

Oscar frowned. He didn't understand Manning's pious ramble, but it sounded damn depressing. Oscar had no time for anyone else's troubles this morning. He had much to do. "Of course. If you will excuse me?"

The vicar stepped closer and placed a restraining hand on his arm. "You should be prepared for a distressing scene. She was greatly attached to him. She will need you."

"I beg your pardon?" Why must people speak in riddles at this hour of the day? Oscar thought it far from kind, given his current state, that his papa didn't just come out and say what he meant.

"Birkenstock. Surely you've heard by now?" The vicar looked about him then glanced at Oscar's clothes. "Were you out all night?"

Oscar felt like a scolded schoolboy again. It wasn't that unusual to be coming home at this hour and in this state. Hell, he was practically a novice when it came to debauchery. "What of it?" Oscar asked, belligerence making his voice louder than he intended. Fierce pain resumed its assault on his head, reminding him of his somewhat delicate state. "What do you mean, Birkenstock? Heard of what?"

"He died," Manning said simply, hands spread before him.

"Dear God, Agatha. Excuse me."

Oscar pushed past his father and rushed for home, despite the fact his head threatened to split in two. How could he have chosen last night to overindulge? Poor Aggie!

Oscar bounded up the stairs, slapped his palm against the wood, and fumbled for his door key. When the door opened before he could insert it in the lock, he gave thanks for his efficient servant. It was only when a hand curled around his arm and held him back that he realized he wasn't in his own home, or about to gain entry to Agatha's house via the window. He was already *in* her house. Her front entrance hall to be precise. And her butler appeared incensed by his presence.

Oscar shook off the grip. "Where is she?"

"Your mother, my lord?"

"No, not my mother. Agatha. Where is she?"

The butler's eyes flickered upward involuntarily, and then he scowled, tugging at Oscar's arm in a fair attempt to eject him from the house. "I must ask you to leave this instant. The mistress is not receiving callers today."

"She'll see me." Oscar evaded his grip and raced for the steps, ignoring the warning voice behind him. He took the stairs two at a time, but at the top, he hesitated. He'd never explored Agatha's home, but it appeared of similar construction to his. Would she be in her bedchamber or keeping vigil?

Oscar chose the latter and quietly made his way toward what he assumed would be her grandfather's room. His precious girl stood at the foot of the bed, her back toward him, her pale hair slicked into a severe knot, dark mourning weeds already donned to mark the passing. But her gaze remained fixed on the still form lying prone on the bed.

The penny covered eyes unnerved him, reminding him of his nightmares so much he began to quake. At least there was no gaping hole in Birkenstock's head. But the waxy-smooth, white skin did set his pulse to racing. He forced the fear down, forced himself to see the remains for what they were. No threat to him. No example of his actions. Thomas Birkenstock had been an old man. He'd lived a full life and appeared peaceful in death. He could do this.

Besides, Agatha needed him.

Forcing one foot in front of the other, he crossed the room until he stood behind her and slowly wrapped his arms about Agatha's slim form. She didn't resist or react immediately, but when her hands rose to clasp his arms,

Oscar pressed his lips to her temple in a gentle kiss. "Oh, sweetheart, I'm so sorry."

Agatha's shoulders gave a shake, and she sniffed. "It was his time, but I already miss his gruff ways."

He hugged her tighter. "I know. You loved him. And he loved you."

Facing death again wasn't nearly as unsettling as Oscar feared it would be. He could look upon the lifeless face and when he briefly closed his eyes he saw peace, not twisted, painful visions. The nightmare had left him, at least for now, but he hoped it was gone for good.

He scooped Agatha into his arms and carried her from the room. She didn't protest, didn't struggle, only lay quiet in his arms, a rushed breath the only sign of emotion. In the hall, her butler watched them pass with shock clear on his features, mouth agape like a fish at market. Oscar ignored it all and returned Agatha to her bedchamber. He settled down on the lounge and held her against his chest. She was alone now. Deprived of the protection her grandfather could give.

"I thought you'd never come," she whispered.

He kissed her hair. "I'm sorry. I was from home." Oscar removed a few pins from her tightly bound hair, loosening the locks until she looked more herself, less drawn by her grief. "But I'm here now and I'll not leave you again."

Agatha snuggled against his chest, her hand digging into his coat pocket and tugging out his handkerchief. After a short, delicate blow, her fingers clutched at his coat. "You were wearing this last night."

A weary sigh escaped him. "I've yet to go home."

She sat up, hands splayed across his chest. Agatha's eyes were red from crying, her cheeks splotched with angry color, but wariness tightened her eyes. "Where did you go? The Hells?"

He smoothed his fingertips across her damp cheek. "Daventry offered me bed space. We talked quite late."

"Oh?" She sniffed. "You mean you drank quite late. You reek, my lord."

"Sorry." Oscar pulled her against his chest, enjoying the feel of her arms wrapped around his neck. "I should go and change, but, quite frankly, I'd not like to leave you alone."

Agatha stilled in his arms then began to pull away. "I'm not alone."

He slid his fingers along her jaw gently. "I know your grandfather is still here, but I'd like to stay. Let me. Please."

Word would spread and everyone would know by now that he'd run to her front door and barged into a house in mourning. The whispers would reach Penelope eventually.

The sense of rightness swelled as he held her in his lap, offering comfort during her time of need. He wasn't going to leave her. Not again. Lord Thorpe would sue him for breach of promise, and Oscar would marry Agatha. If the Carrington name was dragged through the mud in the process, he could not regret it.

Movement at the door caught his attention. He turned his head and met his mother's shocked expression. Her expression turned to a glare. Once upon a time, that look would have cowed him. But those days were over. He could not please everyone, and it was high time he tried to please just one. He stroked his hand down Agatha's back, thankful she could not see the disapproval in his mother's face. She'd be embarrassed, and Agatha had nothing to feel guilty about today. She needed him as much as he needed her.

When Oscar pressed his lips to Agatha's hair, she snuggled deeper into his arms. His mother took a step back, her hand rising to her mouth to hold in a gasp. *Yes, Mother, I'm holding the woman I love. Can you tell that from where you stand?*

Apparently she could, because her eyes filled with glittering tears and she turned her head away to give them privacy.

In his arms, Agatha stirred and looked up. She always managed to make him feel a better man than he was. He had to tell her about his mother at the door. But, oh, how she looked at him with such longing. Regardless of his mother's presence at the door, the dead body down the hall, and the scandal of the situation, he dropped his head to press a gentle kiss to her lips. She smelled delicious, warm, and in every way his.

He kept his kisses light, undemanding, offering his love, strength, and anything else she wanted to take. When their lips parted, her contented sigh proved she'd needed him.

"My mother is at the door," he whispered, holding her still when she would have jumped from his arms. "It's too late to hide anything, precious. No more lies. No more secrets. Agreed?"

Agatha blinked up at him then her eyes softened. She cupped both hands to his jaw and returned his tender kiss. "No more secrets."

~ * ~

All this time. Poor Thomas had thought that no one could win his granddaughter's interest, but that was because her heart had already been claimed. How blind they had both been. Estella pushed the cold cup of tea away with a weary sigh. How her son had come to be so intimately involved with Agatha Birkenstock she didn't know, but she grieved for the girl.

Her heart was bound to be broken by his marriage.

"Am I disturbing you, Mother?"

She looked up. Oscar's face was filled with contrition and uncertainty—exactly the same expression Lynton had worn yesterday. She closed her tired eyes, willing the day of shocks to be over. "No. Of course not."

When she opened them again, Oscar was perched on a chair opposite. "I am sorry for your loss, Mother. It must be difficult."

Estella drew herself upright from her slump. "I should have expected it. He wasn't a young man any longer."

"No. No, he wasn't." Oscar shuffled in his chair. "Manning said you were quite disturbed by his death. Can I do anything for you now?"

"Lynton said that, did he?" Bitterness over Thomas' death added a bite of anger to her words. Lynton would likely be happy to have Thomas out of his way.

Oscar merely shook his head at her. "Despite whatever history is between you and Manning now or in the past, Mother, he was truly cast down by Mr. Birkenstock's death. As are we all."

Estella took in a steadying breath. "Forgive me. It has been a long day and night."

"Agatha was exhausted and fell asleep quite quickly, but have you been here all night?"

Estella nodded. "She sent for me not long after I arrived home from Daventry's dinner. You, I imagine, must have been well and truly in a fog by then."

Oscar looked down. "Perhaps not the best night to sample Daventry's wine cellar as extensively as I did, but I am here now and intend to stay."

"You cannot stay here." She shook her head. "Think of her reputation. Or what she might still have, that is, after your unseemly arrival."

"Her reputation is my only concern, and I promise to correct the damage I've done as soon as possible."

Estella's mouth fell open. He couldn't mean to marry Agatha Birkenstock, surely? He was already to wed. "But what about Lady Penelope?"

Oscar's face twisted into one of distaste. "I rather expect her father will sue me for breach of promise. I really couldn't care less for my own reputation, should he savage me to society. Penelope can go find another gullible gentleman and force a match on him."

"Oh, Oscar," she cried. "What a mess you're making. We may never recover from this."

Oscar sat forward with his hands upon his knees. "As indelicate as this is for me to say to you, I'm planning to improve on my father's efforts to be happy. I'll marry Agatha and move from the city. If we can find a big enough place, and funds permit, we will take the orphanage children off the trustee's hands and raise them ourselves."

Estella fell back in the chair. He would throw away everything they had both worked so hard for, their position in society, a supremely beneficial marriage, and all for love?

She stared at him.

"Don't look so surprised, Mother. You raised me to be a gentleman, to do the honorable thing. I should have married Agatha months ago, long before Lady Penelope made her accusation. A lie, by the way. I've never even held Penelope's hand."

Estella gulped. "Is Agatha with child?"

"Unfortunately, not." He grinned. "But give me time and I'll report happy news in the near future, I'm sure."

"Oscar, this is no joking matter. This is serious."

"And it's about time I was serious and lived up to my obligations." He stood and prowled the room. "Agatha will be my wife, and to make us both happy, we will have the orphans with us. If you cannot bear to lose your position in society because of my decision, you are free to disown me as loudly as you dare. But if you make a scene before Agatha, I will never speak to you again."

Estella gulped. She barely recognized the affable gentleman in the son before her. He reminded her too much of Lynton. "Oscar, I like Agatha very much, as you well know, but have you really thought this through?"

Her son set his hands to the back of a chair. "I've thought of little else since signing that blasted betrothal document. I made a mistake then, but I'd be a bigger fool if I didn't marry her. I love Agatha with my whole heart, and I won't make the same mistake my father did. I'm not afraid of what people will say. The bigger scandal would be never to marry her at all."

Twenty-Four

OSCAR HURRIED UP the front steps of his townhouse, anxious to greet his unexpected visitors. He'd spent the last few days in Agatha's home, mostly holding her when she cried, and had thought little of the outside world. But he should have completed his assessment of the orphanage by now. He regretted his failure to deliver his findings to the trustees, not have them demand a meeting like this. He could have worked while Agatha rested. She might have found the puzzle of straightening the orphanage finances a relief from missing her grandfather.

As he crossed the threshold of his drawing room, he drew to a sudden halt at the unsmiling faces of the trustees from the Grafton Street Orphanage. Each gentleman curled their lip at his arrival. Were they that angry with him over the delay? He'd have to think quickly to appease them and maybe they would grant him a little more time. "Gentlemen, to what do I owe the pleasure?"

They glanced between themselves then Lord Carter stepped forward. "Never in all my years have I had to engage in conversation with a gentlemen of such depravity. If it were not for our pressing business, I should have no cause to call on you at all."

Oscar blinked at the startling statement. He glanced around those present, seeing varying degrees of violence in their expressions. All this because he was late? Perhaps they hadn't come for the accounts, after all. "How have I offended you?"

Lord Carter set his hands to his hips. "By taking up with that . . . that . . . oh, I can scarcely say the words. Her own grandfather, a man ever conscious of his place in the world, still lies at rest within the house and yet you frolic with the girl, no doubt on his very death bed too."

The gentlemen closest to Lord Carter looked everywhere but at him. Oscar shut his mouth. But he was shocked to his core. "There has been no frolicking, as you put it. Miss Birkenstock is a very good friend and is deeply distressed by her grandfather's death. I am giving comfort, not debauching her. But you may set your minds at rest. It is my intention to marry her and restore her reputation."

"We couldn't give a fig for the girl. If she hasn't the sense to boot you from the house, then she deserves every ill that comes to her. We, my colleagues and I, are concerned with more important matters."

"And what exactly would matter more than your mistaken assumptions about me and Agatha Birkenstock?"

Lord Carter held out his hand. Mr. Manning, his dear newly discovered papa, stepped from the rear of the group where Oscar hadn't spied him before with a paper in his hand. Manning didn't meet his eye. Carter took the paper, gave it a little shake, and then handed it to Oscar.

He unfolded the note and read.

"You will find everything in order. You are not now, nor have you ever been, intimately involved with the Grafton Street Orphanage. We thank you for your interest, but are unable to accept your contribution to the scheme."

Oscar raised his head from the ridiculous bit of paper. "But this is a lie. It is a well known fact that my family has been intimately involved for the past years. You would not have Lord Ettington's financial support if not for our association."

Carter glared. "I hardly think you can claim credit for that. Lord Ettington is a marquess, a benefactor to many charitable causes, and a superior gentleman not given to associating with rabble. We would never desire an acquaintance with a fellow of your low moral character. We must think of our reputations. They could be irreparably harmed by the taint of your association. It pains me to give the cut direct to any woman, but I shall cross the road to avoid Lady Carrington from this moment on. So should any good woman in society, if I had my way."

"Don't you dare!" Their decision and accusations stunned him. Oh, he'd known he'd endure a loss of status by marrying Agatha, but this was so far beyond what he'd imagined. He was appalled that they would turn against his mother like this.

"You are hardly in a position to tell us what we may or may not do." Carter snapped his fingers imperiously until Lord Brooke held out another paper for him to take. "This concludes our business. Good day."

Oscar opened the note. A one thousand pound promissory note stared back at him. Was that how much his family had contributed over the years? The sum was astonishingly small. He folded the note carefully and tucked it into his pocket as the trustees filed out. He didn't bother to look at them. They were right, of course. His actions with Agatha had placed him in an indefensible position to be involved with the orphans. He had not behaved as a gentleman should and would be seen as a bad influence. But Mother?

He looked up. His father stood opposite him.

"I should, by rights, have something scathing to say about your behavior. However, that would be like calling the kettle black. As it is, I've a mind to call them out for the slight they intend to cast upon your mother. Unfortunately, if I say a word they, and she, may never speak to me again. There is too much at stake to have that happen yet."

Oscar raked his fingers through his hair. This was a catastrophe of the worst proportions. "They are right, Father. I am completely in the wrong here."

Manning's breath hissed out. "Your mother told you?"

"Of course she didn't. Would Mother ever admit to any scandal?"

Manning chuckled suddenly. "No. No, she wouldn't."

The older man looked Oscar over. He returned the intense scrutiny, recognizing the familiar angles that had puzzled him before. How had he missed connecting the similarities?

He'd missed them because his mother had never given him cause to suspect her of infidelity while his father lived. Behind closed doors, she had always been scathing of women who cuckolded their husbands. The man he'd called Papa had agreed right along with her. Only now Oscar knew that his papa had been weak and easily led astray by other women. How chagrined Mother must be now. Especially since she'd unwittingly done the same as her unfaithful husband had.

Oscar smiled at his real father. "I hardly know what name to call you."

"Lynton will suffice." His eyes glittered with unshed tears, and he quickly looked away. "Did I hear correctly that you will be marrying Miss Birkenstock?"

Quite choked up, Oscar took a moment to collect himself before he answered. "As soon as possible. However, if I cannot obtain a special license, we will be traveling to the border without delay after the funeral. I have done far too much damage to both Agatha and now my mother to wait for the banns to be called."

"Good man." Manning clapped his hand on Oscar's shoulder. "I may be able to help you with the special license. Staines can add pressure to my request if it becomes necessary."

Oscar settled himself to a chair, quite done in by the events of the morning. But one thing still puzzled him. "Why did he visit my home the other day?"

"Staines? Isn't it obvious?" Lynton laughed again. "He loves his family."

Oscar squinted up at his father. "And the nephew needing a new house? What nephew?"

"He meant you." Lynton pursed his lips. "Oscar, you will soon learn that my brother is a terrible force to turn once he has chosen to act. Although I cannot claim you openly as my son, he will ignore all of that to provide for you. He loves being the head of the family and lording his opinion over all of us. We have disagreed over my taking orders these last twenty years. I should suggest, for a peaceful life, that it is in your best interests to let him have his way. Or at least consider that you will likely lose. He's probably considering properties to purchase for you even now. I do hope you like Oxfordshire. No doubt he'll find a property close to home."

Oscar took Lynton at his word about the property. He only knew of Staines by reputation and by all accounts he was not a man to gainsay. But he could very well be against his marriage to Agatha. After all, her grandfather had been in trade; he held no title as Lady Penelope's father did. What would he say about Oscar marrying a woman with no elevating connections? Would he care that he loved her?

He paced the room—worried. Perhaps he'd have to flee to Scotland to marry after all. He would do well to make plans for it just in case. Yet, inspiration struck. "Lynton, I wanted to ask, and Agatha wanted this too. Would you consent to marry us, should we obtain a special license?"

If Lynton agreed, it might influence the duke's decision to support the marriage. But Lynton remained silent. Dread churning his stomach into knots, Oscar turned around. A single tear flowed down his father's face before he brushed it quickly away.

"I should be honored."

Oscar sagged with relief. "Thank you." He grinned. "Now, I should like to return to Agatha next door. Will you join us so we might share the good news about you officiating?"

"Ah, no. I'm afraid I shall not be able to see either you or Agatha until the funeral. I have some pressing business to attend to over the next day that cannot be delayed. Please pass along my regards and affections to your mother and Miss Birkenstock. I shall see you all very soon."

When Lynton hurried out the door, he took Oscar's optimism with him. It seemed that despite the fact that he would gladly make amends for ruining Agatha, some things were unforgivable—even to a father.

He strolled out his door, along the street, and climbed the stairs to Agatha's house.

Agatha's butler greeted him with a scowl. "Lady Carrington is waiting in the drawing room."

Poor man. The butler was quite put out with him, too. Laying Birkenstock to rest and marrying Agatha couldn't come soon enough. After that, someone, besides Agatha, might actually smile at him again.

"What did those old windbags want?"

Oscar grinned at his mother as if he hadn't a care in the world. He hadn't come up with a kind way of saying they had been shown the door because of his scandalous actions. He would break it to her gently after the funeral. "Nothing too serious, Mother. Just some paperwork to look over."

"I expect they think I've deserted the enterprise. I'll call there this afternoon."

He sat beside her and took up her hand. "No need. They were quite adamant that you take all the time in the world. No point upsetting the children from their current routine."

"Oh," she whispered. The silence stretched. "They don't want me to return, do they?"

He drew his wise, wise mother into his arms and gave her a hug. "Saying I'm sorry doesn't seem enough, but I am. I had not anticipated they would condemn you, too, because of my actions."

She sniffed. "I suppose if I had disowned you, as you gave me leave to do, they would have tolerated me. But I worry for Agatha. Being here so often lends her what little support I can."

"She appreciates it, even if she has not shown how much. In time, her grief will lessen and she'll be more herself around you."

His mother gave him an amused glance. "Agatha and I are not such strangers that I would easily take offence. She is much caught up in her grief and I would be a poor mama-in-law to deny her time to cry. Was Manning with the trustees?"

"Yes. Lynton was among them."

"And?"

Oscar drew her into his arms again and squeezed. "Oh, Mother. Your love life is a bigger mess than mine. My father sends his affections and regards to you and Agatha. I did remember my manners and asked him to call on you here, but he had other business to tend. We will see him at Mr. Birkenstock's funeral and after."

"After?"

Oscar settled back in the chair and crossed his legs at the ankle. "Yes, of course. Agatha and I want him to marry us, and he has consented."

A deep frown line creased her brow. "Then he hasn't left the church yet."

"No. He never said anything about it. He's consented to obtain a special license for us, with the duke's assistance if it is required. Once he has that, I expect to be wed as soon as possible."

His mother huffed, a bitter sound. "Should have known he'd pretend to be leaving the church to get on my good side." She stood. "I'm going upstairs to sit with Thomas."

Before she reached the door, Oscar called out. "I say, Mother, does Lynton really have property in Oxfordshire?"

"He did once. Why?"

"Because he claims the duke will want me to live there. If that happens, will you come and live with us?"

His mother swayed, and then righted herself. "Two women under the same roof makes for a disharmonious household, Oscar. I shall be all right on my own. Excuse me."

Twenty-Five

A COLD WIND blew through the church yard, hurrying more than one mourner across the grounds toward the grave where Agatha wept at Oscar's side. For all his lower birth, it seemed Thomas Birkenstock had been well liked. There were faces here Oscar didn't recognize. Some he did. The Earl of Daventry was here, a bookseller from Bond Street stood beside him. At the back of the crowd, Oscar spied Leopold Randall trying his best to keep his presence as unobtrusive as possible and still pay his respects.

Lynton Manning kept the graveside service brief, his words uplifting despite the sad occasion. Oscar appreciated that for Agatha's sake. She was taking the loss of her grandfather very hard. Her loss of appetite and lack of decent sleep shrouded her features with sorrow.

Her cousin was not in attendance. He had send word of his coming, and then sent a terse note later to decline. That he shunned his own cousin's funeral was Oscar's fault. Rumors had spread that he had all but moved into the Birkenstock townhouse and Arthur's note had been scathing of Agatha's character. He wanted her out as soon as possible. Her dowry and the allowance that her grandfather had arranged would not be paid.

They had become the scandal of the year.

Oscar shifted his weight from foot to foot. Winter was coming, if today's chill was any indication. Agatha's black-gloved hands kept clenching and unclenching until he could bear it no longer. He reached for her restless fingers and captured them in a tight grip. Agatha swayed until she leaned against his shoulder. She really should not have come, but he couldn't persuade her otherwise. And because Agatha was here, so too was his mother.

Oscar doubted they could live this lapse of etiquette down any time soon.

More than a few mourners frowned at Agatha, but not the people who loved her best. They knew how hard she grieved for Mr. Birkenstock, how easily tears had flowed over these last few days.

Lynton concluded his sermon and closed his prayer book as the coffin was lowered. His gaze flickered to their joined hands, then he circled the grave and led Agatha a little away from the other mourners to speak with her privately. As always, Oscar followed, but not too close— ready to offer support if she had need of him.

"She managed that far better than I expected," his mother murmured.

"Yes, but she trembled the entire time." Oscar glanced at the muttering crowd. "She'll need to rest when we return home."

His mother offered him a weak smile. "Well, the worst is over now."

The worst wasn't over. "We'll see."

The mourners lined up to say farewell to Agatha. She did well, accepting everyone's condolences, offering thanks for their coming in soft tones. Randall tipped his hat to her, but made no attempt at conversation. Oscar gestured to his mother to take his place with Agatha, and then moved away from the crowd.

"Taking quite a risk with the lady's reputation," Randall remarked as they shook hands. "I should warn you that there is more than one person outraged by her presence and your behavior. You might find yourself out of favor with society."

"We are already firmly out of favor." Oscar shrugged. "It cannot be helped."

Randall rubbed his chin. "I'm leaving London in a few days."

"So soon?"

Randall crossed his arms over his chest. "So far my search has come up empty. Even in the most unsavory of places. I take it you've had no luck, either."

Oscar had forgotten Randall's concerns in the wake of Birkenstock's passing. He winced. "I'm so sorry. With everything that has happened, I have let you down."

Randall stared over Oscar's shoulder. "I'll take the risk and return home to request an audience with the young duke. Perhaps the current duchess will be more forthcoming than her predecessor. One can only hope. Don't worry about me—your lady needed you more."

Oscar turned and spied Agatha alone by the graveside. He searched the lingering mourners and could see no sign of his father anywhere. His spirits fell. Manning must have been more upset with him than he'd let on. If memory served, he'd not spoken one word to his mother either.

His heart ached for Agatha. What a great mess he'd involved her in. She said little on the subject. Her sorrow consumed her. However scandalous the Carrington's might be now, Randall was correct. He'd done the right thing to put her first above all else. Society and their impatience be damned.

He turned back to Randall. "Leave your directions at my home before you go, and be sure to send a letter to let me know how you get on at Romsey. If I don't hear from you, I'll make the trip south. I swear it."

Randall nodded with a quick dip of his head, but his eyes glassed. "Birkenstock was right about you. You are a true gentleman."

That cut. He'd not done the right thing by Agatha before, not by any stretch of the imagination. But he would now. She was the only thing worth living for, and he would soon set her reputation to rights. "Safe journey, Randall."

Randall stuck out his hand. "Best of luck to you both. Take care of her."

"Count on it." Oscar strode over to where Agatha stood with Lord Daventry at her side now. He drew Agatha's arm through his and moved her away from the grave again. He dipped his head to better see her expression. "All right, precious?"

Agatha let out a weary sigh. "I am now."

Oscar turned to Daventry. "Might I impose upon you for the use of your largest carriage in the near future? We may need to take a long trip fairly soon."

Daventry's eyes narrowed. "How long a trip?"

Oscar thought it through. He'd never traveled to Scotland before, but he did think it a long and tiring journey. If they stopped frequently, Agatha's spirits might be lifted by the fresh surroundings. "I think we should return in about a week to ten days."

"A border wedding? Surely it shan't come to that." Daventry set his hand to Oscar's shoulder and squeezed. "But about time you made an honorable woman out of her. Congratulations."

"Thank you," Agatha murmured, turning her face into Oscar's shoulder to hide a blush.

Daventry smiled. "I was starting to think I'd have to call you out for not proposing marriage to this forbearing young woman. Lilly will be thrilled that you are to wed, but not that she will miss the wedding. However, my carriage is at your disposal as soon as you need it. Call on me day or night."

"Thank you." How he'd been lucky enough to have such good friends astounded him. They were very forgiving of his flaws. But then again, Daventry was not entirely a saint where his wife was concerned. Oscar guessed that Daventry had tested the waters with Lilly, so to speak, before actually proposing matrimony.

When Daventry departed, taking Oscar's mother with him for the journey so he and Agatha might have privacy, Oscar wrapped his arms around her. He rested his chin on the top of her head. "We should be going, precious."

"I know, it's just..."

The clank of the mortsafe being carried toward the open grave sounded behind them. He couldn't have Agatha stay to watch it being lowered. She could have nightmares from witnessing that. Oscar kissed her cheek. "You have done everything a dutiful granddaughter could do and more. He would be proud of you."

Agatha sniffled. "I don't think he would be proud of the way we are behaving, and in public, no less. Where is my mind? My sense of decorum?"

"Misplaced with mine. Don't fret about it." Oscar curled his arm around her waist, lifted her from her feet, and set her in the direction of their carriage. "Once we are married, the whispers will die down and another scandal will rise up to take our place."

But he still worried how long it would take. The whispers and stares aimed at Agatha and his mother bothered him a great deal more than he let on. No one called on his mother. Neither of them received invitations to entertainments. The only company they had kept was with each other and the Earl and Countess of Daventry. Not even his new father came to call.

After tonight though, things would change. He had waited long enough. He would ensure Agatha got a sound night's sleep and then tomorrow, if Lynton failed to arrive with news of a special license, they would depart for Scotland.

He hoped Agatha wouldn't be too disappointed about the long trip and marrying without friends beside them in Scotland. But their life would be free of scandal once the words were spoken to join them as man and wife. And after that, they would see how well they were received by society.

With his arm draped around Agatha's shoulder, he moved them toward the waiting team. Agatha clambered inside, a deep sigh passing her lips as she sank into the well-padded seats. Although she looked comfortable sitting alone, Oscar pulled Agatha into his lap as soon as the carriage lurched forward. "I love you."

Agatha cradled his face. Tears began to fall again, but Oscar had some hope that they were tears of happiness, not sorrow. She pressed their lips together, urgent, desperate, and so full of her own love that Oscar's heart raced.

When she drew back they were both out of breath. "Are you vexed with Mr. Manning for rushing off?"

"Well," Oscar shuffled her on his lap until he was more comfortable. "Lynton did not speak to me today about the special license, as I expected. I'm wondering if he can obtain one at all. I want us married, and soon."

Agatha frowned. "And if he cannot obtain a license then you want to marry over an anvil?"

Oscar smoothed his fingertips over her cheek until the frown lines disappeared. "It may be necessary. I wanted to be prepared, just in case." He winced at the image Agatha's words evoked. An anvil wedding would hardly be any young woman's dream. Agatha deserved far better than a rushed affair far from her friends. "Will you forgive me for that?"

She smiled. "Your mother will be disappointed. But I will not. Not if you really want to marry me."

Oscar set his head against Agatha's and drew in a deep breath. "Oh, my precious girl, of course I do. Whatever did I do to deserve you?"

A soft laugh escaped her. "You are kind to me when I need you most. Exactly as you were when my parents died and I'd come to live with my grandfather. You made me love you then, and nothing has changed except my love grew stronger."

Humbled by her words, he held her snug against him for the short ride to Berkeley Square. They were meant to be this way—together against the world. Nothing would separate them. He'd see to that and make her smile every day.

When the carriage stopped, he helped her out and led her gently up the stairs, shielding her from the staring faces of their neighbors. Once inside, he kissed her cheek. "I'll have tea sent up if you like."

She nodded and wearily trudged up the stairs. He'd join her later and sleep in her bed tonight rather than the chair he'd occupied since her grandfather's death. Maybe if he held her through the night, she wouldn't seem so sad come morning.

There was nothing he could do until evening. He turned for Agatha's little corner of the house to resume reading the book he'd started the day before.

Before he got there, however, her butler cleared his throat. "Might I have a word, my lord?"

Oscar smiled, hoping to get Agatha's servant on side. "Of course, George. What can I do for you?"

"I wanted to enquire about a position, my lord."

Oscar blinked. "A position? Are you not gainfully employed here?"

George drew himself up straighter. "For the time being, my lord. However, it has come to my attention that you have an opening, and I would much rather remain employed here in Town, or wherever Miss Birkenstock resides."

"An opening? I don't have an opening in my household."

"Then you have not been home as yet?" George winced. "I, ah, hate to be the bearer of bad news, my lord, but your butler decamped today for a position in another household. And then most of your household staff left as well. At present, you have one pot boy running your house. The gossip about the departures is racing up and down the street."

"Oh, for Heaven's sake."

George smiled hesitantly. "Those were my exact words. Inexcusable behavior, if I may say so."

"You may." Oscar looked over Agatha's butler. She had never spoken a bad word against George and they *would* need someone to manage their household efficiently. As long as George here could get over his dislike of their present situation, there was no reason not to employ the man if he were in earnest. "What about your position here?"

"We think, the staff and I, that Miss Birkenstock will be more comfortable with familiar faces around her. We worry that she's not herself. If you should accept my application for the post of butler, I have several other household staff candidates to put forward to replace the servants you've lost."

Amused by this turn of events, Oscar raised a brow. "And what happens with Agatha's cousin? Won't Arthur Birkenstock be somewhat put out with you all for leaving?"

George tugged on his waistcoat. "He should not have withdrawn his financial support from Miss Birkenstock. He should have honored Mr. Birkenstock's last wishes. We are certain Mr. Birkenstock would have wanted his granddaughter well cared for after his passing, and she is not."

Oscar winced. "Not yet. But I will do my best to correct the situation."

George smiled suddenly. "That is what we believe too, my lord. When should you like me to begin in my new post?"

The sooner the better. If the gossip was spreading the way George claimed, then he was unlikely to find suitable replacements of good character at short notice. "Possibly from tomorrow. I will discuss the matter with Agatha after she has rested, but it is my hope that she will be my wife by tomorrow night. With her agreement, you may take up your new duties as soon as convenient. Wedding or not, I do hope to remove Agatha to my home tomorrow. Arthur Birkenstock was most keen to have the house back."

"Very good, my lord." George smiled. "On behalf of the staff, we should like to congratulate you on your wise decision to marry Miss Birkenstock. She is a remarkable woman."

Oscar nodded. "She is truly remarkable, but I'm surely not wise. Not yet, at any rate. Fate is responsible for my good fortune, George. Never doubt that."

Twenty-Six

CHAOS REIGNED AROUND Agatha as the servants of her household removed themselves and Agatha's possessions to Oscar's home next door. The noise of closing up the house was really quite deafening after the peace of the last few days, and although they still were not married yet, she looked forward to the change of location. As Oscar put it, either here or there, they would create scandal until they were wed. But she had to move anyway. Cousin Arthur wanted her gone from his house, so she had agreed to move from the only home she could remember. It was almost done.

She heaved a sigh as she stepped out into the rear gardens. It was quiet out here. Peaceful. A temporary reprieve from the demands of the world. She wove her way through the kitchen gardens, amused with the gaping holes in the earth. Cook must have unearthed her favorite herbs that could be transplanted with ease to Oscar's kitchen garden. But the holes worried her. Arthur might get his nose more out of joint that it already would be over the loss of his London servants. He loved order as much as her grandfather had. So, seeing a shovel left lying carelessly on the ground, she picked it up and refilled the holes.

She patted the soil down hard with the back of the shovel then leaned upon it as she gazed around. She had spent most of her life here in this house, in the very tiny garden, and although she was only moving one house away, she would miss it very much indeed.

Agatha carried the shovel to the edge of the garden and set it against the wall where it would be out of the way. No one would stumble upon it here in the corner where she'd once dreamed pixies lived. A rambling vine grew over a sturdy frame, and she smiled at the memory of how often she'd played beneath it, thinking she'd be hidden from everyone's sight.

But she knew now that invisibility was impossible. Her grandfather had watched over her even when she'd thought he'd been occupied elsewhere. He'd had eyes in the back of his head, he'd said at her surprise.

Agatha quickly wiped a tear away. She couldn't keep crying like this. Her grandfather was gone and no amount of tears would bring him back.

He would hate to think of her so sad.

She had to let go of the past and face the future.

Agatha looked up at the house then shifted her gaze to Oscar's rear windows. He stood at one, watching her reminisce, worry creasing his features. Agatha raised her hand, and when he waved back, her heart gave a happy flutter. Soon they would be married and after her mourning period was over, and society forgave them, they would settle into a comfortable life together in London. Would society accept their marriage?

She would hate it if Oscar came to regret his decision.

A scrape of sound turned her around. She peered at the rear garden, but couldn't detect any sign of company. But the rear gate hung open, just enough that a passing scoundrel with thievery in mind might peek inside and find something useful to steal. Even though this was no longer her home, she didn't like the idea of strangers in Arthur's home. He might be ashamed of her, but she'd never wish him ill. He had enough trouble with his shrew of a wife. Elizabeth Birkenstock would have been the one to convince Arthur to disown her.

Agatha rushed toward the gate to close it for the last time. As she set her hand to the open gate, a dirty hand closed over her wrist and she was wrenched through it. Stunned, before she could even scream out a protest, she was tossed over a broad shoulder and carried off down the lane.

Behind her, glass shattered as Oscar called her name. Agatha struggled and fought, but the hands holding her were merciless. As she drew in a deep breath to scream loudly for help, her captors threw her into a darkened carriage. Her head hit the wooden side hard.

Lights danced before her eyes. Stunned, she made no greater sound than a moan. The carriage lurched forward and picked up speed. Without breath, head spinning in pain, she couldn't cry out more than a whimper. Agatha scrambled frantically, but there was no escape. Her hands and feet were bound, and before she could yell, a cloth was pressed over her mouth and tied around her head.

She couldn't make a sound but to whimper.

Once her eyes had adjusted to the dim light of the carriage interior, she whimpered again. Toothless, her attacker from the park, grinned at her. "Pretty missy," he said.

By daylight, he looked infinitely worse. His slack mouth gaped, his bent nose dripped, and his skin was coated in dark grime. Not even a thorough dunking in the Thames would make much difference.

The carriage turned a sharp corner, and she was thrown hard against the other man. She turned to get a glimpse of him and shrank back as soon as she had. He was huge. As big as the villain that had attacked her in the park last time. He leered at her, then his gaze moved on to his partner.

Agatha shivered in fear. She'd never get away from them. Not unless Oscar ran faster than any living man.

The brute caught Toothless by his shirt and hauled him close. "Now remember, no touchin this time. Were gettin hard coin, and we isn't allowed to muss up the merchandise. They want her undamaged."

Toothless gasped for breath. But when he was released, his hand darted out and snatched Agatha's gold cross from her neck. The replacement that Oscar had given her dangled before her eyes a moment, then he slipped the precious possession into his pocket.

The brute cuffed him across the jaw. "Better not've put a mark on her neck or I'll give ya hell for reducin our profit. They want her presentable. Figure they got men lining up for a new thing to poke at."

Toothless laughed soundlessly, his hand covered his groin, and he crudely rubbed himself. Agatha closed her eyes. Why?

Why her?

Why now?

But she had no answers, unless all of society had turned against her to save Oscar from her clutches. If she was gone, he'd be free and could reclaim his place in society. He could even marry Lady Penelope, if she'd still have him, and be free of scandal.

The carriage slowed and turned into a side street. It was dark here and stank of things she'd rather not know about. They moved at a snail's pace then stopped. Agatha shivered from the chill seeping into her bones. What now?

The carriage groaned as the brute lumbered out. He turned, caught her bound hands, and wrenched her toward him. Agatha tried to peer past him to determine where they were taking her. Desperately, she hoped she could escape. She had to try. But when the brute tossed her over his shoulder again, her head hit the alley wall and she saw nothing else.

~ * ~

Oscar cradled his bleeding hand against his chest as he limped back toward home. He'd lost Agatha. Despite his best efforts, the carriage had been too quick, the drop from the first floor had stunned him, and by the time he'd reached the lane entrance Agatha's carriage was at the end of the street. He'd run as hard as he could, yet he'd still lost sight of them within two streets.

He was going to punish whoever was responsible for taking Agatha from him. He would not rest until she was safe again and those responsible had paid with their lives.

He limped into his house to find it in a greater uproar than when he'd left.

His father had arrived, and so had his mother. He'd hoped Lynton would call not an hour ago, but right now the sight of his father and mother were not helpful in the least.

His mother cried out at the sight of his bloody hand, her hand at her throat.

Lynton hurried forward. "For Heaven's sake, boy. I leave you alone for a few days to conclude my business, and you get into a huff and smash windows. What's gotten into you?"

Oscar winced as his father pried his hand from his chest to inspect it. "My hand is nothing. Agatha has been taken."

They both clutched at his arms. "What? Why?"

"I don't know." Oscar moved his fingers to check his hand still functioned the way it should. "I think it was the same ruffians that accosted her in the park last week. They were quicker than last week, and better prepared. Had a carriage ready in the lane this time. I couldn't keep up."

Lynton turned his hand over carefully. "Essy, lean against the wall like a good girl before you faint."

For a change, his mother didn't argue.

Lynton met his gaze. Concern and worry clouded his features. "This isn't too bad, but it will need to be cleaned and bound to prevent infection."

Oscar shook his head. "As long as I can still shoot, it can wait. Then, once I have Agatha back and safe again, you can do whatever you like with it."

Without waiting to see if he agreed, Oscar strode to his bookroom. He needed his pistols and to decide what to do. He couldn't do that with his father fussing and his mother about to faint from the sight of blood at any moment.

He wrenched open the drawer that contained them and inspected them carefully. Primed and ready to fire. Thank heavens.

Lynton hurried toward him. "What the hell are you doing with them? Put them down."

He stared at his father and shrugged. "I intend to get my Agatha back by any means necessary. If I have to murder someone again, I certainly will not hesitate."

"Murder?" His father's eyes grew wide. "For God's sake shut your mouth. You're not thinking clearly."

Oscar ignored the warning. He *was* thinking clearly. He was attempting to remember every detail from when Agatha put her hand on the gate until he'd lost sight of the carriage. Two men inside with her, another two whipping on the dark carriage, but no crest or identification of any kind on the doors. All he had to go on was that skinny, toothless fellow and his burly companion. Would such a filthy combination be easy to find?

"What the devil is going on? Why is he bleeding? Redding get in here!" The Duke of Staines hurried forward and pushed his brother aside to make way for his servant.

Although Oscar would much rather be on his way, he let Redding inspect the wound. Could Staines help him? The duke was known to have his fingers in many pies of the unsavory variety. Perhaps he could be useful.

Redding demanded supplies to dress the wound, but George, who'd hovered nervously behind the Duke of Staines when he'd first arrived, had them already.

Redding nodded his thanks. "This will sting, my lord."

Oscar gritted his teeth as brandy was poured over the wounds. The pain amplified his anger. He would make them suffer if one hair on Agatha's head was harmed.

Staines set his hands on his hips. "I have yet to hear an explanation."

Oscar scowled. "Someone has taken my future wife. Agatha was abducted not thirty minutes ago."

Staines drew closer, peering over his servant's shoulder, his hand resting lightly on Redding's back. "Be as quick as you can, Redding. We'll need your expertise to find her before any harm is done."

Redding nodded, but ignored his master's lingering touch while he cleansed the wound and then checked for embedded glass shards.

When he was done, Oscar flexed his fingers a bit. There was some pain, but the firm bandage helped. "Thank you."

Redding met his gaze. "Everything you remember. From the beginning, my lord."

So Oscar told them everything he remembered, and when pressed, about the first attempt in the park. When he was done, he glanced between Redding and his new uncle. But they moved aside to confer in private.

His mother approached him and laid her hands over his uninjured arm. "So brave, my Oscar. You should have told me."

"Not brave, Mother. Utterly desperate. I couldn't bear to lose Agatha then, and I certainly cannot now." He kissed her brow. "Excuse me, I must go."

"Be careful. Bring her back safe, and send word to me here if you are delayed."

"I will." Oscar untangled himself from her embrace, tucked his pistols into his coat pockets, and approached his uncle. "I'm ready."

"As am I," his father agreed.

Staines looked at his brother. "You stay here in case our girl finds her way home. Keep Essy calm if you can."

"But . . . "

"No buts." Staines clapped Oscar on the back. "Redding has an inkling, and his inklings are surprisingly accurate. Come on. We have a bawdy house to wage war on."

"Damn it," Lynton argued. "Stop mollycoddling me. I'm not a child."

Staines approached his brother and set his hands on his tense shoulders. "No, you are still a man of God, and as such you should not be put in a position to fire upon someone, should such an action be required. You have no experience with any of that, and I'd rather keep it that way. I may not have agreed with your choice of profession, but I envy you your pure heart. If it helps, you can sermonize at me later as much as you want. We three can manage and do what becomes necessary."

"Despite them taking Agatha, I fear this has something to do with Oscar." Lynton clutched his brother's arm. "He could be in danger, too."

"Oh," his mother moaned, as she tumbled to the ground in a faint.

Lynton rushed to her side and pulled her into a sitting position on the floor.

Staines pinched the bridge of his nose. "Now why did you have to say that out loud? I thought you had better sense."

"Oh, do shut up," Lynton grumbled as he swept his fingers over her cheek until her eyes fluttered open. She met his gaze and a tender smile turned up her lips. Seeing his mother in Lynton's arms seemed right. She'd certainly been lucky in love to have Lynton's continuing devotion. They could do very well together. Lynton only needed time to plead his case. But he couldn't do that if Oscar placed him in danger pursuing Agatha's abductors.

He walked out, but heard his new uncle quite clearly. "Brother, do look after dear Essy for us. I'm sure you can still work your charm to make her forget her troubles. We'll be back before you know it, so don't get too carried away. Oh, here, I arranged for two special licenses—not just one as you requested. Do be a good fellow and make the loss of six cases of my finest brandy worthwhile. I do love double weddings."

Twenty-Seven

"COME AWAY FROM the window, Essy. It is far too soon for any news."

Although Lynton was right, Estella didn't want to leave the window. Not when a special license for them to marry rested nearby. Staines, that meddling old fool, had gone too far this time. She wasn't about to marry Lynton just because the duke demanded it, or because he'd made it incredibly easy to do. The Duke of Staines failed to understand that she was in mourning for Thomas. She had not meant to find comfort in Lynton's arms after she'd fainted. Staines had misunderstood their familiarity and leapt to the wrong conclusion.

Besides, given the scandal's embroiling her family, Lynton should wish to be miles away from them. What was he doing here now? He hadn't been interested in speaking with either her son or her at Thomas' funeral. That public slight would give more credence to the stories told by wagging tongues. If not for Staines' order, would he have slunk away already?

"I cannot help but worry about my son and Agatha."

Lynton sighed loudly. "We both worry, but Oscar has Staines and Redding with him. He is in good hands. Redding will protect them both and bring Agatha home again very soon. He has unlimited sources in the city. He'll find her as quick as he can."

Estella hugged herself. "Why does Staines keep such a man with him? If Redding is as dangerous as you let on, then should he be with my son?"

"Redding is a fine man, a perfect match for my wild brother. He keeps him in line and keeps those who would exploit him at bay. You don't want to cross Redding. He almost died once to save my brother from harm. Staines rescued him in return and has had Redding as his shadow ever since."

Estella nodded. That did explain Redding's near constant presence behind the duke. "I'd not heard of that incident. Your brother is very lucky."

"It was years ago, just after I'd taken orders. Redding has my eternal gratitude for keeping my brother at least partially respectable all these years." He chuckled suddenly. "The quirk of Redding's eyebrow can squash one of my brother's mad schemes better than any sermon I could deliver. I rest easy knowing he is there."

Estella bit her lip. She longed to ask Lynton a question about the earlier conversation, but worried he might take offense once the disturbing subject came up. She didn't want to wait for news alone, but Oscar's mention of murder worried her. He seemed—very little like the son she'd raised today. Yet if she discussed the matter with Lynton, she'd get an idea if he had any intention of forging a closer friendship with her son and whether he would be a continuing presence in her life. Oscar had seemed to take the revelation in his stride, but Estella found the notion of having made love to Lynton an uneasy one.

She took a deep breath, prepared to be abandoned at any moment. "Did you catch, by any chance, Oscar's mention of murder?"

Lynton stood and approached. Her skin prickled as he closed the gap between them until he rested inches from her back. "Staines told me yesterday about an unfortunate incident involving Oscar. I take it that the boy has not confided in you?"

Estella shook her head, panicked that her son should be a murderer.

Lynton sighed, ruffling the hair at her nape with his breath. She shivered. "Redding uncovered a recent incident involving Oscar, Lord Daventry, and his new wife. Although you may not like it our . . . our son did a very brave thing. Do you want the details?"

Estella's heart raced. No wonder Oscar was so thick with Daventry this season. "He will tell me when he is ready, but I appreciate you reassuring me. He's been so black in his moods lately that I didn't know what to think."

Lynton's hand settled on her arm and stroked over her skin lightly. "He's had a lot to reconcile, I imagine. He wouldn't be the man he is if he could take a life without contemplation."

"And today?" Estella shuddered. "If any harm comes to Agatha, I don't know what he'll do. Did you see his expression? He frightened me, Lynton."

Lynton set his arms about her. "Shh. He is still the same boy you raised."

Although she should resist him, his embrace comforted her more than she could let on. The warmth of him seeped through her gown and warmed her. She laid her hands on his encircling arms and allowed him to weave their fingers together.

"I should apologize for my brother again."

Estella waited for him to continue, but he said nothing more. His breath puffed across her ear lightly, and a tingling of desire curled within her. Again, she should fight her attraction to Lynton Manning. But it was hard to do when he was so quiet about his seductions.

She closed her eyes and inhaled. He smelled so good. Clean, like a new forest after rain. Slowly, Lynton turned her in his arms and he eased her against him. "I should apologize, but I won't."

Estella opened her eyes to find Lynton smiling at her, a little, knowing smile that lifted the corners of his mouth and fixed her attention on his lips. The slow burn of desire sped up. As his hands stole over her back, she willed them lower. Unfortunately, he didn't comply. But he pulled her against him.

The hard ridge of his erection pressed against her belly, and her lips lifted in a smile. "Are you attempting to seduce me, Lynton?"

His lips pursed. "If that were my intention, I'd be under your skirts already. But I won't do that until you consent to be my wife. I dishonored you once, Essy. A regret I have harbored all my life."

Estella drew back. "You regret me?"

His hand swept down her back and over her bottom. "I regret not fighting harder to win you from Carrington before you married him. I regret not making love to you openly that night. And I especially regret not courting you the minute Carrington's body was cold in the ground. I feel like I've missed your whole life."

Manning's hands kneaded her bottom and Estella shuddered. "My life isn't over yet."

He grinned suddenly, his hands stilled. "No. But since you haven't consented to share the rest with me, I may still miss out. Marry me, Essy. You may scold me and make me earn my place at your side, but do not send me away." His hands moved again, curling her tighter against him, raising one of her legs in the process. "Not when we can feel like this together."

Lynton kissed her suddenly. Estella moaned and opened her mouth to him. A hot rush of sensation gripped her as they wrestled to touch any part of each other they could. She teased his tongue until he growled at her, and gave up the fight against him and her desires. She did want him in her life and in her bed.

She had been very good at lying to herself.

He ground his hips against her as they kissed until Estella thought she'd go mad. Poor Thomas had never made her feel like this, not even on his most amorous day. She drew back, gentling Lynton with her fingers over his lips. He kissed them, then drew them into his mouth and sucked. The unexpected suction drew her senses higher. He circled his hips against her. Her body tightened unexpectedly. She shook. She gasped. She buried her face at Lynton's throat to hide her embarrassment.

He forced her gaze back to his. He smiled like the devil himself. "Good to see I haven't lost my touch."

Although still astonished, she smiled back and curled her arms about his neck. "Gracious. How did you?"

"Not quite the saint you thought me." He laughed suddenly. "Believe me, I have years of fantasies to prove with you. Marry me so I may seduce you properly."

He kissed her flaming cheeks gently while Estella struggled to think. If he could do that and not think of it as a seduction, she was in terrible straights if he did. She stared across the room blindly as his kisses progressed to her neck.

Clearly, he'd employed the last few years wisely, not perhaps as saintly as one would expect. She dropped one arm down his back until she reached his hip, and since there was space between their bodies, she laid her hand over his impressive erection.

Lynton hissed. "That was a 'yes' to marriage, Essy. Don't think I won't hold you to it."

Estella met his gaze as she moved her hand. Lynton shuddered and swept her to a couch. She cupped his face between her hands as he hovered over her. "Oh, yes."

~ * ~

Agatha opened her eyes for the third time to see the same sagging ceiling suspended above her. She had so hoped this was a dream, not a nightmare come to life. But judging from the coarse sounds filtering into the room, she was in a house of ill repute somewhere. The masculine groans and the banging of a bed frame against the wall behind her head reminded her, once again, that she was unable to get free.

She tested the bonds that held her hands and feet in place again. They didn't give her the slightest hope of a successful escape, yet if she called out and assistance arrived, she might be in more trouble. They'd taken her gown and she lay clothed only in a thin chemise. The position they held her in should excite any man with a heartbeat who should walk through the door.

She lifted her head to see the closed door. So far, she'd seen no one but her two abductors. She didn't remember anything after the carriage pulled up in the lane. She didn't remember this house or being stripped of her black gown and corset. She desperately hoped that the door was locked.

She lay back down. There was nothing to be gained by panicking. Nothing could change until that door opened and either savior or sinner passed the threshold. She desperately wanted Oscar to walk through that door.

Footsteps approached, and keys rattled in a lock. Agatha raised her head to see who came near. It was a woman she didn't recognize, but guessed to be the abbess of this crumbling establishment. The woman who'd hired thugs to abduct her was a well-dressed older lady, a woman who could walk on the street and be called elegant. She shut the door behind her and came closer. "You're awake at last."

Agatha nodded carefully, mindful of her aching head.

"Good. Tell me your name."

Agatha frowned and kept her mouth closed. Shouldn't the abbess know who she was? Agatha had assumed the woman had abducted her. Was that not the case?

She looked around the room. Nothing in her line of vision gave her any clue to where she was except for the rhythmic thumping against the wall. The peeling paper was old and faded, as was the quilt beneath her body. The window was covered by fading drapes, so she couldn't see the world outside or guess at the time of day. The house seemed old, possibly one in a poorer part of London. Yet this woman was stylishly turned out. She looked as if she'd just returned from a carriage ride during the fashionable hour with friends. But her gaze held no warmth. She seemed immune to Agatha's helpless situation.

The woman frowned. "It is not like my friend to gift me with a girl with no logical explanation. I have a busy house to run, and should not like the inconvenience of dealing with irate family if you are not the fancyware you should be. Who is your father?"

Agatha kept her lips closed. If she answered honestly, she'd be signing her own downfall. There was no one legally bound to care for her now. Not even Oscar.

The abbess' cold, dry hands skimmed over hers. "Soft. A lady of leisure?"

The woman inspected her exposed skin. Agatha suffered the indignity of the cold touch without response for as long as she could, but when the woman lifted her chemise to look beneath, she bucked to get away.

The abbess frowned. "If you're clean, I can ask a higher price for your first gentlemen caller. There is many a man who would take one look at you as you are and demand a whole night in this bed." The abbess tested the bonds at her ankles and hands. "It is not usually my way to resort to such precautions, but Prewie was adamant that you should not get away. I will have to ask for more particulars about you before we proceed."

Prewie? Did she mean Lord Prewitt? But why would he bring her here. She had done nothing but turn aside his scandalous offer to share his bed. Why would he retaliate so cruelly like this?

The thumping against the wall ended with a harsh groan.

The abbess smiled. "Another satisfied customer. Do excuse me? I need to attend to my customer and see that his companion survived that onslaught." She tapped her finger against her lips. "I will never understand why rakish gentlemen try to be good. It only leads to unnecessary frenzy in the bedchamber once they get there. Bad for business to always be replacing broken girls. Unfortunately, you all have a short working life. Make sure you enjoy what you can of it."

The abbess glided out the door and locked her in again. Agatha thumped her head against the mattress in frustration. Prewitt? Did he do this because she would not accept his advances, or to avenge himself against Oscar for failing to marry his sister-in-law as promised? Either way, it didn't matter.

Oscar would never think to look for her here.

No one would.

Twenty-Eight

OSCAR GRIPPED REDDING'S coat and pulled him closer. "Are you sure this is the place?"

"Hands off my servant, boy," Staines growled.

Redding escaped Oscar's grip and grimaced. "Yes, unfortunately. My sources say she was brought here around midday. The two thugs who grabbed her are well known, well enough known to be avoided at all costs. They were paid by the abbess and are currently arse deep in rum down by the docks. That's two less. But we have Mrs. Leyton's footmen to contend with still. She does not employ small men."

Staines straightened his footman's coat. "How many inside?"

"Enough to be a problem. Two or three apiece."

Staines winced. "We could mount a frontal assault."

"And likely get you shot?" Redding laughed softly. "I don't think so."

The duke folded his arms across his chest and pouted. "I am not a magnet for stray bullets, Redding."

"Despite all evidence to the contrary." Redding chewed his lip, his eyes glued to the distant bawdy house. Staines couldn't seem to let his servant get the last word and continued arguing.

This situation was worse than Oscar had feared. In a bawdy house, Agatha could be made to do many an unspeakable act, and no one would help her. They would turn a blind eye to her distress, or likely cheer some bloody scoundrel on. Oscar clenched his fists, fighting his growing frustration. Outnumbered or not, he was going to get Agatha out of that place. She must be terrified.

He glanced at the duke and considered what his chances were of getting past Redding to gag him. The duke and his footman had been bickering like this all afternoon. Although they were discussing and throwing out ways and means of rescuing Agatha, Oscar could not quite make up his mind how to take them. They behaved like an old married couple, which was ridiculous since the duke was a well known skirt-chaser. Yet there was an intimacy between them that neither man tried to hide. They seemed genuinely fond of each other, despite the differences in their social positions.

Redding sat back in his seat and met the duke's gaze. "How amorous are you feeling today, Your Grace?"

An amused grin crossed the duke's features, interest and more behind his smile. "We're on a mission to rescue the damsel in distress, Redding. Now is hardly the time for experimentation."

Oscar quickly looked away. He did not want to leap to conclusions, but they made it ridiculously easy to do so. Heaven help them if any member of society noticed this close friendship and listened to their banter. The duke and his servant could get themselves arrested merely on the suspicion of unnatural affection. The duke's reputation, and his entire family, could be ruined as a result of an unfounded rumor. If it were proved true, they could both lose their lives.

Redding sighed and gestured toward the bawdy house. "There are women in there, Your Grace, and if memory serves it's been quite a while since you've selected a new woman."

The duke chuckled. "Why, Redding, I had not realized you paid that much attention to my personal life. But you are correct. I feel a certain yearning even as we speak."

A resigned expression flittered across Redding's face as he turned away. "Doesn't the Hunt Club need new blood to replace that girl who went and got married?" Redding held out his hand for one of Oscar's pistols. "You are known to personally interview potential candidates, are you not?"

"That I am." The duke held out his hand for the other, but Oscar didn't oblige him. "Redding is a genius. You will wait here, my boy. We have a better chance of getting her out without you with us. Redding has an inkling this abduction is directed at you, personally, and that Agatha is the innocent party in all of it. I know your blood yearns for revenge, but I can walk in there and demand entry to any woman's bed with Redding at my heels without anyone raising a fuss. He could probably watch me bed the girl and it wouldn't be remarked upon."

Redding rolled his eyes. "Surely you do not need an audience to get a rise, Your Grace."

The duke barked a laugh, but didn't seem to have a ready answer for a change. Redding's grin appeared and disappeared as the silence lengthened.

Could Oscar trust the duke to bring Agatha to him unharmed? Did he even know what she looked like?

The duke eased Oscar's pistols from his grip and handed one to Redding. "Blonde hair, blue eyes, face of an angel. Answers to the nickname precious?"

Oscar nodded numbly. Was there anything about his life that Staines could not find out? Surely some things were private?

The duke chuckled. "You sleep on the left side of the bed and prefer one particular sexual position. The . . ."

Redding clamped his hand over the duke's mouth to shut him up. "Enough now. If you say any more, the boy will likely never speak to you again."

When Redding dropped his hand, the duke was grinning. "You see why I keep him on, Oscar. Who else would dare keep me in line like that? We will return with your Agatha as quick as we can. Stay in the carriage and keep out of sight. We don't want you noticed, or they might not let me have her."

Oscar opened his mouth to protest.

The duke held out a staying hand. "Shh, boy. Trust me."

Redding spoke to the driver and they moved off. As the building came closer, Oscar's panic doubled. It was a mean place. Too coarse for his precious girl. He hoped Staines could get her out. He prayed for it with all his heart.

The coach stopped and Redding stepped out. After a long wait, Staines followed and rushed up to the front door with an eager spring in his step. The door closed and his carriage moved away. They circled the block as the driver normally would and stopped in a side lane to wait for the duke's return.

Oscar slid to the window closest to the brothel and peered out. He could see scarcely one window from here. He wasn't nearly close enough. He'd get out and wait. He set his hand to the door as one of the footmen jumped down. The groom opened the door and pushed him further into the carriage.

"Here now!"

The groom ignored him, flipped open a concealed cupboard and poured a drink. He handed the crystal glass to Oscar. "Redding insisted."

A drink could settle his nerves.

Oscar took the glass and swallowed it down fast. As he handed the glass back, the groom pulled something long from his pocket. Oscar's dueling pistol sat on the groom's lap. A silent threat.

The groom shrugged. "Afraid Redding insisted on this, too, my lord. Mrs. Leyton's bawdy house is no fit place for you. The duke would never forgive himself if you were hurt. Best to stay here as Redding likes you."

~ * ~

"She's lovely. Very soft skin, but I'm after someone a little purer on the eye. Someone who might cause a ripple of envy on my arm at the theatre. I want everyone mad for her name and for an introduction. When they find out she's the latest acquisition for the Hunt Club's stable, we will be inundated with applications, all of which I must reluctantly refuse, and thus retain our popularity. You, of course, know what a reputation for exclusivity means in our world. I intend to finish the year with a triumphant roar."

Agatha heard the deep voice outside her door and cringed. *Don't come in. Don't come near me. I cannot be that woman.* She'd rather die than be any man's whore. She held her breath, but the footsteps didn't move on.

"Well, that does make your pocket book heftier. Wouldn't mind that myself." There was a painfully long pause. "If you want purity, then I've got just the lass for you. Mind you, she could be trouble. The pure ones always are. But if the price was right I'm sure we could come to an arrangement. This one is worth double the previous girl."

Agatha's door knob jiggled. She stared at it as it began to turn and could not look away as the abbess entered the room, two finely dressed gentlemen hard on her heels.

One of them, the tallest, hissed.

The other stared at her foot. "How utterly delightful."

Despite not wanting to react, Agatha squeezed her toes together. A flicker of anger crossed the shorter man's face. One of his hands curled into a fist.

The tall man moved closer to the bed. He tested the bonds at her ankles, yet did not, thankfully, touch her skin.

The shorter one turned his back on her, one arm behind him, fist still clenched. "She's perfect, breathtaking, but I do think she should be inspected. Redding, be a good chap and take a look at her teeth."

Redding winced. "Of course, Your Grace. I should have thought of it sooner."

Agatha stared at the shorter man's back. A duke? Good God she would never get out of this with any of her reputation intact. While the duke haggled with the abbess, the Redding fellow moved closer. He met her eyes as he reached for her face.

Agatha shifted her head from side to side.

The abbess appeared beside the bed. "You'll need a firm hand with this one. She's somewhat feisty."

The duke drew the abbess away again. "I do like a feisty woman. So much more fun to have around. Now about the price."

Agatha whipped her gaze back to Redding just as he captured her jaw.

"Don't fight me now, precious," he whispered. "Open your mouth like a good girl so we can get you home."

Precious? Only Oscar called her that. Why would this gentleman know or use the name? He didn't say another word. His grip softened.

She let her jaw slacken. Redding gently pried her mouth open and made a show of inspecting her teeth. But he whispered, "Go along with whatever the duke does and says. Don't fight us too much."

Redding sat back. "She has all her teeth, Your Grace."

"Excellent. And her breath?"

"Quite fine, too."

"Well." The duke returned his attention to the abbess. "I'll take her now and Redding will deliver the funds this evening. I cannot wait to begin."

The duke seemed almost giddy with glee. He swung about, his hand falling to the binding on her ankle.

The abbess put a staying hand on his arm. "Half now to secure her. Half later. You can take her once you've paid me."

The duke's smile fell. "I so hoped you would indulge me, Mrs. Leyton. Redding?"

Redding stood and put his hand behind his back. But Agatha could see what the abbess couldn't. Something bulky hid beneath Redding's clothes. "Yes, Your Grace?"

"The abbess strikes a hard bargain, but requires payment before we can take the girl. Do be a dear fellow and pay her. You know I loathe handling money."

"With pleasure, Your Grace."

Redding hurried forward, removing a pistol from the back of his trousers. The duke lunged for the abbess at the same time and slapped a hand over her mouth. "You should have been kinder to me, Mrs. Leyton. I do not like being thwarted."

Mrs. Leyton squawked behind the duke's hand, her eyes round as saucers. Unfortunately, they closed to slits after a moment. Her eyes darted around the chamber in a way that made Agatha afraid.

Redding hurried to close the door then turned to Agatha. He tore his coat from his shoulders and laid it gently over her. "Oscar sent us."

Agatha closed her eyes. Despite her best efforts, tears squeezed out. Redding untied her hands and feet and drew her upright. She clutched his coat tightly about her and looked for her own dark gown. But it was gone. Nowhere within sight.

Redding and the duke glanced at the abbess. Redding stared at Mrs. Leyton, his jaw clenching and unclenching in a disturbing way. "I think I will enjoy this."

"Oh, no, Redding." The duke countered. "The joy will be all mine. Come muzzle her while I do the honors."

While Mrs. Leyton struggled and squirmed, the duke stripped her of her gown and held it out to Agatha to slip on. Then, while Agatha was contending with the larger garment and her shaking hands, the pair of them forced Mrs. Leyton into the exact same predicament that they'd found Agatha in, but with one additional detail—they gagged her so she couldn't cry out.

Redding approached. "May I finish dressing you, Miss Birkenstock?"

Numbly, she nodded. Everything had changed so fast, but why were this duke and his servant rescuing her on Oscar's behalf? She didn't know either of them and couldn't remember Oscar mentioning this duke either. Redding buttoned her as fast as any maid she'd ever had, and when he was done he led her to the duke's side.

The duke held his arm out to her.

Puzzled, she frowned at him. "Who are you?'

He grinned rather impishly and wound her arm through his. "Someone who really shouldn't be crossed." He looked sadly at the woman twisting violently on the bed. "Mrs. Leyton would do well to remember this incident for future reference. I look after my own. Don't get involved with my family affairs again or I will crush you out of business. Is that understood?"

Mrs. Leyton's gaze flew to Agatha and a small sound, a muffled whimper, escaped her throat. Family? Agatha looked up at the duke as he patted her hand.

"Come along, my dear. We have nicer environs to frequent. You must come to dinner soon."

The duke swept her from the room and down the main staircase as if he made the short journey every day. But at the bottom, Redding was struck and slumped to the ground with a groan. His pistol bounced uselessly across the floor.

When Agatha looked around, she spied Lady Prewitt standing between her and the door—pistol pointed at Agatha's head.

Twenty-Nine

OSCAR THUMPED THE side of the carriage and glared at the groom blocking the door. "It's taking too long. What could be taking them so long?"

The groom sat up, alert once more. Oscar cursed his lack of foresight. If he'd stayed quiet, he might have been able to get past him and away before he could be stopped.

The groom waved the pistol in his direction. "Now, your lordship. Don't be taking that tone with me. I got orders, you see, and one does not cross the duke's man unless one wants to seek employment with the fishes."

Oscar scowled at the weak, cautious man. If he did not hold a pistol, now aimed exactly at Oscar's chest, Oscar would have been out of this carriage ten minutes ago and inside the building to find Agatha. However, he couldn't do anything to help if he sustained another injury. His hand ached enough as it was.

He still hoped to convince Redding's lackey to be reasonable and let him have his way. But the man appeared utterly opposed to crossing the duke's man. They'd spoken at length since the duke's departure, and he'd not conceded one point in Oscar's favor. Damn foolish loyalty.

Oscar slumped in his seat, imagining the retribution he would bring against the duke's man should they not return with Agatha within the next five minutes. He pulled out his pocket watch to mark the time. A little before three. Three o'clock seemed a goodly time of day to shoot someone.

As he tucked his watch away again, a carriage passed the end of their lane.

Oscar sat forward as the gleaming Town carriage pulled up before the bawdy house steps. A single lady stepped from it. An elegant lady he recognized only too well.

Yet he had trouble believing his eyes. "Lady Prewitt?"

She swept up the staircase and disappeared inside without a glance left or right. What the devil was she doing visiting a brothel in this, or any, part of Town? Then he remembered. The Prewitt's had some small connection to Mrs. Leyton that he'd not liked and had refused to indulge that day in the park. At the time, he'd dismissed the woman. Now, it seemed he should have paid more attention.

Redding could be right. Perhaps he'd brought this revenge upon Agatha by not marrying Lady Penelope. A woman scorned was a dangerous woman. But a woman with low and unsavory connections would be a greater danger, indeed.

The groom whistled. "Now that changes matters somewhat." He held out the weapon to Oscar. "You'd better go, milord. That one isn't right in the head. I mean, who would be when her husband's shagging her baby sister right under her nose? Disturbs the mind more than a bit. Even turns my stomach, and I seen a lot working for the duke."

"I knew something was going on between that pair," Oscar growled. All of his suspicions had been vindicated. Prewitt, huh. That explained his possessive presence beside Penelope and his reluctance that they be alone. Prewitt could have Penelope, but he'd go retrieve Agatha now.

The footman climbed out and held open the door. "Don't kill 'er. It's harder to hush up that kind of thing in London than in the country. Too many witnesses to pay off in Town."

Oscar hurried for the bawdy house door, pistol tucked beneath his coat. The two footmen allowed him to pass without question. To them, he must have seemed like an eager gentleman come for a fuck and little else. He hoped everyone else he passed assumed that.

He slowed his steps once he entered the house. He'd never come here before and had no idea of the layout. Could he ask the butler to direct him to the newest acquisition? Probably not a wise question to ask, given that he wasn't a regular customer. But the butler was no where in sight to direct him. The foyer was empty.

He eased forward until he heard voices.

"Lady Prewitt, what an unexpected pleasure to see you," the Duke of Staines purred.

Oscar glanced around the corner just as his uncle tugged Agatha behind his back. The duke's man was on the ground at the base of the stairs, hand raised to his head in obvious pain. When Redding removed it, the bright stain of blood coated his fingers and the side of his face.

Oscar's pulse hammered; his breath grew labored.

He checked on Agatha again. So far she looked unharmed, but Lady Prewitt's wildly swinging pistol arm gave him pause. It reminded him too much of his previous encounter with a deranged man at Lord Daventry's estate. He drew back, breath catching in his chest. This was his nightmare come back to life. Only now Agatha was in the middle of it, and he had to save her.

Redding groaned and when Oscar checked again, he had dragged himself to a seated position. Redding met Oscar's gaze across the room, but made no other gesture to show he'd recognized him. Was he dazed?

"Are you all right, Redding?"

Redding groaned again. "Yes, Your Grace. It's just a scratch. Always happens around you. I should be getting used to it by now."

"You're slowing up there, old fellow. By the way, there's still a pistol aimed at me. This is no time to be getting comfortable on the floor. Really, Red, I hardly ever do anything to deserve such an indignity."

Redding set his hand to the floor. "Don't call me Red."

Lady Prewitt hissed. "It's aimed at her, if you would just get out of the way. I've got nothing against you."

Oscar risked another peek and his world slowed. While he'd been regaining his senses, Redding and the duke had repositioned themselves. He now had a clear shot at Lady Prewitt. He just needed the wits to pull the trigger and fire upon another human being again.

Oscar flexed his hand around the pistol and drew in a deep breath, hoping the duke could talk his way out of this.

"At my little Agatha? Dear lady, what has she done to deserve such hostile treatment?" The duke's soothing tones had little effect on the hostile woman.

Lady Prewitt drew herself up tall her grip on the pistol firming. "She's after my husband. I won't share any more of him."

"Lord Prewitt?" The duke glanced at Agatha.

Agatha shook her head violently. "No. No, of course I don't want him."

Lady Prewitt sneered. "That's what she said, too. Now see what goes on. They think I don't know, but I've got eyes. I know where they creep to in the dead of night. It stops with her."

Redding climbed slowly to his feet but rested against the wall, putting himself further out of danger. "If that were true then we might all be afraid. As it is, you'll not pull that trigger."

Lady Prewitt looked Redding up and down and sneered. "And why is that?"

The duke pushed Agatha two steps further back. "Because, my dear, you've lost."

Oscar pulled the trigger.

A puff of smoke wafted before him as Lady Prewitt collapsed to the ground, pistol spinning far from her reach. She held her bleeding arm against her chest as she screamed in pain at the wound he'd inflicted. Oscar swayed. The pistol fell from his fingers with a loud clatter.

Agatha ran to him and jumped into his arms. "I knew you could save us. I knew you could."

She kissed him and hugged him and told him many flattering things that were profoundly good for his ego. He hugged her against his chest and collapsed against the wall for support.

What if he couldn't have pulled the trigger?

That didn't bear thinking about. He set his hands around Agatha's face and kissed her full on the mouth.

"Redding? We need to get this pair married, don't you think?" The duke approached, supporting his footman as they crossed the room. He leaned his servant against the wall beside Oscar and inspected the cut on his head. "Red, there's a fair bit of blood leaking from your head."

Redding brushed his hands aside. "It'll stop directly. Don't fuss. Mr. Branxton will be waiting impatiently to perform the ceremonies. I'll deal with my wound later."

The duke looked set to argue until Redding pointed at the woman crying on the floor. "Also have to deliver her back to her husband with an explanation. You should enjoy that, don't you think?"

"Immensely." The duke grinned. "Are you all right, Oscar?"

Oscar squeezed Agatha tightly. "I am now, Your Grace. I'll bring Lady Prewitt to the carriage. Agatha, go along with His Grace. I'll join you in a moment."

Agatha shook her head stubbornly. "I'll help you."

Together, they got Lady Prewitt's wound bandaged enough to slow the flow of blood, and supported her between them as they followed the duke and Redding, listening to their banter once more. Lady Prewitt stumbled along without saying a word.

"Rather forward thinking of me wouldn't you say, Red, to arrange that vicar fellow?"

Redding clutched his head. "Don't know if I'd go that far, but if you insist."

The duke slung his arm around his footman's back to support him for the short walk. "Oh, I do, I do."

Redding faced the duke. "Carrington should be saying those words. You cannot do everything for him."

Staines chuckled. "Carrington I trust to comply with my wishes, but I do long to hear my brother say them.

But let's dispose of Lady Prewitt first, and then we shall have a nice wedding to enjoy."

The grooms on the carriage sprang into action at the sight of their battered party. Redding was helped into the carriage muttering 'of course, Your Grace' to another of Staines' self-serving pronouncements. Did he never stop talking?

Lady Prewitt said nothing at all as she was pushed inside, too.

Agatha tugged on Oscar's sleeve and drew him a little away from the carriage. "Which duke is that?"

"The Duke of Staines." Oscar set his hands over hers and squeezed. "My uncle, in truth."

She frowned. "But you never told me you were related to a duke before. I thought you wouldn't keep secrets from me."

"This one is a new secret. I had planned to tell you after we were wed in case you had second thoughts about marrying into such a scandalous family."

Agatha clutched at his lapels. "Exactly how are you related to the Duke of Staines? I don't remember reading anything of that in the peerage."

Oscar cupped his hand around her face and lifted her lips to his. "And you never will."

He quickly kissed her.

Agatha scowled. "So you are not Lord Carrington's son? Not Lord Carrington at all?"

"Oh, I am still legally Lord Carrington, but my father was, in fact, another man." He could see the question in her eyes. "Would you believe the very proper Mr. Lynton Manning is my real father? I tell you now, I could not at first."

"Oh."

"Oh, indeed. Lynton also loves my mother quite madly. The duke has only just learned of my parentage and is adamant they be married with haste."

All of a sudden, Agatha laughed. "Oh, dear. We really are quite tame, are we not, in comparison, Oscar?"

"Tame for now. But I have such great plans for tonight." He set his lips to Agatha's, longing for the moment when they could be alone again.

A throat cleared behind them and they turned. The duke had stuck his head out the carriage door. "Children. Let's get you married first and then you can resume your private assignation. There's always a welcome for new family. Don't hesitate to get her with child when it's convenient. But Redding and Lady Prewitt are drenching my carriage in blood. Can we please move along?"

Oscar escorted Agatha to the carriage and squeezed in beside her. "So you like children, Your Grace?"

"Oh, yes. Manning delivered me seven just yesterday. He's adopting the children from the orphanage as his own." The duke laughed suddenly. "One hopes he tells your mother about it after the wedding, or I fear she'll faint with shock."

A tear fell down Agatha's cheek. "He's taking all of them? Why?"

"The orphanage closed, my dear, and, given the scandal you two stirred up, Lynton had to talk fast to secure their care." The duke took up her hand and rubbed soothingly. "But not all will live with him. Seven is too grand a family for a man of his age with a new wife. I thought perhaps you would consent to raise little Betty, Mabel, and Kitty. The little scamps pleaded to see you before they were removed to my estate, and then the others joined in and created a tearful uproar. I am currently overrun with little ones."

Agatha turned to Oscar, a plea in her eyes. He nodded. "Those three, or all if you have no objection, Your Grace. I'll speak to my father about it."

Agatha hugged Oscar then turned her tearful gaze on the duke. "Thank you, Your Grace. Your charity toward the orphans proves the nasty rumors about you are false and completely untrue."

Redding lifted his head from the squabs. "Don't count on it. He's hardly a stranger to scandal. It runs in the family."

While the duke and Redding resumed their squabbling, Oscar pulled Agatha hard against him. "I could have lost you."

She smiled softly and set her fingers over his lips when he would have continued to voice his fears. "No chance of that. I know everything about you, Oscar. Like cupid's arrow, your aim is true."

Agatha kissed him, and although the duke cleared his throat, Redding coughed, and Lady Prewitt sat mute across the carriage, they did not stop kissing until they had to. Exactly long enough to say 'I do'.

Epilogue

OSCAR THREW ANOTHER log on the fire and held his hands out to the blaze. It was a perfect night for seduction. He'd been thinking of getting Agatha alone and away from the children all day. He was so desperate for her, he ached.

"It's hardly fair, you know."

Oscar smiled as he got to his feet and admired his wife's sleek bare back. "Nonsense, it's just the right size for us. Trust me."

His gaze drifted lower. Agatha sat at her new pianoforte, naked and playing a soft tune just for him. But at this rate, he'd never be able to keep his hands empty of her for long. Her body was a delight, and he could never get enough of her.

"But it's far too big for us to use all of it."

Oscar moved so he could see her breasts. Although covered by her unbound hair, the peaked buds of her nipples peeked through the strands. His mouth watered. "Agatha, you've got to believe me. This is perfect. You just have to be prepared to make the adjustment."

Agatha continued to play. Although she shivered, he wouldn't call a halt to their games yet. She'd never played in the nude before, and the sight delighted him. She squirmed on her bench and pressed her knees together.

Perhaps they should try this another day during the summer.

Oscar set his hands on her shoulders. Her skin was cool. "Come to bed, precious."

Agatha flattened her hands over the keys so that her prized possession made a discordant sound. "We have to talk about this. How can we take over Lord Lynton's home? It's unfair of you."

Oscar knelt beside the pianoforte and brought each of her hands to his lips. "For the last time, it was his idea to keep the children together rather than dividing them between two houses. They are all happy as larks upstairs in the nursery after a day rambling around the estate. My father and mother are content at the dower house."

Agatha stood. "They should be here. It pains me that Lord Lynton should leave his home before he got used to living in it again."

Oscar crawled across the floor and set his lips to her knee. Agatha's huff turned to a moan. He kissed up her thigh until his lips were level with her belly. "Have you really seen Lynton and my mother together, not dressed for guests but when they think they are truly alone? The children love spending time with them, but they are better off not walking in on them engaged in an intimate embrace. Honestly, you'd think at their age their appetites would have waned."

Agatha's fingers curled into Oscar's hair as he pressed light kisses to her mound. "They do love each other very much."

"As much as I love you, which is why I agreed to give them as much privacy as they need. Just think of all the nights they missed when they could have been together."

Agatha's palm settled on his head and pushed him down. She was right, much too much talking about everybody else. He had a wife to seduce and he was impatient to get started. He drew a deep breath of her scent into his lungs, and burrowed his tongue between her lower lips. Yet he couldn't reach what he wanted in this position.

Oscar stood, picked Agatha up and stalked with her toward the bed. "Enough about everyone else."

Agatha did try to resist him. When Oscar spread her legs and dipped down for a taste, she did attempt to push him away. "I cannot help worrying over Lady Prewitt in that terrible place. How sad that her husband and sister deserted her that way. It's tragic."

So much for seducing her immediately. She was determined to fret about everyone they knew tonight. He threw himself on the bed beside her and caught up her hand. "What do you want? You couldn't possibly want to visit with her? She could have killed you."

Agatha straddled him. "Perhaps I do. Isn't it worth expending the effort for the sake of her soul?"

She wriggled her hips seductively. Caught under her spell, he nodded absently, but his mind was fixed on sliding his cock into her body. He wrapped his hands about her hips, and then lifted her until her body opened to him.

As he joined with her, he sat up and brushed his lips against hers. "We will talk it over tomorrow or whenever I let you out of bed."

Her fingers tightened in his hair as she began to move on him. "I love you, Oscar."

He moaned as her nails raked his skull, and kissed her fiercely. When he drew back, her eyes were closed, her face lifted high. "I love you and our little family."

She stilled. "Mabel needs new shoes."

Oscar cursed his tongue for bringing up the children at such a moment and threw Agatha over onto her back. He parted her legs wide and wriggled down the bed. As he swept his tongue over her cleft, she moaned and shuddered. He met her gaze along the smooth expanse of her chest, saw the rapid rise and fall of her breasts, and smiled at how easily she could become aroused. They were exactly the same. A perfect, scandalous match. Oscar bent his head again until Agatha forgot everything but him. In fact, she quite forgot anything civilized at all. Which suited Oscar's plans for the night quite perfectly.

About the Author

Heather Boyd is the author of sizzling romance with an historical bent. A fan of regency England settings, she writes m/f and m/m stories that push the boundaries of propriety and even break the laws of that time. Brimming with new ideas, she frequently wishes she could type as fast as she can conjure up new storylines.

She lives with her testosterone-fuelled family north of Sydney, Australia.

For more information visit
www.heather-boyd.com

Made in the USA
San Bernardino, CA
21 January 2014